6

JAMES PATTERSON
& KATHRYN FOX

CENTURY

1 3 5 7 9 10 8 6 4 2

Century
20 Vauxhall Bridge Road
London SW1V 2SA

Century is part of the Penguin Random House group of companies
whose addresses can be found at global.penguinrandomhouse.com.

Penguin
Random House
UK

Copyright © James Patterson 2015
Excerpt from *Murder House* copyright © James Patterson 2015

First published by Century in 2015

www.randomhouse.co.uk

A CIP catalogue record for this book is
available from the British Library.

Hardback ISBN 9781780893914
Trade paperback ISBN 9781780893921

Printed and bound by Clays Ltd, St Ives Plc

MIX
Paper from
responsible sources
FSC
www.fsc.org   FSC® C018179

Penguin Random House is committed to a sustainable future
for our business, our readers and our planet. This book is made
from Forest Stewardship Council® certified paper.

Chapter 1

BRANCHES FROM THE eucalypts and blue gums cracked as they whipped the electrically charged air.

A storm from the east would hit soon and cover his tracks through the dense bushland. The cabin was isolated and close to a river, with a 270-degree vantage of the valley below, but that was in daylight.

Every sense on heightened alert, he scanned the doorframe with his night-vision goggles for the two strands of hair he'd positioned in the jamb days before. Locating both, he exhaled as the door eased open.

The urn over the fireplace was exactly as he'd left it too, the tiny notches in the wood lined up precisely with its rim. He checked his watch. Ninety seconds.

He unscrewed the base of the urn and located the USB device, which he secured inside his zippered jacket pocket.

His watch buzzed with a slow pulse. Someone had infiltrated his perimeter. With no road access from the north, they had to be on foot.

The pulsing sound doubled. Now two people headed towards the cabin. *Cleaners.* Men whose job it was to clean up mess and make sure nothing was left behind.

It confirmed he was a priority. If they had made it here, a hell of a lot of manpower was being invested in hunting him down.

He snatched his backpack and headed for the bedroom. Sliding back a rug at the foot of the bed exposed the trap door.

With the alarm pulsing on his wrist, he grabbed a bowie knife from his pack and dug it into the narrow space between the hatch and floor, dislodging caked dirt.

Summoning all his strength, he grunted and yanked. The hatch gave way. He squeezed through and lowered himself feet first. With a hook and wire he'd screwed into the cavity years before, he reached up, replaced the handle in its recess and repositioned the rug before lowering the hatch.

Sweat dripped from his forehead. He checked his watch again and listened.

No other sensors had been tripped. Instinct told him there were still just two men out there.

On his elbows and stomach the fit was tight, but at least he could propel backwards. After a few metres he removed a rope and screw-top tin from his pack. He unwound the line of rope before topping it with a thin layer of magnesium powder.

Fifteen more metres back and his boots should reach the removable panels at the rear of the wood shed.

The sound of feet clomping inside the cabin was suddenly paralysing. There were two male voices, then glass smashed.

He lit the rope and reverse commando-crawled as fast as his elbows, toes and knees could manage.

Flame ripped along the tunnel to the base of the cabin. As he kicked out the shed boards and escaped the tunnel, yelling pierced the night.

By the time they'd dealt with the flaring caused by the water, he'd be long gone.

Goggles fixed and backpack secure, he jogged along one of the paths he'd previously mapped out, careful to stay close to the gully on his left.

Fifty metres along, one of his motion detectors was attached to the base of a tree. It had already saved his life and could come in handy next time.

As he bent down and unstrapped the cord, something brushed his right wrist. Instinctively, he slapped it hard with his other gloved hand before pocketing the device and running on.

Within minutes, pain tore through his wrist, like a nail had been hammered into it.

He could hear voices in the distance.

Sweat poured from his face as the burning in his wrist intensified. Nausea rose in his gullet but he had to keep moving. He was light-headed.

Wind howled as the storm moved in. The sooner it came, the less likely they'd find him before daylight. He headed off again and stumbled on a rock formation. Reeling back, he staggered, unable to maintain his footing. He reached for something to grab. Anything.

Agonising pain shot through his side as he hit the rocks below. The world went black.

Chapter 2

THE EARLY MORNING temperature was crisp as I stretched aching muscles. Even a punishing run couldn't lessen the grief that today brought. I watched the flaming sun rising above the north and south heads, as a mammoth cruise ship glided into Sydney Harbour. It took me back to my honeymoon when Becky and I sailed home from Noumea.

The spectacle of passing through those heads as the sun lit the city was one of our most treasured memories. It was the moment she told me she wanted to be known as Mrs Craig Gisto.

It had been eight years now, and a song, a smell, even a sound, could still trigger a volcanic release of pain from my core.

If Cal had lived, he would be eleven today.

The car accident that took their lives trapped Cal as an eternal three-year-old and me as a widower. I wondered why there was a word for children who lost parents, but not one for parents who had suffered the greatest loss of all.

After a quick shower and breakfast, I was comfortably heading to the city in my Ferrari Spider. On Military Road,

I stopped at the traffic lights just before the turn-off to Taronga Zoo. Cal's favourite place.

Memories of him hanging off a gorilla statue were interrupted by a call. Jack Morgan. It had to be late morning on the west coast.

'Hi, Jack, what can I do for you?'

The LA-based owner of Private spoke quickly. 'Craig, I'm on a helicopter so we may lose connection. I'm asking for a favour. Eric Moss is the CEO of a company named Contigo Valley.' The background noise made it difficult to hear.

'You're fading,' I said into the hands-free microphone.

He shouted over the din. 'He and his daughter are old friends. Moss was at the top of his field and disappeared two days ago. Emailed a resignation with no explanation.'

'Do you suspect foul play?'

Jack gave directions to the pilot then returned. 'This is a billion-dollar company with international contracts. It needs Moss.'

I knew some of the work the company did with safety and medical equipment. So the CEO resigned on Friday and hadn't been heard of over the weekend. He could have been drinking away his sorrows or celebrating with a young fling.

I braked as a BMW cut into my lane on the approach to the Harbour Bridge.

'Is the daughter high-profile?'

Most of Private's clients were either famous, wealthy, or both, and wanted scandals kept out of the tabloids.

'She's special, Craig. I'm asking you to do this for her. Her name's Eliza Moss. She owns Shine Management.'

The phone crackled again.

'I've been a big supporter of Eric Moss,' Jack continued. 'Trust me, this isn't like him. Eliza and the company are his life. He wouldn't walk away without a fight. And he'd never do this to his only child.'

I wondered what sort of daughter panicked when her father didn't contact her over the weekend. But if Jack thought it worth looking into, I'd do it, despite this week's heavy workload.

'Thanks, Craig,' he finished. 'Let me know if I can help in any way.'

When the line went silent, I replayed the conversation in my mind. Jack mentioned Eliza was special to him. I wondered how special.

After pulling into the car park just after seven am, I took the stairs to street level.

First thing I saw was shattered glass.

The ground-to-ceiling door to Private had been smashed.

Chapter 3

I STEPPED PAST the two young men working on the glass repairs and was greeted by our receptionist thrusting forward a handful of messages. Collette Lindman hadn't been with us long, and seemed overly eager at times, but had skills that I believed would come in handy one day.

'These are the important calls on the machine. And there's a married couple waiting in your office. They were supposed to see Johnny at eight but came early to beat the traffic and had a good run. I couldn't leave them in the waiting area with all that broken glass and without the door, it's been pretty breezy –'

Collette barely drew breath. First thing was the door, which she still hadn't explained.

'What happened? I didn't get a call.'

'Oh, that? I didn't want to bother you. The security company phoned me at home and said our door had been smashed by vandals. Anyway, I rang the glass repairers, who came straight out. They said other businesses had breakages too. I hope it was the right thing to do. Before you ask, the door was shattered but unopened. No one got inside.'

Given the amount of high-tech equipment in the place, that was one positive. It was difficult to take it personally when other businesses had been affected.

I stepped further inside so the workmen couldn't hear. 'Who exactly are the people in my office?'

'Mr and Mrs Finch. It's heartbreaking what they've been through. I didn't think you'd mind, under the circumstances.'

Getting to the point was not Collette's strong suit. 'That's fine. What are they here for?'

'A background check. I assured them the name "Private" means their information stays that way, 'cause they seemed pretty nervous about confidentiality.'

I felt a pounding in my head. 'You did the right thing, Collette. The police will need the security footage from last night. We'll have good images of the door being hit and who did it.'

She hesitated. 'That's another thing I didn't want to bother you with yet.'

'Tell me now.'

'The computers are down. I mean, that might be why there isn't *actually* any vision of what happened overnight.' She touched my arm. 'Don't worry, I've called the technicians. They'll be here in a couple of hours.'

Technicians would take far too long. Without computers we couldn't work.

'Get Darlene to come in early. If she can't fix the problem, she'll know who can.'

I took stock of Monday morning so far: a favour for Jack Morgan, a smashed door, no computers and an anxious couple in my office, all by seven am. Cal's birthday was shaping up to be one hell of a day.

Chapter 4

I COULD SEE the pair through the glass wall to my office. The man paced while his wife sat twisting the rings on her left hand.

I entered, introduced myself. The husband was late forties. The cut of his suit, along with the white shirt and pale blue tie, suggested middle management, or a small business operator.

'Gus. Finch.' He shook my hand vigorously. 'And this is my wife, Jennifer.'

I greeted the woman, who wore a crimson silk shirt with a black skirt. She had to be at least ten years younger than Gus.

I took a seat at my desk. Finch sat next to his wife and held her hand.

'How can we help you?' I asked.

'We want a background check on someone. A potential employee.'

With the computers down, I opened a journal and started taking notes as Finch began rattling off his requirements.

'You should check she is healthy, no mental illness, has no criminal past, and that includes charges for DUI. I don't just mean convictions in case she got off on some technicality, I'm talking charges, any history of affairs . . .' He ticked off the list on his fingers. 'Doesn't abuse drugs or alcohol, is clear of any sexually transmitted infections, has a mortgage to show she's committed to staying locally and isn't in more than $200,000 debt.'

This was clearly no ordinary pre-employment check, unless the job was for a childcare worker. The mortgage question threw me. Not many nannies in Sydney had paid off mortgages to the last $200K. Nannying jobs were something students or new graduates sought.

His wife added, 'And we have to know she's a good mother.' She squeezed her husband's hand, pale grey eyes boring into mine.

'Yes,' Finch confirmed. 'If we're going to trust her with our children.' The inflection in his voice went up a notch at the end of this comment. He was lying, and he wasn't very good at it.

Today, I didn't really care to know why. 'Agencies routinely do employment checks and they charge a lot less than us. To be honest, you'd be better going through one of them.'

Finch slapped an envelope on the table. Hundred-dollar notes spilled out.

'We want *you*, not anyone else, to do the check. You guarantee confidentiality.'

I didn't like people assuming I could be bought. Not everyone has a price. Whatever they wanted kept secret didn't sit right.

Maybe it was just my mood, but it didn't seem worth the hassle.

'That isn't how we do business, Mr Finch. I'm afraid we can't help you.'

I stood to usher them out the door.

They remained seated.

'Walk away and you'll regret it,' the man said calmly. 'You do the right thing by us and we can boost your business. Turn us away and I can guarantee Private will suffer.'

Chapter 5

I SWUNG AROUND. This guy had picked the wrong day to tick me off. 'I don't answer to threats.' I took a step forward. 'Or deal with liars.'

Finch now stood and his wife quickly stepped between us. The guy was volatile and she knew it.

'I'm sorry,' she interjected. 'We're not being truthful. I – we – can't have children so we're looking at a surrogate.'

Suddenly the couple's questions made sense. I relaxed a little.

Finch's bluster evaporated. 'We didn't know if you'd agree to help us if we told you the truth. We have to know if she's likely to extort us for more money, and that we won't be dragged into legal fights down the track.'

This was obviously difficult for them, but there was no point continuing the conversation. Commercial surrogacy was illegal in every Australian state. Carrying a baby out of kindness, known as altruistic surrogacy, *was* permitted but fraught with potential legal complications.

'We didn't mean to threaten you,' she added. 'It's just that there are many of us in the same situation and we could bring you a lot of business. Most of us would pay whatever it took to have our own children.'

'We work closely with law enforcement,' I explained, 'and what you're proposing is illegal. You're obviously planning on paying for this baby. I'm sorry.'

'Mr Gisto.' The woman touched my arm. 'Do you have children?'

The question stopped me cold.

'I've had eight miscarriages and we had a daughter, Caroline . . .'

'Stillborn,' the husband almost whispered.

She held my gaze. 'We've tried everything natural, multiple rounds of IVF. And now my husband's too old at forty-eight to adopt. This isn't a whim. We can give a child a wonderful life.'

It was impossible not to feel for what they had been through, but I was responsible for this business. I certainly couldn't let emotion sway my decision.

She paused. 'Doctors have told us it isn't possible, so we are turning to a surrogate who says she just wants medical costs covered. That's all.'

A stranger becoming pregnant and not wanting anything in return sounded risky.

'We could have gone to somewhere like India or Thailand, but that doesn't seem right.'

Not to mention the practice was outlawed there now too, I thought. We moved back inside the office. 'How did you hear about this woman?'

'Her name's Louise Simpson. She advertised on a surrogacy website. We just want to know if she's genuine.'

A background check could only give her credit rating and criminal history. She would have to approve of them accessing her medical information, and I told them that.

'We understand. But this is our last chance,' Mrs Finch pleaded.

Despite reservations, I agreed to help.

Chapter 6

HE WAS WOKEN by burning in his wrist and forearm, and a deeper, bone-like pain in his right shoulder. He took a gasp and inhaled smoke, as sun peeked through the canopy directly above.

Disorientated, he struggled to sit up. Sweat dripped off him. He cradled his right arm, which provided some relief. The shoulder was out of its socket, down and forward. Then he remembered something had brushed him when he'd reached for the sensor device.

Peeling off the right glove, he saw the curled-up body of a spider. A centimetre long, black with a red patch on its back. A red-back.

The welt on his wrist was unlike anything he'd experienced before. Hospitals had antivenom, but it had to be administered quickly to be effective. That wasn't an option given the nearest hospital was two hours by road. He moved his other limbs and ankles. The shoulder had taken the brunt of the fall. It had to be put back in place. Then he could at least get to safety and take his chances with the bite.

The sound of a distant siren echoed in the valley. The cabin had gone up in flames and the flames must have spread to surrounding bush. The 'cleaners' should be long gone, but the area would be swarming with locals and emergency services volunteers, and the police.

He pulled himself to his feet and took some breaths. It was now or never. With all the strength he could muster, he ran and slammed his shoulder into a tree. Pain exploded through his shoulder and arm as he suppressed a scream. A few seconds later, it eased. The shoulder was in place but he could feel the lymph nodes under the arm were swollen and tender. The poison was spreading.

Using a spare shirt as a sling, he struggled to recall everything he'd ever learnt about red-back spiders. No one had died from their bite in years. But if the toxin didn't kill, it could debilitate and affect nerves for up to a week.

Either way, the odds of making it through today were worse than even he'd imagined.

Chapter 7

WITH THE FINCHES sorted, I could concentrate on more pressing issues. Johnny Ishmah had begun trying the computers and backup systems, starting at reception.

The young investigator was completing a degree in criminal psychology. Brought up in a rough part of the western suburbs, his school mates included the son of a leading underworld figure. Those contacts had proved helpful more than once.

Dust swirled into the entrance as two men manoeuvred a large pane of glass towards the door.

I asked Johnny what he had so far.

'I ran a virus scan on the entire system. Nothing showed up. The cameras didn't record because Collette's computer was shut down.'

The video feed was accessed on her station. One of her tasks was to fast-forward through the footage each morning.

I turned to Collette, who was anxiously picking at bright red fingernails.

'Could you have accidentally shut it down instead of logging off last night?'

'No. I did what I do every night. Log off.'

Whatever happened, the footage didn't exist.

Next to arrive was Darlene Cooper, her usual immaculate ponytail and wrinkle-free shirt and jeans replaced with a baggy top and crinkled pants. Nothing about today seemed routine.

'Sorry, boss. I came as quickly as I could.'

I explained the situation and she told us not to turn anything on until she'd had a chance to update the virus library. Meanwhile, I went to find Mary in her office. She could start on the Finch job.

After filling her in, I suggested she use her phone until online access was restored. Instead, she stood, arms folded across her chest. The former military police officer and kickboxer was formidable at the best of times. The stance emphasised her biceps and was designed to intimidate. 'You can get someone else.'

Her reaction took me completely by surprise. My most experienced investigator and right hand in the business, Mary Clarke pulled more than her weight in the agency.

'Today's not started well. We need to function even more efficiently as a team. None of us gets to pick and choose cases. The others are tied up with the computers –'

She stood, arms still folded, like a bouncer blocking a night-club entrance. 'You don't need to remind me about teamwork.'

That was true. Mary had put herself on the line many times, including for my safety. I closed the door so we could speak in private.

'Is there something going on I need to know about?'

'I don't want to be a part of this. Johnny can do it.'

Darlene interrupted with a knock. 'Thought you'd want to know. I updated the virus library and tracked the source to Collette's computer. Going through the log files, the system shut down at midnight.'

'It was programmed to switch us off in the night?' I asked.

'Could have been in an email attachment or a bogus web link. I'm still running diagnostics, so if you give me an hour, I'll do a full sweep of the backups too.'

I wondered how long it would have taken if Darlene wasn't on the job. And what sort of thrill led people to design viruses which destroyed strangers' computers. Our business relied on confidentiality and with high-profile clients we needed to guarantee information security.

Right now, that was at risk.

'Can you double-check for spyware? We can't afford to have anyone access the systems.'

Darlene looked from Mary to me, obviously sensing the tension. 'On it.'

I thanked Darlene and watched her leave.

Mary's finger was already poking my chest.

'You ever dare question my loyalty again, I'm out.'

She pushed past me and slammed the door.

Chapter 8

MARY'S REACTION LEFT me stunned. She was the calm, measured one of the team.

I followed her into Kent Street where she continued to weave through workers heading to their offices.

I just missed colliding with a man in a suit, eyes down on his phone. 'What's really going on?'

She kept walking. 'I won't be a party to buying and selling babies.'

'What the hell is that supposed to mean? It's one background check, an hour's work, maybe two.'

The pedestrian lights went green and we crossed, passing behind a taxi blocking the intersection. She stopped at the other side.

Frustration mounting, I tried to understand her problem. 'What am I missing here?'

'You let Cal affect your judgement.'

Mary could hit hard, and with precision.

We stood on the kerb in silence as a wave of people swept past, juggling coffees and briefcases.

Mary spoke first. 'I know today is his birthday.'

We were on the corner outside the Queen Victoria Building's Market Street entrance. A homeless man with a cardboard sign sat begging for spare change.

'I'm not seeing your point, Mary.'

'This couple come to you with a sob-story about wanting a child. Like they have a God-given right to breed.'

So that was it. Mary had a problem with surrogacy.

A woman with twins in a double stroller approached. We stepped out of the way, beside a cart that sold snacks and magazines. I ordered two coffees and some fruit.

Mary wasn't finished. 'What happens if the surrogate is carrying twins? These people target poverty-stricken women in South-East Asia. They act like it's mail order, and they have every right to a refund if the result isn't to their liking –'

I'd never seen Mary so worked up about a single issue, and she hadn't even met the Finches to form an opinion of them.

'I get it. And it's tragic when that happens. Sometimes you have to trust your instincts and believe in the good in people. A woman is volunteering to become pregnant, for no profit. Isn't that between her and the Finches?'

'Do you really think a stranger will risk her health and her own family for nothing? This is baby trading no matter how you spin it.'

'OK. You don't agree with what the couple is doing. But if we only accepted clients whose life choices we agreed with, we'd be out of business.'

'Today you let emotion override reason. Once you start doing that, Private will suffer.'

'Mary, this is one background check.'

The vendor handed over the coffees. Mary took a cup, a concession of sorts towards peace.

'I just hope this one doesn't come back to bite us.' She had the final say and headed back to the office.

I gave the other coffee, banana and apple to the homeless man and looked up Eliza Moss's company on my smartphone. She worked just a block away.

I decided to make a detour there before facing any more complications at the office.

Chapter 9

SO FAR, I HADN'T found much on Eric Moss, CEO of Contigo Valley. The name sounded more like an orchard than a development and training organisation. From a quick search, again on my phone, there were no public scandals. Moss had never married.

I headed into the Market Street building, scanned the directory and took the elevator to the thirty-fifth floor. Inside double doors to the left was a glass desk with a twenty-something woman poring over photo proofs.

Behind her was a giant canvas print of female rock climbers, giving those below a hand up.

The young woman looked up.

'I'm here to see Ms Moss.'

'You must be the private detective.' She gave a megawatt smile as she came out from behind the desk. 'Eliza's working in the conference room. At the end there. You can't miss it.'

I moved to where she'd pointed. In the room, two women sat at one end of a long wooden table surrounded by computers and diaries. The one at the end spoke assertively into a phone.

'There is *no way* the budget can reach to ten! Eight thousand or we'll have to cancel.' After a pause, she nodded and gave the thumbs up to her colleague, who smiled. 'Ramone, you are a genius. I'll make sure all our members know how incredible you are.'

I wondered if Ramone would stay in business long if he dropped his prices so easily.

Off the phone, the pair high-fived and paused when they saw me.

I entered the room. 'Craig Gisto. Jack Morgan said we should speak?'

The negotiator tapped the other lightly with a finger. 'Can you give us a few minutes?'

'Of course.' The colleague collected some paperwork and excused herself. 'If you need anything . . .'

'We'll let you know.' Eliza remained sitting and gestured for me to have a seat. There was no hint of despair or anxiety about her father.

'Thank you for coming. Jack speaks highly of you.'

'He mentioned you were concerned about the whereabouts of your father.'

She stroked the face of a diamond-encrusted watch on her left wrist. The only other piece of jewellery was an infinity ring on her right hand.

'He is supposed to have resigned – by email – last Friday and hasn't been seen since. He would never leave Contigo. He turned it from a handful of search-and-rescue volunteers into a multibillion-dollar organisation with an international reputation.'

I studied her face as she spoke. Blonde, shoulder-length hair with a cowlick on one side of her fringe, pale green eyes, enough make-up to look natural but highlight her fine features.

The woman from the front desk interrupted us with a document in hand. 'I'm sorry, but the florist wants to know – Singapore orchids dyed blue or violet?'

Eliza Moss waved her in.

'Blue.' Eliza initialled the page and clicked off her pen. 'We recruit for over a thousand companies, working to increase women's representation at executive and board levels.'

'Dyed orchids?' I asked.

'We're holding a major charity fundraiser at the Park Hyatt tonight and I need to make sure it's a success. A lot of people are taking note of how we do.'

Being the boss meant travelling a fine line between delegating and micromanaging. I wondered if she was an overly protective daughter or justified in raising the alarm.

'Is it possible your father simply went away for a few days? Wanted to have some time out after making a rash decision? Or maybe spend time in a new relationship?'

The list of possibilities was endless, especially with middle-aged men who had resources at their disposal.

'There's no woman.' She was adamant. 'He'd have told me. His work is everything. He even sleeps at the company base, near the Blue Mountains.'

I sat forward. 'Does he have any medical history or a condition that worries you if he goes without treatment? Physical or –'

'Why does everyone assume someone who commits themselves to work is either lonely, depressed or suicidal?'

I suspected she was referring to comments made about her. 'You've already flagged this as aberrant behaviour, for him. We need to know his routine before pinpointing when and what changed.'

'And how to find him. I'm sorry. This is just . . . He's very private. We both are.'

In my business, private was a euphemism for keeping secrets. Eliza obviously idolised her father. If I started digging . . .

'I need to explain something before we start. In the course of an investigation, we may discover information you didn't expect. It could change your impression of him and possibly alter your relationship.'

She thought for a moment and came back to the watch.

'He knows I'd worry, so do what you have to. Keep me completely informed. I'll pay whatever it takes. Just find him.'

Chapter 10

'I'LL NEED MORE than we have so far,' I said as there were further interruptions by staff. I wanted her complete focus. 'Is there anywhere quieter we could speak? To clarify personal details.'

'Here suits me better,' she said, matter of factly. 'I can handle any last-minute issues. Like I said, tonight's important.'

I didn't have a choice. Over the next half-hour, punctuated with queries about song lists and raffle items, I gained a picture of Eric Moss. An only child, focused and driven by the desire to excel in his field.

I was surprised to learn that Contigo Valley was a non-profit organisation. And tax exempt. There weren't many with turn-overs in excess of hundreds of millions. Greenpeace was the only one that came to mind.

Funded by donations, loans and occasional government grants, Contigo raised revenue by developing and selling new trauma devices, safety equipment and retrieval vehicles. They were awarded large supply contracts both in Australia and overseas.

'Bushfires, tsunamis, floods, landslides, man-made disas-ters. My father increased survival rates for victims and emergency service workers. A device for giving life-saving fluids to injured soldiers has changed protocols in emergency departments and the combat field. Contigo even trains soldiers from China and the USA.'

I could see why Jack Morgan, a former US marine, had invested in the company. It was a cause close to his heart. Still, I needed more about Eric Moss the man.

According to Eliza he was fit aside from a few extra kilos, didn't smoke or drink and only reluctantly attended work functions. He avoided the media, leaving that to the chairman of Contigo's board, Sir Lang Gillies. It sounded as if Moss enjoyed his own company more than other people's. At fifty-eight, he was a workaholic.

'Any conflicts with colleagues or subordinates?'

'Only with Lang Gillies. Dad's been feeding his ego for decades. The old man spends his life on company junkets, in the social pages, collecting awards for work Dad did.'

'Why keep someone like Gillies on?'

'He has influential friends and Dad prefers life out of the spotlight.'

That made sense. Sir Lang and his third wife were regulars on Sydney's social circuit. Lang was politically connected, having made his money as a property developer in the most corrupt period in the state government's history.

I took notes. 'So Gillies received the resignation email on Friday?' Moss's departure should have been big news in the business community.

Eliza's eyes shone with a new intensity.

'The old man is lying. Lang told me Dad felt like a change. And how he'd wished Dad well.'

'You don't think that's what happened?'

'No way. Dad would never have left, let alone like that. Besides, Lang knows that without Dad the organisation would fail. And . . .' she poked the table with her index finger, 'no one else has seen the resignation email.'

I agreed that Gillies's disinterest in Moss's plans was questionable.

The receptionist interrupted again, this time for a call.

Eliza held out her hand for the phone and covered the mouthpiece.

'I've put together a list of places Dad goes, where and when he was born, where he lived, anything that might help.'

As she took the call, I flicked through the two-page document. It made Moss sound like a saint.

'No trappings of wealth despite the potential to command millions in salary.' I read further. 'Drives an eight-year-old Toyota four-wheel drive.'

Eliza put the phone on the table with a thump. 'Dad has never gone more than a few hours without calling back. No matter where he is. If he's on a training exercise, he has a satellite phone with him.' She bent lower to lock eyes with me. 'Something's really wrong.'

Clomping heels rapidly approached. Another young woman tapped a clipboard and Eliza nodded.

'I'd appreciate if you keep me informed, regularly. Is that all?'

I was taken aback by the curt end to our conversation. She'd just raised the issue of foul play involving her father then closed off any chance of further discussion. As I stood and pushed my chair back in, she remained seated. A queen holding court with minions at her disposal.

'Thank you, Mr Gisto,' she said, shaking my hand.

I was unceremoniously dismissed.

Chapter 11

BACK AT THE office, Darlene had managed to restore all computer function. The virus had been isolated to the reception computer, which was lucky in the grand scheme. The new glass was fitted and Collette had cleaned the foyer. It was as if the morning's distractions had never happened.

I found Johnny in his office. The check on Louise Simpson was straightforward. An insurance company was stalling on compensation for an industrial accident that killed her husband, Vincent, eight months ago. She had two kids and lived modestly in Killara, in a home with a mortgage currently paid by her late husband's parents. She was a cleanskin, without even a parking ticket to her name.

My one concern was the group where Louise Simpson advertised.

'What about the surrogacy site the Finches found her on?'

Johnny flicked through some papers. 'It has a firewall up, so I couldn't find out who runs it. If you want me to, I can, but it'll take more time.'

'There must be legitimate organisations you can run it by.'

Johnny was already ahead. 'I contacted the two best known

surrogacy groups, whose reps work with state governments on clarifying the laws on overseas surrogacy that at the moment differ in every state. They both vouched for the content and advice on the site.' He pulled it up on his 24-inch screen.

'Apparently it's the only one that offers to connect people with altruistic surrogates in this country. It also connects couples to agencies overseas that deal in commercial pregnancies and navigate visas, birth certificates, documentation of legal parents, and other bureaucratic nightmares. From what I can see, the hopeful parents are pretty vulnerable every step in the process.'

I wondered if the Finches had been burnt overseas, which was why they were turning to a local surrogate. Either way, it didn't matter. Johnny could send through the information he'd collected and invoice the Finches. We need have nothing more to do with them or their life choices.

I was relieved. At least something today had been straight-forward. I needed Mary on the Moss case right away. We'd start at Contigo's city office in Martin Place. If Lang Gillies had lied about the resignation, Eric Moss's disappearance had just become our top priority.

Chapter 12

THE WALK TO Martin Place was quick and silent. On our way to the MLC Centre, Mary stopped short of the revolving door and looked back at a memorial to the victims of the 2014 siege.

She had been directly across at the Channel Seven studios interviewing a client, an hour before the gunman entered the café.

'You couldn't have changed the outcome,' I said, 'if that's what you're thinking.'

She shrugged and pushed through the door.

Contigo Valley's central office was on the sixty-fourth floor of prime Sydney real estate. Prominent legal chambers, international finance corporations, a Russian bank and the US Consulate all shared space in the building. It was a stone's throw from State Parliament as well.

We were greeted at reception by Eric Moss's personal assistant. In his mid-twenties, Oliver Driscoll was around 170 centimetres with hair shorter at the sides than on top and dark-rimmed glasses. He quickly led us to an outer office with an interconnecting door.

'This is where we work.' He opened double doors into a larger room. A white shag-pile rug filled some of the void between a nondescript desk and sofa. The desk was conspicuously clear apart from a closed A4 portfolio diary in its centre.

'How long have you worked with Mr Moss?' I asked.

'Two years.' He seemed focused on the piece of rug. 'I can't believe he just walked out. Without telling me.'

'Have you cleared out his things or is this how Mr Moss likes to keep it?'

'Eric's fastidious. He writes everything in the diary. Calls, meetings, functions. I don't get why he'd ever leave it behind.'

Mary wandered around the room. 'Does he have a problem with computers or smartphone calendars?'

'He's just old-school and likes to have everything written down.'

Mary wondered, 'Doesn't that reduce efficiency?'

'In the afternoons I fill in his upcoming appointments. If he's at the base, I phone him and he writes it all down. He always has it with him.'

I moved around to the desk. 'May I?'

'Sure.'

I opened the diary. It had functions organised for the next six months. Fundraisers, training courses, and a list of everyone he called. From the volume of calls listed each day, Moss seemed averse to emails as well, yet that was how he'd chosen to resign.

The assistant hovered. 'If Eliza is asking you to help, she must be worried too.'

'Too?' I looked across at Driscoll.

'Something stinks. Eric would never walk away. This was his life, and we were like family. He'd work from six in the morning until midnight. Even slept on the fold-out couch when he was in town.' Driscoll moved to the other door and opened it. 'This is his bathroom.'

A toothbrush and razor were still in place in the shower recess.

Mary quietly checked out the bookshelf then tried to open a credenza beneath the desk. It was locked.

'Do you have a key?' she asked.

'No. Eric is the only one with that. Why would he keep an office key and leave his personal belongings? None of this makes sense.' Driscoll sat on the sofa, face in his hands. I had to wonder about how close the assistant was to his boss.

'Did Eric have problems or disagreements with any of the staff?'

Driscoll shook his head. 'He gets on with everyone, knows everyone's names. Even kept paying one woman who had cancer and ran out of sick leave.'

He smoothed his skinny trousers. 'Eric believes you can tell a man's character by the way he treats people who can't further your career.'

It sounded as if Moss and his daughter shared philosophies.

I sat beside him.

'How are the staff taking the news?'

'Donors are panicking, groups are cancelling training camps . . . It's exactly what Eric wouldn't want to happen. And none of us wants to work for –'

'Driscoll!' a voice snapped.

The assistant sat to attention. 'Quick, hide Eric's diary,' he whispered.

Mary dropped it to the floor and pushed it under the desk with her feet.

Chapter 13

I RECOGNISED THE distinctive cravat and striped jacket from the social pages. Sir Lang Gillies, chairman of Contigo's board.

'You should have told me Eliza sent visitors.' He made no attempt to hide his disdain.

'Craig Gisto, Private Sydney, and this is Mary –'

'I know who you are and you have been misled.' He turned and limped on what looked like a bad hip. Mary and I followed with the assistant close behind.

'Mr Moss's daughter has asked us to find her father. If you know where he might be –'

'The Bahamas, Noumea? Have you tried Tasmania, the Midlands?' He waved arthritic fingers in the air. 'He always talked about going there for a holiday.'

I stepped into line with him, past a couple of offices with staff answering phones.

I decided to be non-combative in my approach, despite the obvious animosity towards us. 'We understand the timing and manner of his resignation was surprising.'

'How so? The man was free to leave without notice. He's no doubt taken up a more lucrative offer. And before you ask, it wasn't my place to question him. I didn't care to know.'

'How many years was he with Contigo?'

'I've been on the board for twenty-seven years. So a couple more than that. We built this organisation into what it is today . . .'

If that was the case, it was unusual; no golden handshake, no farewell, no drinks. Not even a media release.

'. . . into a world-class research and development centre.'

We moved into an office. Mahogany bookshelves housed rows of photos, reaffirming Sir Lang's importance to the world. Framed images of him with prime ministers, celebrities and a US president.

Gillies made sure we noticed. 'Impressive,' I said for his benefit as he plonked himself into a high-back leather chair behind a desk the Queen would have been proud to own. The assistant and Mary lingered in the doorway.

'Is there any other reason you can think of that might have prompted Eric Moss to change jobs so suddenly? I mean, a quarter of a century with no changes, then,' I snapped my fingers, 'he's gone in a flash. Without telling the people he's closest to.'

Gillies opened the financial newspaper on his desk and looked up, as if bored by our presence.

'I cannot discuss Moss's work with you due to commercial in confidence.' He reached into a drawer and pulled out some glossy brochures. 'These should tell you all you need to know about what we do. Now, I have an organisation to run. Oliver will show you out.'

I took the promotional material and entered the corridor.

'And, Oliver, bring me Eric's diary. I'll be personally handling all his appointments and calls.'

'I'll have to search for it, Sir Lang.' The assistant seemed defeated. 'Is there anything else?'

'There'll be significant restructuring in this office. Let the staff know that anyone breaching confidentiality by speaking to these people will be the first to go.'

Gillies really ticked me off. He was beyond arrogant. Anyone with a heart would want to make sure Eliza's concerns were allayed.

Unless he had something to hide.

Chapter 14

I WASN'T ABOUT to be railroaded by Lang Gillies. I popped my head inside his door and asked if he objected to my using the bathroom on the way out. He grunted, but could hardly refuse.

Mary seized the opportunity to distract the old man by pointing to a photo of him in military uniform proudly displayed on his desk. I stepped back into the corridor and left her standing at ease by the picture, hands clasped behind her back.

'Where did you serve, sir?'

The old soldier couldn't resist the urge to brag. And Mary could keep him talking with her knowledge and experiences in the military. It bought me a few minutes with Oliver.

'If Eric's in some sort of trouble, maybe I can help,' he volunteered.

Thankfully, Gillies's threat hadn't intimidated the man who worked closest with Moss.

'Any idea what sort of trouble Eric could be in?'

Oliver scratched his neck. 'The guy's a monk. Doesn't drink, smoke, gamble, take drugs or date. It's offensive the way

Gillies's acting like he didn't ever exist. He's *got* to know where Eric went.'

This could be the only opportunity I had to ask. 'Were you two having an intimate relationship?'

The assistant smirked. 'You think Eric and I were an item? God no, he's way too serious for me. Besides, he was married to this place. From what I can tell, he wasn't interested in either sex. It was like he was asexual.'

I asked Driscoll if he could tell me who looked after the accounts.

He hurried back to his office and wrote down the name of the chief financial officer who Moss dealt with. 'She's fond of Eric and due to retire in a few months. She won't have much to lose by talking to you.'

He collected Moss's diary. The information was only in hard copy, nothing electronic. Once Gillies got it, any leads would be kept from us.

'Any chance I can get a quick look before you hand that over?'

'Better than that.' He glanced around to ensure no one was in earshot. 'I'll photocopy it first.' He held the diary to his chest.

I couldn't walk out with papers now and it was unlikely I'd ever be allowed back in.

'Can you courier the copies to our office?'

'I can't see me getting away until late. Maybe I can drop them off before I check in with Eliza.'

'How well do you know Miss Moss?' I asked.

'Sometimes when we were working late, Eliza would bring dinner and eat with us. They're both really good people.'

We left the office with the diary still in Oliver's hands.

As he closed the door behind us the assistant said, 'Lang Gillies may come across as a buffoon but he has a lot of powerful friends. You'd never want to cross the vindictive SOB.'

Chapter 15

FROM THE FOYER, I called the financial officer's number.

Renee Campbell listened as I introduced myself and explained that there were concerns about Eric Moss's whereabouts.

Oliver Driscoll, however, had beaten me to it.

She agreed to meet us in Martin Place in five minutes and suggested a café that made great flat whites.

As the coffees arrived, a small woman in her late sixties approached. She had short, wispy grey hair and wore a pink crocheted vest over a navy skivvy and skirt.

She took a seat and thanked us for meeting her.

'I can't believe he's gone.'

'It sounds like his leaving shocked almost everyone. Do you have any idea where he went?'

She stared at the coffee. 'No. I couldn't believe it when I heard he'd resigned. We were supposed to meet that afternoon.'

'Was there a problem with accounts?'

She wrapped both hands around the cup and took a sip before answering.

'Not really. I couldn't locate the receipts for a table at a charity ball. I happened to mention it to Eric in passing. He said he had them in his office and told me to come at four o'clock the next day. He's so lovely; he put half an hour aside so we could catch up over a cuppa.'

Mary glanced at me.

'How much were the tickets for?'

'$10,000. It's like petty cash. Last year we turned over four hundred and seventy million dollars from donations and revenue.'

I downed my drink and asked if Moss had much to do with the finances.

'Not routinely. Although he was adamant he handle some of the accounts himself, which he kept locked in a safe in his office.'

'Didn't that seem odd to you? No checks and balances?'

'Not for us. Some of Contigo's contracts deal with defence departments and international governments. They involve issues of national security. Oh, and Eric kept watch over Sir Lang's expenses. The old man takes his wife on every imaginable junket, first class all the way, claiming he's promoting the organisation around the world.'

Donors may not be thrilled about all the first-class travel in a non-profit organisation. I asked if Moss ever confronted Gillies about the spending.

'No, but he kept his own record. It was easier to run the place efficiently without Sir Lang around to interfere. Gillies is a figurehead but he does bring donations in through his rich cronies.'

I wanted to know about Moss's salary package and what sort of payout he would receive after that many years of service.

It was all conjecture at this stage but I had to consider the common reasons for sudden resignation. If he took a better offer, that salary could narrow the companies who could afford him.

'Could Eric have been headhunted by another company?'

Renee Campbell scoffed. 'You obviously don't know the man. Money means little to him. He costs Contigo about $40,000 a year and doesn't even receive it.'

'In expenses?'

'No,' the older woman chortled. 'That was supposed to be his salary. He has every cent of it put into a trust for Eliza. She'll have access to it on her fortieth birthday, or her father's death. Whichever comes first.'

It sounded like an odd arrangement. I was curious. 'How much is in it now?'

'Due to investments, it's around one and a half million, I believe.'

I had to wonder about Eliza now. Family members had killed for a lot less. The devoted daughter could have been an act. If Moss had been killed, and I could prove it, she was suddenly a lot wealthier.

Chapter 16

BACK AT THE office, Mary went over the Contigo brochures.

It was all we had until we got hold of the diary photocopies. The locked cabinet in Moss's office could answer a lot of questions. That was, if Moss or Gillies hadn't emptied it first.

As far as I was concerned, the circumstances of Moss leaving were suspicious. Lang Gillies was determined to make sure our access to all of Contigo's records was blocked. There had to be something significant in the organisation's books. Why else would Moss disappear after a minor discrepancy was discovered? Were the two events even related?

I decided to look into Contigo's contracts. The website looked like it promoted an exclusive resort. Situated on thirty-five hectares just west of the Blue Mountains, it could have been a stunning rural retreat. There was little practical information apart from mention of training facilities for rescue workers, emergency retrieval operations and disaster simulations.

I ran a check on Lang Gillies first. Gut instinct said he was hiding something. On top of that, he was the last person known to have seen Eric Moss.

Gillies held dual UK and Australian citizenships and was knighted two years earlier for a life of service to the community. Prior to that, he used the title 'Dr' after being awarded an honorary doctorate in humanities from the University of Wollongong. The son of a High Court judge, he joined the air force and flew cargo planes. Interestingly, there was no record of him serving in Vietnam, despite his *Who's Who* entry citing him as a pilot during the war.

My guess was that his father's connections had kept him far away from conflict zones. Marrying the daughter of the state's longest serving governor wouldn't have hurt either.

From what I could gather, Lang started a cargo business in the 1970s then found his way on to the boards of charitable organisations. Ones his father-in-law happened to be patron of. He joined Contigo's board twenty-seven years ago and had benefited ever since.

And Gillies had not only picked up a knighthood but also collected an honorary doctorate on the back of Moss's work.

From what Oliver Driscoll had said, Moss was private and married to his job and wanted little remuneration or acknowledgement. The men couldn't have been more different.

I wondered how Gillies's expense account sat with someone like Moss. The CEO had to be independently wealthy to sacrifice a salary for all those years. More than that, he had to be very committed to the work they did there. I couldn't help suspect he'd had a falling-out with Gillies. The old man certainly wasn't mourning Contigo's sudden loss.

And then there were the secret contracts and accounts in Moss's safe. What could be so confidential that no one else in the organisation was permitted to know about it?

Chapter 17

I CALLED JACK Morgan and left a message for him to ring me, then I went to check on the rest of the team. Darlene was extracting DNA from a series of forensic rape kits for the police. It was a service I wanted Private to supply for free as the police laboratories were often backlogged for more than six months at a time.

Johnny was involved with the case of a trade union official accused of using work funds for brothel visits. A few of the credit card receipts resembled the official's. Others were nothing like it. He was scanning the signatures of all the union executives and superimposing handwriting to identify potential suspects.

I stopped in on Mary who had the Contigo brochures open across her desk.

'Sir Lang Gillies made my flesh crawl,' she said. 'No wonder he's so close to the powerbrokers in both political parties.'

I turned around a chair and straddled it. 'What have you got?'

'I've been looking into his family-owned companies. He and his wife are silent partners in a series of shops in Circular Quay with Alby Slade.'

That made Gillies a lot more powerful than I'd imagined. Slade was one of the 'silent puppeteers' behind a number of politicians. Rumour had it he was responsible for deposing two state premiers who dared question the legality of his business dealings.

'Slade's been up before the Integrity Commission, the Independent Commission against Corruption, he's alleged to have threatened investigative journalists among others.' Mary added, 'And Gillies is in business with him.'

'Maybe Moss thought the Slade business would tarnish Contigo.'

Mary sat back, hands clasped behind her head. 'The work Moss did was topnotch.' She swung a notepad around. 'These are some of the things his team has produced.'

One was a device that injected fluids directly into bone.

'This lifesaving device can be used by soldiers in the field. It goes into the shoulder or shin, and can deliver litres of fluids, like plasma, in minutes. They've been snapped up by armies from just about every nation. Victorian paramedics and hospitals are trialling them next month.'

Sales like that were lucrative. 'Does Contigo own the patent?'

'Yep. Its returns have already paid off bank loans used to develop it.'

Moss's work wasn't limited to small items. His team modified the capacity of aerial-firefighting helicopters, credited with saving thousands of houses in bushfires over the last decade.

'Flame-retardant clothing, emergency retrieval training. They even came up with a new foam formula for the helicopters to dump on chemical fires.'

Mary was justifiably impressed.

'Any idea what those secret contracts were about?'

She took back her notes. 'Contigo was contracted to work with the government on something highly secret. A buddy in Defence said it was so secret, rumours were circulating about everything from digestible drones to transformer tanks. He seemed to think it involved counterterrorism.'

'How much was the contract worth?'

'My contact thinks it had to be over eighty million.'

I blew out a whistle. 'That's a lot of money to keep track of in a paper ledger.'

'Another source, at the fraud squad, says they've been asked to investigate a number of not-for-profit organisations.'

'Contigo Valley's on their list?'

'Yep, but they're being pressured to hold off on that one. Someone in the government doesn't want them investigated. They're tendering for a number of federal defence contracts. Any hint of scandal will affect Contigo's chances.'

'And boost any rival's.' I stood up and stretched my back. 'Do you know how they got on the fraud squad's radar?'

'You'll love this. An anonymous caller phoned their office.'

We needed to find out who had reason to want Moss out of the picture. With government subterfuge, this case just got a lot more complicated.

Chapter 18

I STOOD AND turned the chair back around. Mary cleared her throat.

'Craig, about this morning –'

I raised a hand. 'You don't have to –'

'No, I was way out of line.'

She got no further as Collette burst in, red-faced. 'You two need to see this!'

We moved quickly into the conference room and Collette turned on the curved screen.

A news bulletin showed crime-scene tape around a suburban home. A woman had been brutally murdered in Killara.

A banner across the bottom read Fiddens Wharf Road. 'It's the same street as Louise Simpson,' Collette said.

The potential surrogate for the Finches. I noticed Mary's body tense.

Johnny and Darlene joined us as an image of a blue Toyota Corolla in a carport appeared. Its number plate was pixellated.

My heart began to pound as I asked Johnny what car Louise Simpson drove.

Johnny's eyes fixed on the screen. 'That exact make and model.'

Chapter 19

THE YOUNG REPORTER pressed her earpiece and relayed what she knew. 'We understand that at approximately four-twenty this afternoon, a woman's body was found inside the home by an elderly neighbour. This gentleman noticed the front door was wide open. That's when he made the shocking discovery.'

The network's 'serious' news anchor, Bruce Davitt, pushed for details. 'Has the man been able to help police piece together what happened?'

'Bruce, ambulance officers are on the scene and we understand they're treating the neighbour for shock. Police are standing by to interview him.'

'Do we know anything about the victim or how she died?'

'As yet, the victim's name hasn't been released but I can tell you that homicide detectives have arrived.'

On her laptop, Darlene had pulled up the Google street images of Louise's address. My heart sank. The reporter was across and down the road, but the house looked similar to the one on Darlene's screen.

Bruce Davitt announced that residents in the suburb

of Killara were shocked at the gruesome discovery. As we watched people walking dogs recoil with predictable horror at the mention of murder in their neighbourhood, I phoned Deputy Commissioner Brett Thorogood.

His phone went straight to voicemail. I asked him to ring me urgently about the Killara homicide victim. Johnny, meanwhile, tried to reach the Finches. His olive skin blanched when he heard a prerecorded announcement. The number was not connected.

'I emailed them a couple of hours ago with the information,' he said. 'It had the Killara address in the report.' He tried emailing again. This time his message bounced straight back.

My phone rang. It was Brett Thorogood.

He immediately confirmed the dead woman's name.

Louise Grace Simpson.

Chapter 20

TWENTY MINUTES LATER, Darlene and I were at the scene. Thanks to Private's arrangement with the police to share resources, we were allowed in.

Darlene donned plastic overalls and headed in first with her collection kit. I assessed the scene from the outside. The front yard contained potted native plants. A wooden carport housed the Corolla. Around the side of the house, a bathroom window was slightly ajar. The soil was damp but there were no footprints or signs of entry.

The backyard was larger, with a glassed-in verandah. A magnetic board on an easel stood beside a small plastic table and chairs.

My throat tightened. Two innocent children were now orphans. And my decision this morning may have got their mother killed.

Mary had been right. We should screen clients before working for them.

Through a line of pines, I could make out a golf club's fairway. Squeezing through gaps in the trees, I reached the back fence. On the right-hand corner, on a hinged gate, were dark smears. Blood.

The killer had escaped over the back fence. Someone on the golf course could have seen him. I called Johnny to find out who could have been playing those holes in the hours before the body was found.

I photographed the area with my phone. Darlene should swab here when she'd finished. With crime scene officers still inside the house, I told the constable standing guard by the car not to let anyone traipse through the yard. All we needed was for inexperienced officers to tread all over what could be the only evidence to help find the killer.

I pulled shoe covers on and entered through the front door. The lock was intact, with no signs of forced entry. In the corridor a hole had been knocked through the plasterboard wall with blood spatters on the floor. Dark red smears marked the way to the lounge room. It looked like the victim had been hit or shoved into the wall and had bled on to the floor, then been dragged further inside.

The first room on the right contained a neatly made double bed with a floral bedspread. A pine tallboy held silver-framed family photos. Above the bed hung a large wedding photo of the couple gazing into each other's eyes at the beach. The wardrobe doors were open. Female clothes filled only half the space.

The horror had unfolded in the kitchen. The body was slumped forward in a chair. Long brown hair was matted with blood.

The stench in the room was one I'd inhaled too many times. Body odour almost masked the metallic aroma of blood. I wished we could bottle it. Every individual left a unique and identifiable scent at a scene.

Dr Rex King greeted me. I was grateful that a pathologist friendly to us was in attendance. Rex had no problem sharing the work and respected Darlene's abilities. There would be no pissing contest between organisations here.

'Cause of death looks like a knife wound to the lower abdomen,' he said. 'She took a beating first.'

A female detective stood, hands on hips, observing. She introduced herself as Detective Constable Kristen Massey.

I needed to know. 'Where are the kids?'

'How'd you know she had any?' Detective Massey asked.

'She had a four-year-old girl and a three-year-old boy. Husband died in a work accident about six months ago.'

'Then, Mr Gisto, you know almost as much as us. They're still in day care. If we can't locate a relative, they'll spend tonight in the care of the state.'

Darlene looked up at me. 'No signs of a break-in. She either knew the killer or unsuspectingly opened the door.'

The detective said, 'So far, there's no sign of robbery. Her purse and phone are still on the lounge.'

A microwave steriliser with upturned baby bottles sat on the bench. It seemed odd to me she would be sterilising bottles for a toddler and preschooler.

Rex King stepped back. 'I suspect she was systematically beaten before being stabbed – once. I'll need to check on the autopsy table but the blade appears to have passed downward through the lower abdomen.'

Darlene and the forensic technician took more photos of the wound, as I confirmed, 'No signs of sexual assault, then?'

Rex nodded. 'From the position and angle of the blade entry,' he examined the stab wound more closely, 'it's likely our victim suffered a perforated uterus.'

The words hit like a mallet to my chest.

Chapter 21

'WHAT THE HELL do you think *you're* doing?'

I turned to face Local Area Command Detective Mark Talbot. My cousin and I had a torturous history but I thought we'd made peace last year.

'Dr King, if these people are disturbing the scene, I'll –'

'The opposite. They're proving invaluable. Darlene's helping and we'll get faster turnaround if she can put the samples through Private's lab.'

Detective Massey added, 'Mr Gisto knows the background.'

My cousin surveyed the scene and I caught a glimpse of repulsion on his face at the state of the body.

The crime scene technician was now photographing the kitchen. The small space was becoming more crowded by the minute.

Mark bent down to view the body. 'She's wearing a wedding ring on her left hand. I was told she was a single mother.'

'Widow,' I added. 'Kids are in day care apparently.'

Mark glanced around the room. 'You work all that out gawking at a body?'

He was in one of his moods. Even the other detective

seemed wary of him. He turned his attention to Rex King.

'Doc, what do you know so far?'

Rex nudged half-glasses further up his nose with the back of his wrist.

'She sustained a head injury to the frontal region and nose, and there is bruising around her neck. It looks like she was grabbed and slammed into something solid.'

'Like a wall.' I pointed to the hole in the hallway.

'And then she was dragged in here,' Mark commented.

'Tied to a chair and beaten,' Rex explained. 'I can't say whether she was conscious or not, but she was alive when the knife penetrated her lower abdomen. Lividity and body temperature put time of death between one and three hours ago.'

Mark checked his watch. 'That makes death somewhere between one-thirty and three-thirty.' He turned to face me and sighed. 'Why are you here?'

With an index finger theatrically tapping his chin, he delivered his best. 'Oh no, don't tell me. She's one of your conquests.'

Anger surged through my veins. I wanted to ram the smirk on his face right to the back of his head.

Darlene was quickly between us. 'For God's sake. Are you still going on about Becky marrying Craig? This is about *Louise Simpson*, not you.'

Mark stood intimidatingly close to Darlene. 'I can get you kicked out of here in a flash,' he snapped. 'This is between Craig and me.'

I had no idea what had inflamed him again. 'What's your problem? A woman has been murdered and you are attacking *me* over old history.'

'Are you going to tell me how you knew the victim?'

I took a slow breath and explained about Gus and Jennifer Finch. I thought I could see a faint smile appear on Mark's lips, then just as quickly disappear.

'I see.' Mark rocked on his heels. 'You provided two strangers with intimate details of our victim – for payment, of course – hours before she was found brutally murdered. And now you can't tell us where to locate these people.' He moved even closer. 'Hope you get good job satisfaction.'

I lunged at him and Darlene was on her feet again, the other detective blocking us. Mark raised his hands in the air as if surrendering.

'He's not worth it, Craig. He wants you to hit him. Right here, in front of witnesses,' Darlene warned.

I swallowed back the rising bile. Darlene was right. Mark would love nothing more than to report I'd started a fight at a crime scene so we'd never be allowed on one again. Finding Louise's killer had to be our priority.

Rex spoke calmly. 'Detective, a knife is missing from the set.'

A magnetic strip attached to tiles on the wall above the stove contained a series of knives increasing in size. There was a space between the first and third.

That meant the killer may not have planned to murder Louise. Maybe she refused to be their surrogate and things turned sour.

'Right, that place of yours is filmed 24/7. I want the video footage of the couple you saw this morning.'

I sighed. This was going to sound like we had no intention of cooperating.

'The computers went down overnight and we have no vision from midnight until after the couple had gone.'

Mark nodded. 'That's the way you're playing this?'

'Look, we came here to help with the investigation.'

'Or to cover your butt.' He stepped menacingly close. 'You better get a good lawyer, cuz. You're facing charges. Conspiracy to commit murder.'

Chapter 22

A WOMAN'S SCREAM stopped everyone. It was primal, guttural.

Mark and Kristen Massey headed for the open front door. I stayed close behind.

The female detective stopped the woman, who was in her late twenties. 'Ma'am, this is a crime scene. I'm afraid you'll have to –'

'My baby! Where's my baby?'

Mark flicked me a look as if I might know what she was talking about. I remembered the microwave steriliser and my heart drilled.

A young constable was trying to restrain the woman. 'Ma'am, you can't be here.'

She buckled to her knees. 'Zoe needs me. She's just a baby.'

'Wait!' I pushed through as the woman continued shouting for someone to listen to her.

I knelt down with her. 'Was Louise minding your child?'

The woman dug her fingers into my arms. 'Zoe, she's eight weeks old.' Her voice became higher pitched. 'Why won't anyone let me see her?' She locked eyes with mine. 'I just need to get my baby.'

'Something's happened to Louise.' I spoke calmly, and slowly released her grip. 'We didn't know she had Zoe with her.'

Kristen Massey put her arms around the mother while Mark and I raced back inside.

We checked cupboards, drawers, a toy trunk, even the washing machine in case Louise had hidden the child to protect her. The search proved futile.

The baby was gone.

Chapter 23

MARK AND I MOVED outside, now united in our task. The mother was sitting on the brick wall, shaking. She still had the wide-eyed look of hope when we returned.

Her name was Courtney Ruffalo, Detective Constable Massey explained. Louise had been babysitting once a week for three weeks. 'To give her a break. Her husband's a fly-in, fly-out miner in Queensland. He isn't due back until Friday night.'

Courtney nodded, holding back tears. 'Is my baby all right?'

Mark said, 'Is there anyone else who might have picked her up for you?'

There was no proof Zoe had been in the house when the murder took place. Then again, anyone who routinely collected the child would have known to take the steriliser and bottles too.

'Geoff's away. I have a sister. She works at Westmead Hospital and doesn't finish until after three.'

That was at least forty minutes away by car.

We had to consider the possibility that Louise had been killed in order to abduct Zoe.

It could have been unrelated to the Finches' visit. But I had to face reality. The Finches may have killed Louise for the baby.

Mark pulled me aside. 'We'll put out a state-wide alert for the missing child. I'll let the powers know to prepare a media release. We'll need a photo and description of what the child was wearing.'

Courtney Ruffalo had a photo on her phone, taken that morning. Zoe had on a pink cotton jumpsuit with a yellow-and-white flower embroidered on the chest.

Detective Constable Massey spoke quietly to me as I passed her the phone with the baby's image.

'Mark was out of line but he's damn good at his job. He's . . .' She glanced around to make sure no one else heard. 'Just going through a rough time. I'm trying to cut him some slack.'

Today was no joy ride for any of us. Even so, nothing matched what Louise Simpson had been subjected to. 'Are you making excuses for him?'

'No. But he just found out the woman he was seeing was two-timing him. They were about to move in together.'

At least that explained the change in my cousin's attitude. He'd never taken rejection or betrayal well. Seeing me now was like ripping the scab off a deep and painful wound.

'Priority for all of us is finding the child and Louise's killer,' I stressed.

'Let's hope Zoe's still alive,' she added, out of the mother's earshot.

We needed to get a break quickly. The more time that passed, the less chance we had of finding baby Zoe – alive or dead.

Chapter 24

I RANG TO let Mary and Johnny know about the missing baby.

Right now they needed to utilise every possible resource, anything that could give us a lead on the Finches, or the Ruffalo family.

Meanwhile, Darlene began photographing and swabbing the back fence.

Mark and I jumped to the neighbour's side and tried to follow the trail. From what we could tell, the killer had Louise's blood on his torso. In a hole, stuffed beneath some rocks, was a blood-stained grey hoodie. Generic Target brand. One of thousands sold around the country.

We followed the trampled grass until it stopped a few houses down. On the other side of the fence was a red smear. The killer had climbed over the fence here, somehow carrying the baby.

'I'll get the uniforms to canvass the street,' Mark said, frustrated the trail was lost.

I rang Darlene and told her about the hoodie and the extra fence marks. She'd get on to them as soon as she'd finished in the Simpson yard.

An elderly woman peered through the back screen door.

'Excuse me, ma'am,' Mark was in full professional mode, ID in hand, 'can we have a word with you?'

The slippered woman shuffled down the back path and stopped at a gate that opened onto the course.

Mark explained there'd been an incident a few houses down and asked if she'd seen anyone in her yard or noticed any damage to windows or doors.

She gripped the top of her blouse and looked back at the house, explaining she'd been to bingo at the local club and only been home half an hour. Everything was as she left it.

'My children complain about me living so close to the golf course but this has been my home for over forty years.'

Cutting short her conversation, Mark gave her his card and asked her to call him if she remembered seeing anyone or anything out of place.

She toddled back to the house, muttering something about what the world was coming to. We entered through the gate and examined the yard. On the concrete drive was a dark crescent-shaped mark. It could have been blood from the killer's shoe.

Mark ordered one of the officers to cordon off the yard.

'This could be how our killer escaped,' he said. 'We need to test the stain for blood.'

We walked along the street to the Simpson house. Crowds had now gathered outside the crime scene perimeter.

DC Massey had established that Louise's parents were touring the Northern Territory in a Winnebago. Her brother lived two hours north, outside Newcastle. He was trying to call the parents, who could be out of phone range.

'What about the children?' I asked.

'The brother's driving down to get them. Daycare staff will stay until he gets there.'

'Zoe's father?'

'Flying back, gets in at eight.'

I checked my watch. If Louise's parents didn't answer their messages or get to somewhere with phone service, they'd be hearing about their daughter's death on the nightly news.

Vans from all the major stations now blocked the street, with reporters jostling for the best position. Louise Simpson was already a ghoulish spectacle.

There was nothing more for me to do here. Running the gauntlet, I returned to the car without making a comment.

The only way to assuage the guilt I felt was to do everything possible to find that baby alive.

And catch whoever was responsible.

Chapter 25

BACK AT PRIVATE, Johnny and Collette were already working on a computerised composite of the Finches.

It can't have been a coincidence that the security cameras had been down when the pair came in. If they were behind it, the plan to avoid being photographed was elaborate. Planting a virus and smashing a door suggested they knew the layout of our building and which computer operated the cameras.

They could have met us anywhere. In a park, another office, or a shopping mall. Something didn't fit.

I racked my brain to recall even the slightest detail. The man was volatile and reacted badly when he thought he was being called a liar. Then again, he backed down with little persuasion. The woman was either genuine or a brilliant actress. She knew exactly what to say to garner sympathy.

Had they deliberately chosen me, today of all days? That meant they knew my personal history and planned to use me to get the information on Louise. But if they were that computer savvy, they could have found all the information on Louise themselves.

Had someone set me up? Someone who wanted me arrested for conspiracy to commit murder. I kept seeing the Simpson children's playthings through my mind and images of their mother's battered body.

Mary tapped on the doorjamb, with a coffee cup in hand and a ziplock bag of trail mix.

'Thought you could use these.'

I hadn't eaten all day and was beginning to feel the effects. My headache was back.

'It's probably fake but we need to check out the address the Finches gave us,' I said, before sucking back the coffee and popping a handful of nuts and seeds.

Mary slumped in my lounge. 'Already did. It's a vacant block. And there isn't anyone called Gus or Jennifer Finch either. I also tried Angus and Gustav. Nothing comes up on the usual databases.'

It figured. The couple had lied about everything.

The only other lead was the email address used to contact Louise through the surrogacy website.

'They said they contacted Louise through that, which is how they found out she lived on the North Shore.' I sat straighter. 'Could you trace the address the email was sent from?'

Mary pressed both hands on her knees and stood. 'Whoever owns that site is hiding behind a firewall. I couldn't get through but we can try working backwards from Louise's email account.'

'Thanks. Keep me posted. I want to hear any news, no matter how insignificant it may seem.'

I sounded desperate. I was.

Chapter 26

I FOUND DARLENE in our lab.

'Anything solid from the fence or kitchen?'

Her blue eyes had a spark as she pulled a white coat over her jeans and baggy shirt.

'Good palm print on the fence, and the aglet on the cord of the hoodie has potential. Same with DNA from the print on the body's neck.' She placed her camera on the desk. 'I'm more hopeful about what we got with the ALS.'

You could always rely on Darlene. She found evidence that seasoned crime scene technicians missed. Fingerprints on skin were notoriously difficult to capture, which is why she had been using the forensic Alternative Light Source, or ALS, when the opportunity arose.

'Got the best result at 450 nanometres. Amido black's risky but Rex agreed to try it on one of two bloodied prints on Louise's arms. It washed away the first, but we got lucky with the second. Blood on the ridges darkened for what I hope is enough contrast to get a good image of the print. I promised to send through our copies asap.'

'Did they fingerprint the neighbour who found the body?'

'I asked them to. Even though he couldn't remember touching the body, these could turn out to be his. He was pretty shaken up.'

If the killer acted impulsively, I hoped he or she had been sloppy.

'Any sign of the murder weapon?'

'Not yet. The police are searching bins, drains and yards in the area.'

She scrubbed her hands and put on fresh gloves. As she wiped down the benches with antiseptic, she thought out loud, 'If the baby was the target, why beat then stab Louise? I get that she saw the killer's face. But if our clients did it, you and Collette could already identify them.'

As usual, Darlene spoke good sense. The knife perforating the abdomen had to be key. That made the attack personal. Maybe we were missing something. What if another couple had wanted her to be a surrogate and things had gone sour?

I texted Johnny to join us. He was there almost instantly.

'We need to look into Louise's surrogacy experiences, her background,' I explained. 'Zoe's parents need to be checked as well. Make sure the husband was in Queensland and find out if there was any tension in the marriage or questions of paternity, custody, anything you can think of. And anyone who might have wanted either woman to suffer.'

'I'm on it,' he said, looking to Darlene.

She nodded, as if giving him permission to leave. There seemed to be a new dynamic between the two.

Darlene laid out the evidence samples on the clean benches and I left to help Johnny. Mary bailed me up outside the lab.

'Mark Talbot's here. He's got a warrant.'

Chapter 27

MARK AND DETECTIVE Constable Massey stood in the entrance with two uniformed officers.

Mark handed over the search warrant. It was for video footage from the last twenty-four hours along with files pertaining to Gus and Jennifer Finch: addresses, emails, invoices, payments. They also wanted my personal notes.

I explained again how the video had failed to record anything from midnight. But they were welcome to the footage we did have.

'Still find it all pretty convenient,' sneered Mark. 'Mystery couple visits you; you assist them with surrogacy, which is illegal in this state —'

'It was to be an altruistic surrogacy,' I interrupted.

'Unfortunately, Louise Simpson isn't around to verify that,' he retorted.

Clearly, his mood hadn't improved since we'd left the crime scene.

He stepped aside to have a quiet word with one of the uniformed officers. No doubt a power play to make me sweat.

The conversation seemed to amuse him.

When he returned his smug expression confirmed it. 'Your story about other businesses being vandalised doesn't seem to hold true. It appears no one else had any damage last night. Just your office.'

Our receptionist jumped to my defence. 'The repairmen said they had a number of windows to fix in the building.'

I hadn't recognised the glass company as one we would use. 'Collette, where did you get the number for the repairers?'

'In a card that was under the door. I thought they were like, you know, tow trucks. My uncle drives one. He listens to police radio so he can get to an accident first.'

It became clearer now. We'd been deliberately targeted. But by whom? The glass repair company drumming up business? That didn't explain the computer virus.

Mary offered to show Kristen Massey the video recordings we had up until the shutdown. Mark stayed with me.

'You look tense, Craigy boy. Might as well have a seat. This could take a while.'

It was how he worked. Pressing buttons to get a reaction. Just like he did when we were teenagers in the same house. Back then he had the advantage of size and mates to belt me around.

Now he had a police force on his side.

'Don't think this is personal. Try seeing it from where I stand. You meet this couple, who could be serial killers for all you know, then you give them personal info on a young mother who's struggling to bring up small kids while grieving for her dead husband.' He sucked air in through his teeth. 'Within hours she's dead. And a baby she was minding vanishes.'

He wasn't saying anything I hadn't already told myself.

'Work with me,' he goaded. 'There's more. By some dumb luck, you don't seem to have anything to help us identify them.' He waved a hand in the air dismissively. 'The most expensive, highest tech security cameras conveniently don't record the crucial moments.'

'That's exactly what happened,' Collette argued. 'You're making it sound like –'

'You are deliberately obstructing justice? Or conspired to kill Louise Simpson? That would make you an accessory, Ms . . .'

'Lindman,' she answered, voice wavering as her eyes appealed to me.

I needed to stay controlled. 'He's trying to upset you. We haven't done anything wrong.'

Johnny appeared with all the information we had on the Finches, along with everything he'd collected on Louise Simpson. His presence eased some of the tension.

He explained, 'The address and names they provided are fake, the number's disconnected and the email bounces. They didn't pay us. The invoice didn't go through.'

'No surprises there,' Mark mumbled.

Thankfully, Johnny didn't mention the envelope of cash Gus Finch had produced, as there was no proof I'd given it back.

Collette printed out a dozen copies of the computerised digifit of the suspects she and Johnny had compiled. They were amazingly accurate.

She also provided the files on a memory stick.

'Is there anything else?' I asked, trying to appear unfazed.

Mark dumped a number of photos on the reception desk.

'I want you to look at these and never forget Louise Simpson's lifeless face.' He turned to his team. 'That's about it. *For now.*'

Chapter 28

THE THOUGHT I MAY have helped the killer find Louise Simpson began to fester.

I studied the photos back in my office. Mark had done me a favour by leaving them. I could go over the scene and see if we missed anything at the time.

I heard a noise and looked up. Mary was leaning against the doorframe.

'That could have been worse,' she said.

'He's threatening to charge me with conspiracy to commit murder, obstruction of justice.' I rubbed the back of my neck, feeling a wave of fatigue.

'You haven't been arrested yet. We can still prove him wrong.'

I sat back and focused on the ceiling. 'Trouble is, I may be guilty.'

Mary came around and propped herself against my side of the desk, arms folded.

'You didn't beat that woman or stab her to death. If you hadn't given them the address, they could have got it from any computer geek or hacker. If the killer plucked the number from the White Pages, you wouldn't blame Telstra.'

Mary was right. Again.

'This morning I did let emotion overtake logic. Look what it did to Louise Simpson, her kids. And it could cost all of us here at Private our jobs and reputations. Maybe more.'

'All I know is, if you're looking back, you're going in the wrong direction.' She leant closer. 'A mother wants her child back. Louise's family need justice. We can deliver both. Deal with the rest later.'

I splayed my fingers on the desk and stood, grateful to be working with such a professional team. Mary had made it clear this was no time for regrets.

'You're right. We put everything into finding baby Zoe. Non-urgent cases go on the backburner. We'll refund any clients who aren't happy about it.'

'One more thing,' Mary added. 'Collette could use one of your pep talks.'

I'd known Mary long enough to understand what that meant. Mary had noticed Collette was upset, but talking emotions with a colleague wasn't her forte.

'Thanks for the heads-up – I'll go see her. And we need everyone in the conference room. Five minutes.'

Chapter 29

I FOUND COLLETTE in the kitchenette. When I walked in, she quickly fussed over the coffee machine.

'Thought we could all do with a caffeine hit,' she managed.

The red, puffy eyes were impossible to hide. It was easy to forget Collette was only twenty-two and had no experience in the force or the legal profession. She had knocked on the door with enthusiasm and what Becky would have called 'loads of gumption'.

She had drive, and a strong will to learn and take on extra tasks. And she was a good public face for the business. Caring, an attentive listener and a keen observer; the precision of the digifit images confirmed that.

'Rough day,' I said, popping a pod into one of the two machines. 'We've got a staff meeting in the conference room in five.'

She avoided eye contact. 'I'll make sure everyone's hydrated and fed.'

Her hands were shaking, so I offered to help.

'You have a seat at the table and I'll get this going.'

The simple offer was enough to break her resolve.

'I'm so sorry about that poor woman. I keep seeing her face . . . What those people inflicted.' Her voice rasped. 'And the baby.'

Like a pressure valve releasing, she erupted into tears. I handed her the cup I'd made and grabbed some milk from the fridge. So far, I'd been careful to shield Collette from graphic crime scene photos. There was no need to see them in the jobs she did. But Mark leaving the photos had delivered the desired effect.

'The Finches looked so harmless. I mean, I was totally taken in by the story. About how they lost all those pregnancies.'

You and me both, I thought.

I placed a hand on her shoulder. 'You aren't responsible. None of us is.'

She stared at the milk carton. 'That detective thinks we are.'

I didn't want to go into the background, just gave her the essentials. 'Mark Talbot and I have history. It's policing 101. Shake a tree and see what falls out.'

Collette looked up, her brown eyes wet.

'Are we the only tree he's got?'

'So far. Which is why I need you to step up. We all have to.'

She sniffed and wiped her eyes with a hanky.

'I thought you were going to fire me.'

I moved my hand from her shoulder. 'The virus could have happened to any of us, and we both fell for the couple's sob-story.'

'I'm sorry it happened to you, today.'

The comment was unexpected.

'Why would you say that? Have you been talking to Mary?'

She waved both hands. 'No. Before I came here the first time, I did some research. There were articles in the papers

77

about the . . . I mean, your . . . terrible accident. I'm sorry you lost your family.'

I didn't know whether to be offended or impressed by her initiative. I opted for the latter.

'We can't change what's happened.'

'I know.' Her eyes were dry now.

'We're all going to be tied up with finding Zoe and Louise's killer. I need you to get to work on Eric Moss. Everything you can get on him will be helpful. His daughter didn't give me much to go on, just where and when he was born. Johnny can help you access all the relevant databases. If you can get me the basics, birth certificates, passports –'

'I know exactly what you're after.' She smiled nervously. 'I hope I don't let you down.'

Chapter 30

THE TEAM WAS keen to be briefed. I kicked off.

'Finding the baby is, obviously, our top priority.'

I made no mention of the search warrant or police visit.

'Darlene. Anything so far in the evidence?'

She spread out the crime scene photos.

'Louise put up a fight, despite being taken by surprise.'

Johnny scribbled notes. 'Are we thinking she knew her killer then?'

Darlene continued, 'She was in a quiet neighbourhood. No grilles on windows or security doors. My guess is she was pretty trusting and opened the door.'

That didn't help us narrow the suspect list.

'What else?' Mary asked.

'I thought this was interesting.' Darlene referred to images of the face. 'The victim's face doesn't appear to have been fractured.' She pointed to the whites of the eyes. 'Cheek fracture would cause haemorrhages in the lateral sclera.'

We all appreciated that was why one punch, or a 'coward punch' as it had become known, was so dangerous. The face and skull weren't designed to be hit with such blunt force.

'The cheeks, the left one in particular, is reddened and swollen,' Darlene explained. 'There are a couple of parallel scratches on the left cheek too. I swabbed them, which is our best chance for DNA so far.'

Collette appeared with a tray holding a coffee pot, milk jug, sugar and spoons, which she placed on the sideboard, alongside a box of pastries and upturned mugs.

She'd reapplied her eye make-up. You couldn't tell she'd been upset. Johnny winked at her as she sat beside him.

'What did I miss?' she whispered.

Darlene recapped. 'I think Louise was slapped multiple times, not punched, and the killer may have left behind DNA in scratch marks on that left cheek.'

Collette volunteered, 'The woman this morning had long manicured nails. She kept clicking them as she waited.'

'I didn't find any broken nails at the scene,' Darlene said. 'That could explain the slapping. It's something a woman with nails might do.'

'Or a man who wanted to inflict pain without leaving obvious bruising,' Mary added. 'Typical in domestic violence.'

We needed to concentrate our efforts to be most efficient. I listed tasks in order of importance. 'We can't rule out two people at the scene. Mary, can you talk to Louise's brother and track down her close friends? See if she had any previous surrogate pregnancies, and if she told anyone about using that site.'

'On it,' Mary said. 'And if there was a man on the scene, requited or otherwise. Young widows are pretty vulnerable.'

'You read my mind,' I said. 'Johnny, can you go through Louise's phone and bank records? Emails too. Check whether she contacted our couple, visited outside her area. Anything to help us narrow the part of Sydney we're looking at.'

Johnny raised another issue. 'If Zoe Ruffalo had been at the Simpson house on three consecutive Tuesdays, it's possible the baby was the target and Louise was collateral damage.'

I agreed. 'We can't afford to narrow our thinking too early.'

'While I'm at it, I'll look into the Ruffalos and their finances,' he said. 'Miners make good money. It's possible there'll be a ransom demand.'

The police, I knew, were preparing for that possibility.

Mary raised an index finger. 'What about Eric Moss? Can we risk losing time on that one?'

I gestured towards Collette. 'We've got it covered.'

Our receptionist stared at her notebook. No one batted an eyelid.

'How far are we on identifying the origin of the email sent to Louise Simpson? If the surrogacy site is protected by a firewall, can we trace the email?'

Darlene was the one to speak. 'Johnny and I tried that a few minutes ago. Our suspects used a VPN address, so the IP turned up as coming from America.'

'So they're au fait with hiding?' Mary commented.

'Not necessarily,' Collette offered. 'Heaps of people use VPNs. It's how you download shows from American Netflix and Hulu.'

All I wanted to know was whether they could work backwards from the VPN to pin down the local address. Darlene knew that was what I wanted to hear.

'There's a guy I know who can try it for a grand.'

Darlene had some 'interesting' contacts who often challenged technical boundaries of the law.

'Let's get him on it.'

Unless someone identified the Finches from the digifit
images soon, the mysterious computer expert was our best
hope of finding baby Zoe.

Chapter 31

TWO HOURS LATER, there'd been no word about Zoe and no ransom call. The police had set up at the Ruffalo home, around the corner from the Simpson scene.

Our friendly deputy commissioner had given us the information gleaned from Zoe's mother. We took that and collected more. Nothing stood out as particularly useful.

Geoff and Courtney Ruffalo appeared happy to their neighbours, owed six hundred thousand on a mortgage but paid their credit cards off on time. There were no withdrawals from bank accounts apart from small, consistent amounts of cash each week and direct deposits to pay the regular bills. The husband wasn't in debt. There was always the possibility of an affair with a colleague at the mine.

They'd been together eight years and married for three.

Courtney Ruffalo and Louise Simpson met at the local park and struck up a friendship. When Zoe was born, Louise offered to babysit while Geoff was away. The new mother used that time to attend a postnatal yoga class.

The instructor confirmed Courtney was in class at the time Louise's body was found.

I remembered how challenging Cal's first few months were, especially for Becky. When days and nights all blurred into one.

I felt a deep ache in my chest and took a slug of Chivas Regal that lived in the locked top drawer of my desk, in the flask Becky had given me on our wedding day. Right now it was the closest I could get to her and Cal.

But we still had to find baby Zoe.

I placed it back in the drawer.

In the lab, Darlene was busy processing samples. There was no word yet from her mystery friend.

Johnny and Mary were collating information. I decided to see how Collette had fared with her assignment.

I found her at her desk, face red and flustered.

'Everything all right?' I pulled up a chair by her side.

'I don't know,' she said. 'You may want to sack me now.'

Before I could ask why, she blurted her explanation. 'I haven't found anything yet.' She nervously checked her watch. It was nearing nine o'clock.

'You must have found something in two hours.' I couldn't hide my frustration. Time was critical and I'd given her basic facts to gather.

'I couldn't even find a clear photo.' She began to tear up again. 'I promise I tried. I promise, I'll be in super early tomorrow.'

Today had been tough on all of us, including Collette.

'You should go home and get some rest.'

Collette looked relieved. She picked up her phone and bag and let herself out the new glass door, locking it behind her.

The pounding in my head returned. Collette's task had been simple. Any of the others would have had a dossier on Moss by now. I began to wonder if I'd overestimated her potential.

I checked my phone for any messages from Brett Thorogood and Jack Morgan. Nothing so far.

Sitting at reception, I started with the list Eliza Moss had provided. Friends of her father, where he'd lived, been born.

Movement on the surveillance monitor caught my attention. A man greeted Collette. He was stocky, muscular. He had his back to the camera so I couldn't see his face, only the bunch of roses he was hiding. He reached forward and kissed her on the cheek as he presented the bouquet.

As far as I'd seen, Collette's relationships were frequent and short-lived. This one appeared to be in an embryonic stage.

I flicked through what Collette had recorded so far. There were question marks against passport, registration of birth, bank account.

While the others worked on identifying the mystery pair, I made a strong black coffee and prepared for a long night.

Chapter 32

I STARTED WITH the usual databases. There was no one with a name even resembling Eric Moss born on or around the date Eliza provided.

Even allowing for misspellings, typographical errors and flawed transcribing, his birth wasn't registered in New South Wales. Definitely not in the small town of Jerilderie or the nearby, larger town of Deniliquin. Jerilderie, in the state's west, was famous for being raided by the country's most notorious bushranger, Ned Kelly.

Searching the electoral rolls, there was no Moss registered in Echuca, Victoria, or Moama across the border, for the decade he and his parents supposedly lived there. Eliza had made a note about her grandfather drowning in the Murray River when the paddle-steamer he crewed for the sawmill caught fire. A quick search of cemeteries in the area proved futile. There was no record of Eric's mother, Margaret, or grandparents living or dying in the area.

Eric Moss didn't appear on the current electoral roll. He hadn't requested a silent listing. From what I could tell, he had never voted, enrolled or been married.

He wasn't listed in *Who's Who*, despite being CEO of the largest Australian-based non-profit organisation. Infopedia only mentioned him in a page on Sir Lang Gillies, with no accompanying link to his name.

I began to wonder if records for Moss had been wiped. Or if they had ever existed. No tax file number, no Medicare number and no digital imprint. Scores of articles on Contigo Valley quoted Gillies and mentioned Moss in passing. He was rarely photographed without dark glasses.

What struck me most was he didn't have a passport or driver's licence.

The man known as Eric Moss was a ghost.

Chapter 33

I DECIDED TO do what I should have done with Gus and Jennifer Finch and double-check who our clients were and what they claimed to be.

I refused to be played again so this time I searched for Eliza Moss. An abundance of photographs of her appeared in business and social pages. She talked with pride about her father, but there was no mention of a mother.

She claimed she'd been born in Lithgow, not far from Contigo Valley. Only there was no birth record for Eliza Moss. By now, my patience was at breaking point.

What were these people playing at? If they wanted their true identities to be secret, it was beyond bizarre that they would both hold high-profile jobs. I had to wonder what sort of fraud the two could have been perpetrating. Was Moss siphoning money from Contigo or its donors? One thing was certain, I wouldn't be party to it.

I headed back to the lab to check on Darlene's progress. She was in the middle of attempting to highlight a fingerprint on the aglet from the blood-stained hoodie.

'I tried cyanoacrylate in the fume cupboard,' she said. 'It didn't pick anything up. Now I'm adding a fluorescing agent.'

The fume cupboard was a way of highlighting latent finger-prints. The work was tedious and fiddly. It took someone with Darlene's patience and experience to develop new ways to improve the technique.

'If there's a partial, you're hoping ultraviolet light will show the definition?'

Darlene smiled, the full-dimpled version that was reserved for someone appreciating her ingenuity. 'You *so* get me.' Her attention quickly turned to the remaining specimens. 'I'll let you know the second I find something.'

Next stop was Mary and Johnny. They hadn't made much progress on the IP address. I suggested they go home, get a few hours' sleep and come back early.

Mary stood up and stretched her back, cracking the joints in her spine and neck. 'You should grab some kip too,' she said.

'I'll stay here on my office couch.' It wouldn't be the first time. Anyway, after the door being smashed last night, I'd be more comfortable if Darlene had someone with her in the office.

Johnny offered to stay but there was little point. He agreed to keep working a couple more hours, though. There was something important I needed to do.

I headed out to confront Eliza Moss.

Chapter 34

I PARKED BY The Rocks at Circular Quay and walked along the promenade. The night was clear with a slight hint of a breeze. Summer crowds were out enjoying the best of the harbour. It still amazed me how stunning the city could look, particularly at night with the iconic Bridge and Opera House lit up.

I'd lived in a few great cities but this one always felt like home.

It was almost ten. Eliza's function would be in full swing. I was now calm enough to challenge her without emotion.

I breathed in the sea air and entered the Park Hyatt through the bar.

The noisy ballroom was decked out in full Mardi Gras splendour. Colourful streamers, ornate masks, beads and brightly coloured candles adorned the banquet tables. The residual aroma of spicy Cajun wafted from the 'Spice Palace' buffet as a jazz band played to a full dance floor. On the perimeter of the room, people jostled around carnival stalls offering temporary tattoos, fortune tellers and voodoo instruction. The atmosphere was electric, not the usual dull, charity event.

I spied Eliza at a table near the centre of the ballroom and wove my way through overly merry revellers. A street magician I passed seemed affronted that I wasn't interested in his card tricks.

My client sat amid a sea of wealth, at a table with a couple of recognisable faces, and some barely identifiable ones thanks to overzealous cosmetic work.

She saw me approach and interrupted her conversation, without getting up.

'You have news?' Her piercing green eyes looked up at me.

'We need to speak in private.'

A minion delivered her a glass of wine. 'Things wrap up in about half an hour. Can this wait till then?'

I wondered what the hell this woman was playing at. She seemed more interested in holding court than finding her missing father. I didn't like being used or made a fool of. She'd contacted Jack Morgan and misled both of us. Given she was going to profit in the event of her father's death, she could leave her workers to 'wrap up' for her.

'I need to see you in private. *Now.*' I was sharp, exactly as I'd intended.

She suddenly seemed rattled. 'OK. There's a staff room we can use.'

As I waited, she pushed back from the table and led the way out of the ballroom – in a wheelchair.

Chapter 35

ELIZA TOOK US to a room provided for her event staff. A four-seater table and a television mounted on the wall were all it could accommodate. The TV was on with the sound muted.

Inside the room, she moved straight for a bar fridge and pulled out two small bottles of beer.

She manoeuvred to the table and offered me one. I declined and sat opposite, regretting judging her for 'holding court' when she was wheelchair-bound. Still, I was reeling from the day's events with the non-existent Finches, and now the phantom Eric Moss. My pulse raced with anger at having been conned – again.

She twisted the cap of her beer and drank from the bottle before ripping open a bag of corn chips on the table. 'Help yourself.' She took a couple of chips and waited for me to speak.

'There's no word on your father.' I placed both elbows on the table. 'But you probably already knew that.'

She swallowed hard. 'You must have something by now.'

'I get the feeling I wasn't expected to, given the "facts" you provided. About yourself and the man you call your father.'

There was a moment's silence. 'Are you serious? What's got into you?' She slammed the bottle on the table. 'Is this about my chair?'

'I don't appreciate being lied to.'

She threw her head back and laughed. 'That's pretty rich, calling me a liar because I don't wear my disability like some neon sign. Shock, horror. I acted normal and you treated me like I was. Now you sit there, all sanctimonious, accusing me of being dishonest.' She looked me up and down, exaggerating every movement of her upper body. 'We're all disabled. You hide your emotional scars with swagger and self-importance. Let me guess. Your parents divorced, leaving you with commitment issues –'

My anger seethed. She had no right to lecture me on family. Attacking me just proved her dishonesty. I'd wasted enough time on Eric Moss, whoever he was. I stood to leave.

'Lies have a way of unravelling.' I didn't bother to hide my irritation. 'Did you think I wouldn't find out the truth?'

'You assumed I was like you. I just didn't assault you with my differences.' She took a few more, slow sips. 'People treat me differently once they know. Case in point, you.'

'This has nothing to do with your wheelchair.'

'Now who's the liar? Why is it an issue then?'

'Because you and your father both seem good at covering up who you really are.'

'If you want to know, I act that way so people will take me seriously. I wanted to prove to my father I was independent. It's why I started my own business, to show everyone I could be a success.' She gulped what was left of the beer and wiped her mouth with a serviette. 'Well, actually, that part's not entirely true.'

The comment took me by surprise. Judging by tonight, she excelled at what she did.

'I have a Master's in business studies and my resume landed me countless interviews. Only the moment a prospective employer saw the chair, they'd start mentioning someone they knew who had cancer, or a footballer who'd become a quad-riplegic in an accident.' She picked at the label on the bottle. 'I could see them suddenly panic about insurance, workers' comp, and whether the toilet in their inner-city terrace office would have to be refitted.

'Now, I ditch the chair for meetings with clients so they treat me like an AB person.'

'AB?'

'Able-bodied.' She made a point of enunciating the phrase.

'Which is why your staff keep coming to you for signatures and advice.' I felt foolish for misreading her manner. Even so, I still had to confront her about the lack of documentation for her and Eric Moss.

'There's something we need to get clear. Your father isn't who you claim he is. He doesn't exist in terms of Medicare, the electoral roll, or any other usual records.' I ticked them off on my hands. 'No passport, no bank account, nada, nothing. I couldn't find a single identifying document.'

'Really?' She landed the empty bottle in the rubbish bin by the wall. 'Tell me. How can someone as brilliant as Jack Morgan be so wrong about you?'

Chapter 36

ELIZA MOSS PULLED no punches in what she thought of my incompetence. I let her vent. In my experience, anger usually stemmed from fear or guilt.

'Jack is *not* going to be happy,' she said, scrolling down her phone contacts. 'I need professionals to find him, not some two-bit amateur. He could have been in the fire for all you know.'

'What fire?'

She looked exasperated. 'You really have no idea?'

I'd been so caught up in the events of the day, I hadn't seen any other news. 'I've been working with the police on another urgent case.'

She pulled up a photo and held the phone so I could see. 'It's off Evans Road, between Katoomba and Blackheath. It made the news because firefighters were concerned it might take Jemby Rinjah with it. Luckily, it didn't.'

I knew of the award-winning ecolodge that backed on to the national park. I took the phone. The cabin was a burnt-out shell.

'They think it was arson.'

I scrolled through a series of photos. Surrounding bushland had been incinerated as well.

'Who owns it?'

'A friend of my father. Dad would go up there sometimes for the weekend, or take the occasional overseas visitor there. He loves all that area.'

'Was anyone hurt?' What I was really asking was if any bodies were found.

She shook her head. 'Reports said no. I just don't think it's a coincidence. It's as if everything he values is being destroyed. His job, his friend's cabin.'

'I'll look into it.'

'Don't bother,' she said. 'I'm getting someone else.'

A TV news update caught my attention with the photo of a baby in pink. The commentary wasn't necessary, given the Crimestoppers number scrolled on a loop across the screen.

Eliza looked up at the TV. 'That poor baby and mother.' She glanced back at me, and must have read the pain on my face. 'How long's she been missing?'

'Eight hours,' I answered, without looking at my watch.

Her tone was subdued. 'That's the other case you're working on, isn't it?'

I rubbed my neck again. 'Let's just say it's been a full day and I can't afford to be messed around. There's no one with the name Eric Moss born anywhere near where you said, or when.'

She leant forward. 'I don't understand. That *is* Dad's full name, date of birth. I even gave you his parents' names, everything I knew.'

I watched her carefully for any hint of lies. 'There's no birth registered for Eliza Moss either.'

She threw her head back again. 'You've investigated me? If you'd told me earlier, I could have saved you the trouble.'

Chapter 37

ELIZA MOSS TOOK a swig from the second bottle of beer before explaining that she was born to a teenage girl who worked in the canteen at Contigo's rural base. The girl had no money or support and no skills to look after a child, let alone one that was – she used her fingers as quotation marks – 'abnormal'.

'In what way?'

'I was born with an unusual neurological condition. My mother was pressured to put me in an institution. Eric didn't want that to happen. He offered to pay for all my medical care, physiotherapy and even new trial therapies. Not long after, he adopted me and my mother left town. No one's heard from her since, not that you can blame her. Unmarried mothers in rural areas were social outcasts back then.'

One of the women I'd seen earlier in Eliza's office popped her head through the doorway.

'Sorry, but I thought you'd want to know. After costs, the night raised . . .'

Eliza's eyes widened. 'Give it to me straight.'

'A hundred and twenty-seven thousand dollars!'

Eliza smiled broadly. 'That's brilliant. As usual, a great job done by all. And thanks for your help, Jules. You are a wonder.'

The colleague blushed, looked at me, then back at Eliza. 'You may as well head off. I'll finish up here.'

'Appreciate it.' Eliza slumped after the assistant left. 'Where were we?'

'You were telling me why I couldn't find your birth certificate.'

'The certificate had my mother's name on it; the father's name was left blank.'

As far as she was concerned, Eric Moss was her father. There was little doubt she also saw him as her saviour. Without him she may well have been left to rot in an institution.

I began to believe she had no idea her 'father' didn't officially exist.

Chapter 38

ELIZA MOSS SEEMED blindsided by what I had to say. She explained that Eric avoided overseas trips. Even so, she'd assumed he had a passport. Her father had always been private about his own family and childhood but once talked about the accident in Echuca and his mother's grief. He'd never mentioned it again.

Eric and Eliza had each other and didn't seem to need anyone else.

In one of their holidays together, Moss hired a boat and crew. They sailed the Whitsundays for a couple of weeks and talked about politics, history and everything else but his past.

'The few times I asked about his childhood, or even my mother, he'd fob me off by saying, "It's not where you're from that counts. Where you're going and how you get there is all that matters."'

Apart from a handful of trips and cabin visits, people usually travelled to see Moss in Contigo Valley. There they could see the facilities and equipment in action. Canberra was a favourite for the pair during school holidays. The museums, galleries and exhibitions were an easy drawcard.

It made sense that Moss didn't have a passport. Even so, it was unusual for a CEO to negotiate major international deals without venturing outside the country.

A text interrupted. I excused myself to check. It was from Johnny.

Gone over Ruffalo's and Simpson's bank/phone statements. No leads so far.

I needed to relieve Johnny so he could go home. Darlene would be working for a lot longer. The broken door still unnerved me. I didn't want my staff put at any risk.

I stood and pushed the chair towards the table. 'I'm sorry but I have to go. Can we talk more tomorrow?'

She placed the second beer bottle on the table and nudged aside the half-eaten chips. 'Of course. I hope it's good news about the baby.'

'How are you getting home?'

Those green eyes challenged me. 'Would you ask an AB woman that?'

I had to concede, 'Probably not. I just know how difficult taxis can be at this time of night.'

'I have a room upstairs as part of the hotel package.' She reached out her hand and we shook again. 'Thanks for the thought, though.'

I felt like we needed to tread carefully finding Moss.

Eric wasn't who he claimed to be and I had a bad feeling his daughter was going to be hurt when we unravelled whatever secrets he was keeping so well hidden.

I texted Johnny to go home and get some sleep. I'd be back in ten.

Chapter 39

JOHNNY HANDED OVER the Simpson file first. Thanks to Darlene, we had the data from Louise's mobile phone and computer. There was no landline in the house.

Some days she made few calls, others were spent in a series of long conversations. Johnny had written 'day care' beside the dates they tended to occur. Louise's brother, the compensation lawyer and her mother were frequent numbers on those days.

There were only occasional calls made to or from the phone after eight-thirty at night. All online activity usually ceased by ten.

Supermarket groceries were home-delivered every Wednesday. A single mother, she kept a routine. Good for the kids, but it made her predictable. And as a result, an easier target for a killer.

The husband, Vincent, had fallen from scaffolding on a construction site and died from a brain haemorrhage two days later. The insurance company alleged that a pre-existing medical condition contributed to his death. Vincent Simpson had contracted hepatitis A while on holiday in New Guinea years before. His liver function was slightly raised at the time of admission. It sounded like a stretch to me, but insurance companies paid doctors big dollars to mitigate payments on medical grounds.

However, their strategy was more likely to be to wear down a widow pursuing a claim. Not torture and murder her.

Still, the payout could exceed three million. Johnny had included a printout of a newspaper article that mentioned the potential amount. That could have made Louise a target for extortion. What if the killer thought the baby was really Louise's and the plan changed when she revealed Zoe wasn't her child?

Possibilities raced through my mind.

Her internet settings were private, and she had less than a hundred 'friends' on social media.

I logged in with the password Johnny had guessed. The kids' names and years of birth.

Photos of two smiling kids filled the posts, taken at parties, swimming and day care. In every one, she held the children close.

One image stood out. Her husband kissing her expanded belly. The comment beneath read 'Missing Vince so much. Happiest time of our lives'.

I went straight in to Darlene to see if she had any results.

She was magnifying images on an electron microscope.

'This hair sample is different from Louise's. They're both brown.' She enlarged the slide further so I could compare them. 'The longer one was broken off. No root. We could only get mitochondrial DNA from it. I took the other from Louise's head. It will take a couple of days to extract.'

I studied the hairs. The broken one was more coarse, and thicker in diameter.

At this stage any DNA was better than none. If we could narrow it down to members of the one family, we'd exclude about four million people in the city.

'Good pick-up,' I said and meant it.

Darlene had managed to enhance a partial print on the aglet from the hoodie and had a striking image of the palm print from the back fence. She was still working on one of the prints from Louise's neck.

'Rex called a few minutes ago,' she said. 'Gross examination's done but the histopathology will be a while longer.'

I braced for what I suspected was coming.

'His first impressions were right. She died of acute blood loss. The stab wound was deep and severed an artery on the way through. It entered above the pubic bone and perforated the uterus, passing above the bladder.'

I said what Darlene didn't. 'Chances are, whoever did this knew what they were aiming for.'

This was no random killing. Louise's murder was deliberate and extremely personal.

Chapter 40

AFTER GOING OVER the files again hoping to find something we'd missed, I managed an hour of fitful sleep on the couch in my office.

Darlene woke me at six am. She was heading home for a shower. As she let herself out, Brett Thorogood slipped in. The deputy commissioner was in dress uniform, cap in his hand, ready for a press conference.

'Rough night for everyone,' he said, knocking my socked feet off the couch and sitting in their place.

I sat up slowly. 'Please tell me you've got good news.'

His face was stony. 'Radio and TV stations are putting out hourly bulletins. Crimestoppers has been flooded with calls overnight after people saw the couple's composite pictures.'

I knew that wasn't all positive news. There would be hundreds, possibly thousands of false leads to keep the police busy for months. Valuable time would be lost chasing crank calls.

'This couple,' he asked. 'Is there anything else you can tell me?'

I'd racked my brain all night for any more details about the pair.

'Craig, give me something to work with.'

I stood up and faced him. 'You know I want to find this child more than anyone else. My team worked through the night.'

Brett calmly rotated the cap in his hands. 'Darlene's contribution was invaluable. I'm trying to protect Private, but you know you aren't the commissioner's favourite. There's going to be a backlash once the shock jocks call for mandatory homicide sentencing and senior heads on platters.'

He didn't have to remind me. A breakthrough could not only save baby Zoe, but also our reputation.

'Her face had minimal trauma,' I explained. 'Gut tells me someone wanted information from her. If they wanted to torture her, they were pretty amateur. Stabbing of the uterus was very specific.'

Brett remained focused on his cap. 'The surrogacy motive is the best we have?'

'Right now it's all we have.'

'Then I'll get the taskforce to hone in on the surrogacy organisations. See if anyone admits to knowing this pair or meeting with them at some stage.'

He stood and I thanked him. Before he left I had one question.

'What do you know about Eric and Eliza Moss?'

Chapter 41

BRETT COCKED HIS head. 'Why would you ask?'

'Eric Moss walked out of Contigo four days ago and no one's heard from him since. The daughter suspects foul play.'

'And you're investigating him?' Brett dropped his cap on the desk. 'The Simpson murder is nothing compared to the Pandora's box you'll rip open with this one.'

The comment was not what I expected. What did the deputy commissioner of police know about Moss going missing? 'How about I make you a decaf while you explain?'

We headed to the kitchenette. Brett had suffered heart palpitations and his doctor had recommended cutting back on caffeine. Greta, his wife, enforced it religiously in addition to a low-cholesterol, low-salt and organic diet.

'Make it a latte and we're on. I've got forty minutes before a briefing.'

I made the coffees while he stood against the bench, talking freely.

'From memory, Eliza spent some time in the US, about three years ago. She and Jack Morgan had a thing for a while, I think, but it fizzled out.'

Brett knew Eric Moss and considered him a decent guy who connected well with people. 'He could have talked the Middle East into peace.' Committed to his business, he'd turned down jobs running a number of organisations for much better pay.

'I had some dealings with him over police training with the retrieval squads. He was spot-on and had innovative ideas about improving our efficiency. From what I could tell, he was a golden boy for ministers, police and defence brass. Sending equipment overseas to help with disasters was great PR; kudos for the state and federal governments to get mileage from, especially at election time.'

He opened a white box and picked up a pastry left over from yesterday. Half went straight into his mouth.

I handed him the coffee.

'Thanks,' he managed, savouring his treat and picking up a chocolate croissant. 'Greta —'

'What happens in Private . . .'

'You always could keep a secret,' he said and took another large bite.

I asked if there was any hint of corruption at Contigo.

He stopped chewing. 'Is that what you suspect?'

I explained how Moss resigned with no warning after the finance officer questioned a small discrepancy. And how Gillies didn't seem keen to have anyone sniffing around the company. He certainly didn't care that Moss had left without any explanation.

'Lang's a classic corporate parasite. He often travels with his wife, only they stay in separate hotel rooms. He orders porn movies and when it comes to checking out, acts outraged at the false charges on his credit card, threatens to tell the media about the hotel scam . . .'

'And gets the charges wiped.'

'Every time.' He drained his mug and placed it in the sink. 'You say Gillies wasn't fazed by Moss leaving?'

'Made out he didn't care to know why. As if Moss was easily replaced.'

Brett frowned. 'Doesn't add up he'd be happy to see his meal ticket walk away. Unless, of course, Moss had something that could bury Gillies.'

That's what bothered me. No one had seen or heard from Moss, and no one but Lang had seen the resignation email.

Brett continued as I walked him out. 'Lawyers, police, defence forces and governments have a lot invested in Contigo Valley. If Moss uncovered corruption, you don't want to be around when that powder keg blows.'

Chapter 42

A COURIER ARRIVED at seven-thirty am with a box on a trolley and instructions to deliver it straight to Darlene Cooper. His shirt had a logo on the pocket: Gene-IE Path Systems. They imported the latest in scientific machines.

Darlene returned with wet hair, and beamed when she saw the delivery.

'I'll explain once we get it in the lab.' She led the way to where she wanted it. The delivery man obliged.

In the conference room, Johnny looked remarkably rested for someone who had managed a few hours' sleep at the most. Mary was sucking on a protein shake she'd brought from home. True to her word, Collette had arrived early, already having collected coffees along with eight egg and bacon rolls from a café down the street.

The smell of the bacon made me realise how long it had been since I'd eaten. We took our seats and I told them first about Brett Thorogood's visit. I didn't need to remind them how much we needed to get a break today.

Johnny was the first with an idea. He wanted to go back to the street address the Finches had provided.

'It's a vacant block,' Mary reminded him.

He wasn't swayed. 'That isn't a coincidence. I really believe they're familiar with the area. I can take copies of the images we made and canvass the streets in daylight.'

It was a good idea. 'You might just get lucky. If you go now, you can catch the neighbours before they head to work.'

Johnny grinned, grabbed copies of the images and squeezed past Darlene on his way.

Darlene pulled on her lab coat, her hair now tightly looped into a bun. 'I'm hoping that machine will help.' She picked up a roll. 'It's a Swift Gene-IE machine that can process DNA in ninety minutes.'

It normally took days to get a DNA analysis with our equipment, which was more advanced and faster than the police labs.

'I didn't think they were available yet,' said Mary.

'Well, not widely,' Darlene declared. 'It's one of only two in the country. And we have it on permanent loan.'

'What's the catch? Does speed leave a wider margin for systematic error?'

'No,' Darlene said. 'But you're right about limitations. It can't extract individual DNA from mixed fluids so isn't any good for rape kits, and it can't detect gender or race at this stage.'

'When will you get a result?' I appreciated that Darlene needed time to learn how to use it.

'The tech's calibrating the machine now. After the printout, the machine compares the DNA to all the others in the database.' She dumped two sugars into her coffee. 'Should have something by ten this morning.'

'How did you manage to pull this off?' I was amazed.

'Quid pro quo. If we like it, we can recommend it to each of the other Private offices for a bulk discount.' She grabbed a serviette and excused herself to get on with the analysis.

For the first time, we had widened our edge on the police resources and we had our tech marvel to thank for it.

Chapter 43

JOHNNY PULLED UP outside the vacant block. The address may have been bogus but the street existed. Two blocks back from the nearest main road and quiet, even for this time of day. Down the road, the shell of a service station had been fenced off. Within a hundred metres, the yards of three dilapidated houses displayed For Sale signs.

He tried the side with an overgrown jacaranda first. In the drive sat a white ute. *Top Job Pipes and Plumbing*. A 1800 number was printed on the back and side.

A man in a blue workman's shirt answered the door. He had a piece of toast in one hand and took the chance to slip past a crying toddler. As the door closed, the child began to scream from inside. The man unlocked the vehicle and placed the toast on the dashboard before turning to Johnny.

'Hi. My name's Johnny Ishmah. I'm investigating Zoe Ruffalo's kidnapping.'

'Yeah, I saw that on the news. Makes you think no one's safe anymore.'

'The police are keen to interview this couple. I was wondering if you could take a close look and see if you recognise one or both of them.'

The man wiped both hands on his shirt before taking the first digifit. 'So you think they live around here?' He looked carefully at the face then shook his head.

'How about the woman?' Johnny swapped the pictures.

'Sorry, mate, haven't seen either of them. We only moved in three months ago. If she is from around here, the codger across the road'll be your best bet. He's about ninety in the shade and sits out there every day.' He pointed towards a red brick house with a half-verandah diagonally opposite. 'Reckon Frank knows all the neighbourhood's little secrets.' He climbed into the ute and wound down the window. 'Hope you find the bastards that did it.'

Johnny was relieved that the public appeals had at least made an impact. Overnight, as a long shot, he had scanned the images into facial recognition ID software. It hadn't paid off. The sketches may have looked accurate but lacked the exact dimensions of mouth to nose, ear contours and forehead size.

He crossed the road and walked into the elderly man's yard. A cat took off from the front verandah leaving white hairs in the cushioned cane chair it had been curled on. Beside that was a wooden chair with tattered tapestry cushions. Against one of the chair's arms, a full metal ashtray stood on a spiral wooden stem base. It had to be from the 1950s. Johnny's grandparents had one similar. The smell reminded him of that house, where smoke had darkened the walls and embedded in all the furnishings.

Above, an abundance of spider webs hung from the guttering. Johnny knocked loudly on the closed screen door. There was no answer. He tried again.

This time he walked around the house, hoping the gentleman was in his backyard. Through the rear window, he saw a still figure.

Slumped across the breakfast table.

Chapter 44

JOHNNY TRIED THE back door. It was locked. He raced around the front of the house and entered through the screen door. The man was facedown on the table, a radio playing by his side.

Johnny tried to feel a neck pulse when suddenly the man took a gasp and snorted. He was asleep.

'Sir! Frank!' Johnny shouted.

He sat up and Johnny stepped back.

'Who the hell are you?' he demanded. There was no sign of fear or concern about a stranger in his home.

'Johnny Ishmah. I thought you were . . . You didn't seem to be breathing.'

'I was trying to hear the race results. Must have nodded off.' He rubbed the stubble on his chin and licked his lips. 'Are you my new carer?'

'No, I was knocking. You didn't answer.'

'Funny thing about screen doors is you can *hear through 'em*.'

Johnny suppressed a smile. 'Sorry, sir.'

'Just a minute . . .' He adjusted something on his hearing

aid. 'No point wasting batteries when I'm on my own. Now what are you here for again?'

Before Johnny could answer, the elderly gentleman picked up a walking stick and slowly lifted himself from the chair. He was stooped, and he shuffled to the front door.

'Well?'

Johnny explained that the plumber across the road thought he might be able to help.

The man stepped onto the verandah. 'Did he now? If you ask me, that kid rules the roost. Carries on a treat every time he goes out.'

Johnny followed and clarified the reason for his visit.

The old man eased himself into his chair and pulled reading glasses from the pocket of his shirt. He gestured for his visitor to sit – on the cat's chair.

Instead, Johnny squatted at his feet and handed over the woman's picture first. The old man breathed loudly as he moved his chin up then down a little.

'I've seen a lot of people in my time but not that one.'

Johnny passed him the man's image.

Frank repeated the chin dropping. This time he grunted on the exhale. A gnarled finger tapped on the page.

'This one. Reminds me of someone.'

Johnny pulled out his notebook. 'Who?'

'This one has more hair. Same beady eyes though.' He lifted his finger and pointed. 'Used to live on that old vacant block. Before the place got knocked down. Fella's been dead years though.'

Johnny sighed. He could try the other houses but suspected they weren't going to give him answers. He thanked Frank and made a move towards the footpath.

'You young people. Always in a hurry. You miss all the good by rushing past it.'

'Sorry, sir, but I have to keep door knocking.'

'I haven't finished. The bloke I mentioned. Well, he had two sons. Twins if I remember, born just after my wife died. 1970.'

That would make them in their forties. Johnny stepped back up, this time sitting on the edge of the cat's chair.

'Do you remember their names?'

Frank smacked his lips. 'Gough and Whit. Have you ever heard such nonsense? Bloody communists. If you ask me –'

It was pretty clear they were fans of the former Prime Minister, Gough Whitlam. If nothing else, they could have been registered members of the local Labor Party branch.

'And their surname?'

'Oh. Let me think.'

The cat appeared and began to meow at Johnny's feet.

'Or where they ended up?' Johnny tried.

'Gough made a fortune out of paper cups of all things. The other one was pretty witless, from memory.' He chuckled and coughed at the irony. 'Became a gardener, I think, up Newcastle way.'

'Do you remember anyone called Gus from the street? He'd be around the same age as the twins.'

Frank rubbed his stubbled chin again. 'Now that rings a bell. They had a cousin who hung around them like a bad smell in summer. My grandkids used to play with them. Don't know what it is with those people but this kid was named Alexandrus. Can you believe it? Alexandrus Wallace. No wonder everyone called him Gus.'

Chapter 45

I ANSWERED JOHNNY'S call before the second ring.

It didn't take long for him to fill me in about the twins' house and Alexandrus Wallace. It was the breakthrough I was hoping for. I searched online. Alexandrus went by 'Alex' now. His company, trading as Al Wallace, restored fine antiques. A further search on antique fairs and I hit paydirt. It was a group shot but, second from the left, Gus Finch's bland face stared back at me. A few shots later, Jennifer's visage appeared.

And we had them.

I rang the business number. A recorded female voice said the office was closed for family reasons and would reopen on the second of next month. The business was located in Dural, forty minutes north of the CBD. A street search quickly showed it was a house on an acreage.

I couldn't make any of this right, but finding the baby was the best start.

Mary was working on Moss's background when I interrupted to tell her about the address for the man posing as Finch. I could use her help if things went sour. She didn't hesitate and suggested we could take her Jeep. I stopped to let

Collette know where we'd be in case anything went wrong and we didn't check in within the hour. We'd call the police on the way to Dural. Collette crossed her fingers and wished us luck.

We headed north on the M2 and encountered surprisingly little traffic until Pennant Hills Road. I decided to wait until we could confirm Wallace was home before letting Brett Thorogood know. We couldn't afford any mistakes. If the Wallaces had already gone, Mark Talbot could accuse me of withholding information long enough for them to escape. The not-so-friendly Area Command could twist it any way he saw fit.

Mary was quiet, concentrating on the road. At a set of lights on Old Northern Road, she spoke.

'Lots of acreages, new and old money out here.'

It was a part of Sydney I hadn't spent much time in. I knew it attracted some high-profile people who shunned publicity and attention on their private lives.

'This whole area used to be orchards.' Mary glanced sideways and cleared her throat. 'I was way out of line yesterday with what I said. About Cal.'

I looked out at striking views of the Blue Mountains in the distance. 'If anyone had the right, it was you. We've known each other long enough to be honest –'

'It wasn't true,' she said.

I disagreed. 'I let my guard down and got suckered.'

'It isn't you I was angry with.' She accelerated around a cement truck in an overtaking lane. 'Surrogates in India are known to have borne kids to members of paedophile rings. Kids are bred for abuse and passed around the rings.'

I knew Mary had survived a rough childhood and that thankfully things had changed once she was fostered by a loving family. She rarely spoke about it.

Opposite a school, cows grazed. Further along, mangoes were being sold from the back of a truck. This area had rural advantages with city benefits. I let her speak in her own time.

'I was angry at a system that gives abusers rights just because they're biologically related,' she finally said. 'After everything they did to us, the courts gave our biological parents legal access. One weekend we were supposed to go for an unsupervised stay. Joanie refused and took off.'

Her hands gripped the steering wheel tighter.

I hadn't known the full extent of the problems in her childhood, but I was aware that her younger sister had died at fourteen.

'The police found her in a neighbour's shed that night. She hanged herself.' Her eyes were locked on the road. 'We'd have been better off if we were dogs. No one would have tolerated that amount of cruelty to an animal.'

Chapter 46

WE DROVE THE rest of the way in silence. There was nothing I could say to defuse her anger.

Mary pulled up about a hundred metres from the address, in the shade of a tree and out of range of the camera positioned on the electric gate.

The home was a single-level colonial style at the end of a gravel drive with pines planted on either side. Lawns looked recently mowed and the garden carefully manicured. To the side and behind the house sat a six-car shed. A stripped wooden chair had been left in the sun.

My pulse accelerated. The sliding access door was open. We had to play this right to get the baby out alive. I called Brett Thorogood using Mary's phone. Mine had zero reception.

I told him Johnny had managed to get a lead on an address in Dural. Our intel said the suspects may be inside. He warned me not to go near the house or approach Wallace. He'd take care of things from here. I wasn't in any mood to argue. It was the safest way of getting Zoe if she was, in fact, inside.

All we could do was watch the house and wait for the posse. But I couldn't sit still. The more information the police had when they arrived, the better.

I stepped out of the vehicle to look for other ways in or out of the property. Fences on either side and at the rear were visible from our position. I clicked photos on my phone.

The sound of a helicopter in the distance made me stop. It was headed our way.

It would alert the Wallaces. Who the hell would compromise the scene with a helicopter? I dialled Brett Thorogood and told him to get rid of the chopper.

As I left a message, Mary reacted. The Wallaces had seen me at the office, but didn't know her. She drove the Jeep up to the gate, lurching the gears as she came to a halt. She slid out and lifted the bonnet before kicking the car.

The helicopter drew closer.

Mary held up her phone in full view of the surveillance camera, as if looking for reception. The chopper remained on course as Mary buzzed the gate.

I watched, out of sight, ready to sprint at the first sign of trouble.

The front door opened and a male figure appeared in a T-shirt and shorts. The cocky walk was impossible to miss. It was Alexandrus Wallace aka Gus Finch.

He moved towards the electric gates and exchanged words with Mary. He had one hand in his pocket the whole time. He reached for something on the side and I tensed. Mary's body language remained relaxed but I knew she was alert.

The gates opened and Wallace casually strolled through. He stopped within arm's reach of her as he saw the helicopter closing in.

Chapter 47

THE WAIT WAS excruciating. I felt completely useless as Mary pointed to somewhere in the distance. Wallace shielded his eyes from the sun and nodded. I guessed Mary had invented a reason the helicopter might be flying by. Whatever she said worked. He was now peering over her engine.

The chopper buzzed closer. Mary moved swiftly and deftly, pinning him against the vehicle with his legs kicked wide apart and arms dragged behind him.

I dialled Brett's number again. This time, within seconds, police cars swarmed the address without sirens. If the wife was inside with Zoe, she could still be unaware of the ambush.

Tactical Response officers in full kit readied their weapons. The scene was about to explode.

The officer in charge spoke into his cheek mike. I had done training with Terry McMahon. He was outcome-focused and fiercely protective of his team. The odds of getting Zoe out just improved.

I sprinted towards Wallace as an armed officer tried to block my way. I produced ID and explained the man in custody was Alexandrus Wallace, the murder and kidnapping suspect. Terry gave instructions to allow me through.

Wallace was struggling against the cable ties Mary had applied.

'Thank God, you have to help me,' he pleaded. 'I came out to help and this crazy bitch attacked me.'

'Clarkey, nice work.' McMahon stood, legs wide, arms folded, smiling at her.

Wallace's head flicked from me to the special forces officer. 'You know each other?'

I stepped in front of him. 'Mary works with me. Where the hell is Zoe Ruffalo?'

Dust and wind picked up along with the noise from the helicopter. It dropped its nose and seemed to pause before accelerating rapidly down to roof level and making a low pass.

Terry McMahon gave orders into his mike. His manner was calm, but his message uncompromising. 'Get that chopper out of here. Now! Shoot it down if you have to.'

An officer waved it away. A weapon pointed in its direction seemed to deter the pilot from making another pass.

'You people are crazy.' Wallace pleaded with Terry. 'I swear to God, I just came out to help someone who had broken down.'

'No,' I said, 'you played me with lies about a surrogate. All you wanted to do was kill her. Was the baby a bonus, or was she the target all along?'

'You are insane!' he shouted. 'I haven't done anything wrong. I want this woman charged with assault.'

'Who do you know this man to be?' McMahon asked me.

'Gus Finch,' I said. 'He presented to my office and I had no reason to doubt him.'

Mary handed over the wallet she'd removed from his back pocket.

Terry McMahon leant in. 'Right now you're under citizen's arrest and I haven't confirmed your identity. For all I know you could have stolen this wallet.'

'That's BS and you know it.' He raised his head and called out, 'I have rights. I want a lawyer. Can all of you hear me? I want a lawyer.'

McMahon leant in closer. 'We'll be storming your house any minute. Our priority is getting the child out alive.' He held the microphone, turned his head to the side and spoke into it. 'Get into positions and wait for my command.'

As armed officers entered the property and spread out, I gave Wallace another chance.

'Tell us where your wife's got the baby. Once they go inside, if there's any resistance, they'll shoot.'

Chapter 48

'YOU'RE CRAZY. WE don't have a child. That's the reason we went to you. To find out about Louise Simpson.'

'You just admitted that in front of witnesses,' I said.

Mary and I babysat Wallace while Terry rang the home number. A few seconds later, he hung up.

'She answered. She's inside.'

'God Almighty.' Wallace tried to free himself from the binds. 'You've got it wrong. We don't have a baby. I'm trying to tell you. I swear that part was true.'

'Then why did you lie to us?' Mary kept one hand on his shoulder.

'Friends we met on the surrogate site told us to. To protect ourselves.' Wallace looked like he was about to cry. Gone was the arrogance. 'Please don't hurt Jen. She didn't do anything wrong.'

'Why would you need to lie if you were going through with an altruistic surrogacy?' Mary quizzed.

He lowered his head. 'It was always about money. To start with, Louise wanted twenty-five thousand. Up front.'

'Did she say she wanted more?' Mary demanded. 'Is that why you hit her?'

'What? No! It was always twenty-five now, twenty-five after delivery. We met her and everything was fine.'

'So what made you beat her? She change her mind? Is that why you rammed a knife into her?'

'I don't know what you're talking about. I didn't hit or stab anyone. Jennifer and I met Louise yesterday afternoon. At Queenscliff Beach. We worked out the arrangements and left. We've even got a medical appointment booked for next week.'

'Louise isn't going to make that one,' I said. 'But you already knew that.'

'I swear to God. Louise Simpson is fine.'

Mary went to the Jeep and pulled out two crime scene photos. She slapped them on the engine in front of Wallace. 'Do these jog your memory?'

He looked at them and turned his head away. 'Why are you doing this?'

'Look closer. Ring any bells?'

'Please,' he begged. 'What does any of this have to do with us?'

'Louise Simpson is dead.' I jabbed at the photos. 'Because of you. Then you took Zoe Ruffalo, an innocent baby.'

'Wait. Is that what you think?' He pleaded with both of us. 'You've got it all wrong. I've never seen that woman before. I don't know who she is, but she definitely isn't Louise Simpson.'

Chapter 49

THE TACTICAL RESPONSE team entered the house simultaneously through the front and back doors. Four more squad cars pulled up. Mark Talbot climbed out and headed towards us, as Terry McMahon checked in with his team.

The woman had surrendered and was in custody. No shots had been fired.

I pulled Mark aside.

'Wallace alleges our murder victim was not the same woman he met as Louise Simpson.'

'Alleges? So now you're a defence lawyer?' Mark sneered.

'I'm just saying something doesn't add up. He had no reason to lie this time.'

'It's called buying time by throwing in something from left field,' he said curtly. 'That's your specialty.'

There wasn't time for agendas here. 'What if there are two Louise Simpsons? Someone else is using her identity?'

He thought for a moment. 'You could be on to something. Now . . . you just have to prove the Illuminati are behind it.'

Mark was revelling in the fact my credibility was at stake. I stayed calm, but stressed my point. 'Wallace says he met someone claiming to be Louise Simpson, with two children, who lived in Killara.'

'And he's an upfront kind of guy, that Wallace, or should I say Finch?'

Yes, Wallace had lied. But he was also a coward, full of bluff. The way he responded to the photos wasn't what I would have expected from a cold-blooded killer who took his time and made the victim suffer.

If the Wallaces hadn't taken the baby, someone else had. And they had diverted all our energies to looking in the wrong place.

Two officers came out with Jennifer Wallace. Her hands were cuffed behind her back. 'Nothing so far,' one said.

Sniffer dogs alighted from another car. The trainer held a flannel blanket, presumably belonging to Zoe Ruffalo, to their noses.

Mark instructed them to search the cars, boots, in every bush, cranny and under every rock on the property.

Fifteen minutes later, the trainer came out. There was no trace of a baby.

Chapter 50

THE WOMAN THE Wallaces met had to be an imposter.

I phoned Johnny and asked him to go over all Louise Simpson's bills and debits again. We were looking for anything to suggest she was a victim of identity fraud.

He knew that meant the baby was still missing and agreed to get straight on to it.

Darlene's new machine was processing the DNA and would have an answer within minutes. I had to get clearance from Brett Thorogood to access the police's DNA database with the Gene-IE.

Mary and I decided to head back to the office. As we moved to the Jeep, someone called my name.

'Gisto. Hey, Craig! Congratulations on tracking down the killer.'

The voice came from the sleaziest entertainment reporter, Marcel Peyroni. I tossed up whether to ignore or answer him.

'Where's the baby? Were you too late?'

'He's an idiot,' Mary said. 'Ignore him.'

'Come on, Craig, you gotta have a comment,' he called.

I couldn't pretend the guy wasn't an arsehole. But I needed to know how this fool had managed to get a TV crew here so quickly. Had someone from the police leaked the news about the Wallaces? His stupidity had compromised the entire operation. If it wasn't for him and his helicopter, Mary wouldn't have had to put herself at risk. And I wouldn't have to suffer the ire of Mark Talbot.

I walked towards him, hand blocking my face from the camera lens. Mary was one step behind. I asked if we could talk 'off the record'.

Peyroni faked a smile. 'Of course.'

His cameraman lowered his lens, but I knew it was still recording.

'You're a regular johnny-on-the-spot,' I said. 'No one from the social pages here. You're in the wrong place.'

'On the contrary. This story has it all. Murdered widow, the fashionable Craig Gisto, Investigator and Scandal Suppresser to the stars.'

The microphone was suddenly beneath my chin. Peyroni had a blog, columns and a TV show. Spiteful press coverage from him could harm the business.

But I had no intention of giving him a sound bite.

Peyroni tried again. 'Do you have any response to the rumours that you provided the killer with all the details to find Louise Simpson?'

I turned away and Mary stepped in. 'The police will be keen to know how you beat them here. Something about obstructing justice, interfering with an investigation.'

Peyroni flashed an ultra-white smile. 'Good old-fashioned investigative journalism. I've learnt a lot studying the great Craig Gisto. Do you have anything to say, Miss Clarke, on his dramatic fall from grace?'

Chapter 51

PEYRONI'S STUNT COULD have put lives at risk. Zoe Ruffalo was still missing, and we were no closer to finding Louise's killer.

The one lead we had was the woman posing as Simpson. The Wallaces were our only hope of finding her.

I needed to get access to them during police questioning but didn't fancy my chances. I phoned Brett Thorogood who, thankfully, picked up.

'Craig, what the hell went down? Mark Talbot is ropable. He says you leaked the address to the tabloid press.'

'How many police knew? Maybe the leak's closer to home.'

Recent raids on potential terrorists had been stage-managed for media. With state and federal elections looming, politicians and police ministers basked in megawatt coverage of high-profile arrests. PR stunts like this reminded the public police were 'winning the war' against crime.

Brett paused. 'It's possible it came from within our ranks but I was very specific. Only those directly involved were notified. Because of what was at stake and the intense media interest. It could have ended badly.' His voice trailed off. 'If it came from someone within the force, their career is over. No matter who they are.'

Mark Talbot wasn't beyond suspicion either.

I described Wallace's reaction to the pictures of Louise Simpson's body. And how he seemed relieved that the dead woman was not the one he had met. Brett listened to my theory about someone impersonating Louise Simpson. With no other leads to finding Zoe Ruffalo, he agreed to see if he could get me in to question the Wallaces. With a warning. If I made any mistakes, the police relationship with Private would be terminated.

Mary and I headed back to the Jeep. She had been on the phone while I spoke to the deputy commissioner. She waited until we were alone inside the vehicle.

'I just spoke to the helicopter charter company. They've had a chopper on hold since yesterday. Booked by Craven Media.'

I pulled the seatbelt across my chest. 'That's Peyroni's employer.'

'The pilot was on stand-by and took a call at eight-fifteen am to fly to this address. Peyroni's team arrived twenty minutes later.'

It was like a heavy blow. That was the time we were on our way to Dural. Before I phoned the police.

'We have to face it,' Mary said. 'The leak came from someone inside our office.'

Chapter 52

MARY STOPPED AT a small shopping mall at the unusually named Round Corner.

'We can get a coffee. Looks like you need some sustenance.'

News of the timing of the leak had rocked me. I still had to decide how to handle it. The day was proving to be worse than yesterday and we still had no idea if Zoe was alive or where she might be. Mary was the only person I could trust right now.

We found a quaint café, called Chat Time, and took a seat in the outside section. The clientele comprised elderly people, mothers with babies and middle-aged women in exercise gear. They were all engaged in conversation at their respective tables. Not an electronic device in sight.

The atmosphere was homely, very different from city cafés. A middle-aged man dressed in a black shirt and trousers greeted us as I checked my phone for messages.

'We don't have wi-fi here,' he said with a natural smile. 'It encourages people to chat.'

The strategy definitely worked. Mary ordered scrambled eggs on toast. I chose a zucchini, eggplant and pesto melt. We both settled on lattes.

Before we addressed the office leak, I wanted to get an update on Eric Moss and his organisation. He'd been missing for four days now.

'Where are you up to with the Moss case?'

Mary sat forward, elbows on the table. 'This guy could be Roy Orbison. In the few photos he appears in, he's wearing darkened lenses. They completely hide his eyes and eyebrows. I couldn't locate one good facial image.'

'What about when he was younger?'

'That's the thing. There are no photos of him before Contigo. I checked the enrolments for schools in the area his daughter said he grew up in. Nothing. This guy had no internet presence.'

The coffees and cutlery arrived.

'It's like he's hiding in plain sight. He gets national hero status, receives top business and citizenship awards, but doesn't appear in any press. He's the legs paddling under the water, out of sight.'

'And Lang Gillies is the duck's head you see on the surface.'

Our food appeared and I realised how little I'd consumed in the last two days. I ate like someone who didn't know when their next meal might be. In many ways that was true. This was going to be another long and draining day.

Mary devoured her eggs, pausing once to wipe her mouth with a serviette.

'I even checked for Throwback Thursday photos, brush-with-fame websites. No one's posted anything of Moss as an adult or child. And he doesn't appear on any politician's websites. Seems he avoided pics with them too. The man was definitely hiding in full view.'

I began to wonder. If he had been hiding for that long, he could have had an exit strategy – in case he was ever exposed.

Chapter 53

BACK AT PRIVATE, a nervous Collette greeted us. We had a visitor who had already shown himself into my office. Two bodyguards waited in the foyer.

One scanned Mary first, with a handheld metal detector, then me.

'Standard procedure, for people Mr Ambassador meets.' He had a southern American twang.

Scanner man stayed guarding our entrance, while the other guard walked us to my office and waited outside with Mary.

'Ambassador Jim Roden.' A silver-haired man of around sixty greeted me. His suit was expensive, I guessed Italian. The tie was silk, with embossed blue flowers on a lighter background. A perfectly folded pocket handkerchief matched. An American flag badge was pinned to his lapel. We shook hands.

I asked if he would like something to drink before noticing the bottle of mineral water from my bar fridge.

'Hope you don't mind, I helped myself. Your receptionist said it was OK.'

I suspected Collette was intimidated by the formality and accompanying muscle.

'What can I do for you, Mr Ambassador?'

He unbuttoned his jacket and crossed a heel over one knee. 'I'm concerned about Eric Moss.'

I sat and leant back. 'Are you a friend?'

'Acquaintance. We've met on a couple of occasions. At a fundraiser and again at the Embassy. He was an impressive man.'

I noted the use of the word 'was'. I wondered what he knew about the disappearance.

'Eric Moss only resigned four days ago.'

'So I hear. My concern is not just personal. Mr Moss has accessed a number of sensitive US facilities during his time with Contigo Valley.'

'Are you worried he's sharing state secrets?'

'We'd like to know what his plans are from here. He has a vast body of knowledge and we'd like to make him a very tempting job offer.'

I found that difficult to believe. He was fishing for information. Somehow he knew we were employed by Eliza. Then again, anyone could have seen us together last night and put two and two together. Word in the business world was leaching out about Moss's sudden departure from the company he'd been loyal to for decades.

I sat forward. 'If I see him, I'll get him to give you a call.'

'Mr Gisto, I'm afraid you don't understand. There may be considerable embarrassment if Mr Moss is not located quickly.'

I decided to do some fishing myself. 'Can you explain to me how someone without a passport or birth certificate gets access to your secure facilities? I'm guessing there are some red faces about that little oversight when a simple web search would have raised alarms.' Unless, as I suspected, all information pertaining to Moss had been systematically removed from the internet.

Roden sipped the mineral water from the bottle. 'I hear you and Moss's daughter have developed a rapport.'

I leant in, uncomfortable about where this was heading. 'I'm not at liberty to discuss clients or investigations.'

'I'm just saying that relationship could be very useful.' He stood. 'International politics can be a minefield. My government would appreciate your sharing relevant information about Moss's whereabouts.'

'Are you suggesting I break commercial confidence?'

'I'm suggesting you consider both our nations' security. I trust you'll keep our communication private.'

I chose my words carefully. 'For reasons of national interest.'

He stared at me for a few seconds. 'Precisely,' he said, without a hint of irony.

Chapter 54

I SAT BACK. He'd caught me off guard. For him to mention my rapport with Eliza suggested someone *had* seen us last night, or she was under surveillance.

Mary saw the visitors out and returned to my office. 'Secret Service. It's all I got.'

Moss had to be in serious trouble if the US government wanted him found asap.

'They're desperate if they came to us for info,' Mary said. 'It's not easy to drop right off the grid. Especially theirs.'

I agreed. Whatever Moss knew made him hot property. If he had planned his disappearance, it was years in the making. I thought of him in photos. The images I'd seen had him in half-profile, with the dark lenses. He was in the habit of hiding part of his face before the advent of facial recognition software. No passport or driver's licence meant there were no documented facial images, front on, eyes captured. He had a strategy all along to avoid being identified. But why? The behaviour dated back to his beginnings at Contigo, when they were a simple search and rescue group.

Mary wondered aloud, 'Maybe he wasn't just working for Contigo.'

From the amount of time he spent there, and the fact he lived on the premises, it was a stretch.

'Or . . .' I said, 'Contigo is a front for something more.' I thought again of the private contracts only Moss had access to. 'Something the ambassador said bothers me. He specifically said they wanted Moss "located".'

Mary sank into the chair vacated by the ambassador. 'No concern for his welfare.'

Eliza was worried about foul play. Roden wasn't interested in finding out. He wanted us to locate Moss, dead or alive.

If he was alive, it couldn't be easy staying on the run from US security agencies.

And if Moss was CIA or an operative for another country, he'd broken a cardinal rule. No complications. Moss had blown that by adopting Eliza and having personal ties. A disabled child was more than a simple complication. Contigo Valley had to be supplying or developing something the US government wanted. Why else would US defence facilities give Moss access then panic when he disappeared?

I wanted answers as to why the US government was suddenly on our back, and why they were using us to get to Moss.

I doodled on my notepad. It helped me think, piece together puzzles. 'Roden mentioned sensitive facilities Moss visited.'

'I know just the person to talk to,' Mary said. 'His personal pilot would have filed logs of times, dates of departures and destinations.'

'Good idea. We need to figure out what he was working on. Whatever contracts were in that locked desk.'

Mary raised the other pressing issue. 'How are you going to deal with the media leak?'

I rubbed my neck again. There was only one thing to do.

Chapter 55

I DOUBTED THE smashed office door was an accident now. We were the only business targeted in the attack and it provided access to plant listening devices. I wouldn't put it past Roden. The visit could have been an excuse to hide additional monitoring devices or modify ones already in place. Roden was unchaperoned in my office before we came back, and the cronie with the metal detector kept Collette distracted. I thought back to the repairmen. They were from a company we hadn't used before. Colette had found the card under the door and they'd answered her call straightaway.

I suspected we'd been set up. I pulled out my phone and checked for their website. The company didn't exist in the Yellow Pages or online.

Whoever smashed the glass assumed a staff member would call the first available glazier. One thing concerned me: the timing. The door had been smashed *before* Jack Morgan rang me about Eric Moss.

Unless Jack's LA office was being monitored, a US agency wouldn't have known we would be involved. It was a stretch at best.

And how did Marcel Peyroni hear about the Dural raid if he wasn't tipped off by someone in our office? If we were being electronically monitored, there was no way a secret intelligence agency would be in cahoots with a tabloid gossipmonger, or risk exposure by leaking news of a raid. That left the question as to whether one of my team was on Peyroni's payroll.

I felt a deep knot in my gut.

I rang an old friend who specialised in technical security countermeasures sweeps. Without mentioning what I wanted, I asked if he'd like to come for a visit and see the offices. He agreed to be here within the hour. I trusted my staff and couldn't believe any one of them would risk lives by notifying a low-life like Marcel Peyroni. I had no answer as to why a third party listening to us would, if only to discredit me and my team.

Mary and I headed to the lab. Darlene had just sent the DNA printout from the evidence beneath Louise's fingernails to the police. The new machine was beneficial but an arrest depended on other factors. We had to show motive, opportunity and compare the finding to a suspect's DNA.

Darlene was frustrated. 'We won't know if Wallace is our killer unless he agrees to a DNA test.'

His lawyer would no doubt advise him to avoid giving any samples that could be used against him until they had enough for a warrant.

Mary reached into her pocket. 'Beg to differ.'

She pulled out a bag containing the severed cable ties she'd used to bind Wallace's wrists.

Darlene's face beamed. 'Give me an hour and a half and we'll know if it was Wallace at the murder scene.'

Chapter 56

GIDEON MAHLER HAD always been slightly eccentric. We'd met in the US when I introduced him to an expat friend. The pair married and moved to Australia. The marriage didn't last but Gideon's services became more in demand. Politicians constantly used him to test their offices for listening devices. Rumour had it ADIA (the Australian Defence Intelligence Agency) had the country's one hundred wealthiest business people under constant surveillance. With trade agreements including China, Japan, Indonesia and Russia, it made some degree of sense – to ADIA.

Gideon was gaunt, sinewy and had deep-set eyes that constantly scanned his surroundings. His first stop was the reception area. He looked under the desk for remnants of dust from holes drilled, checked for any pictures that were even slightly askew, anything out of its normal position. Gideon's assessment cost a premium but our business depended on confidentiality and that couldn't be compromised. I was not about to get Eric Moss killed if we tracked him down.

The smashed door and computer virus on Collette's laptop, which meant the video cameras didn't record that night, had to be related. All I could do was wait. I tried Brett Thorogood and left another message. Once the DNA from the cable ties was back, we'd know if Wallace had lied about being at Louise Simpson's house. Instinct told me he hadn't. If Darlene could confirm that, I needed immediate access to quiz him about the woman he claimed to have met.

I rang Eric Moss's assistant, Oliver Driscoll, to see if he'd accessed the filing cabinet yet. He sounded as if he was in an echo chamber.

'Is Eric OK?' Apart from Eliza, the young assistant and accountant were the only ones who had asked about their former boss's welfare.

'We haven't found him yet, which is why I'm ringing.'

There was an audible sigh.

'I don't know how I can help. I've been given until four pm to clean out my belongings and leave the building. We're not supposed to talk to you, but I'm worried. I can't get the diary copies out.'

I asked him where he was at the moment and if anyone could hear him.

'I'm alone in the bathroom for now. I'm not the only one who's been told to leave. Renee Campbell, the lady you met with, was the first to go. Something is really wrong and I don't understand. I couldn't find the resignation email.'

'Did you manage to get into Eric's personal safe?'

'Sir Lang got a locksmith in but it was empty when he opened it.'

If no one else had access, Eric could have cleaned it out before leaving. Something else was worrying the assistant.

'You think Gillies lied about the resignation?'

'I don't know. But it gets freakier. My flat was trashed. Police reckon it was druggies looking for cash because the flat screen and Xbox One weren't touched. I thought it was my psycho ex, only he's in New Zealand.'

It wasn't a usual break and enter, even for drug addicts. 'Did you have work files there?'

'No. Only stuff on my laptop, and that stays with me. I think something happened to Eric.'

The fear in his voice was clear.

'We're going to find him. In the meantime, can you stay with a friend for a few days? Just until we get to the bottom of whatever's going on?'

'My parents live on the north coast. I can go there.'

I had one more question. 'Have you ever seen or heard of a Jim Roden?'

'Sure, the ambassador's one of Lang Gillies's golf buddies. The old man likes to drop his name and how he used to advise President Bush on homeland security.'

It may not have been Moss working for someone else. I began to suspect Lang Gillies of being more than he pretended.

Chapter 57

GIDEON ENTERED MY office and closed the door.

'I swept the entire place, toilets and bathrooms included. The building's clean.'

That was a relief.

'There's a qualifier on that. I also looked at the computers and phones of all the employees, including yours, as you know.'

Mine was the first I wanted checked. 'And?'

'Good news is the computers are free of viruses and malware, as are your backups. No one called a reporter this morning from their phones or the office, no emails or texts either.'

It was reassuring but didn't explain how Peyroni got the Wallaces' address as soon as we had it. Or why the computer was infected. Or the door was smashed. If that wasn't done to plant listening devices, what was the point? 'What's the bad news?'

'There's spyware on one of your employees' phones.'

I sat back. This was the moment I dreaded. 'Spyware? What sort?'

'The sort that makes a phone a listening device, whether it's on or off. And accesses computers when used as a hotspot.'

Before I heard the name I needed to know. 'Can anyone install it or does it require specialised knowledge? Can it be downloaded remotely?'

He shook his head. 'The person installing it has to physically have the phone.' He pulled a document from his case and handed it across. It was a detailed explanation of this particular phone spyware.

'Anything else?'

'Yeah, two of your employees are dating. Don't know if you have a policy on that, 'cause they're trying to keep it quiet.'

'Did you go through all their texts as you scanned?'

'No,' he smiled, 'noticed them touching hands in the lab when they thought no one was looking. Otherwise, they're clean.'

Johnny had been helping out more with evidence. It was because of Darlene.

'That's one headache we can sort out if the time comes.' It left Mary and Collette. Mary had been livid about me taking on the background check but she always carried her phone and wallet on her. She never put them down. That left one person.

'Your receptionist's the leak,' Gideon said. 'Everything coming in and out of the office has been recorded for a third party.'

I couldn't believe it. Collette? I had trusted her implicitly. 'Any idea who's receiving?'

'Could take a while to find out. Everything's being rerouted.'

'Can you tell how long it's been on there?'

'Again, I'll need some time. Oh, and one more thing. If she didn't actually load the software, it's possible she doesn't know it's there. You have to know what to look for.'

So Collette either knew her phone was a listening device or her phone had been deliberately targeted. Either way, I couldn't afford to trust her from now on.

I thanked Gideon. I had a plan as to how to deal with Collette. We all needed to meet in the conference room.

Chapter 58

BEFORE THE MEETING, I handed each staff member a written note asking them to hand over their phone. All would be explained in the conference room in five minutes. In the meantime, I put the mobiles in my office for Gideon to work on. If the eavesdroppers weren't aware we'd found the software, we still had an advantage.

Once we were all seated around the table, Gideon did precisely what I'd asked. He announced that the phones had been infected with malware. At the moment he had no idea for how long. The software ensured that private discussions were recorded by an unidentified third party. Not just phone conversations, but in-person chats, in addition to texts and voicemail messages. Anything previously thought private was now potentially in the public domain.

Johnny and Darlene exchanged the briefest of looks but said nothing.

Mary rocked back in her chair. 'Hacks or pros?'

Gideon shrugged. 'The software's readily available online, which means a broad net. How they react from here will tell us a lot more. If there are any other "incidents".'

Collette's phone had been to every meeting and with her for every interaction with staff and clients. Like most twenty-somethings, the phone was permanently in her hands or within easy reach to check the latest message. I called it the fear of missing out that meant they were often engaged in social contact but experienced little meaningful interaction.

'Has anyone let their phone out of sight, or had someone ask to make a call, no matter how innocuous they could have seemed?'

I looked around the silent room. 'When you exercise, do you leave it in a locker? When you shower does anyone else have access? I don't care how close they are to you or how much you trust them.'

Mary, Johnny and Darlene all denied the possibility.

'Collette?' I asked.

She frowned. 'I use mine for music in the bathroom, like when I'm getting ready or showering. And I have it strapped to my arm when I go walking.'

'What about clients, visitors to the office? Maybe when you got them a coffee or tea.'

'Always have it with me. Guess it's a habit.'

I suspected Collette was unaware of the software. Now was the perfect time to lie if she knew the spyware would be found on her phone and wanted to divert suspicion.

I handed out brand-new burner replacements and asked if there was anything on anyone's phones they didn't want Gideon Mahler or me to see. No one responded.

'From now on, we use these to communicate for work and with each other.'

Collette remained silent but her eyes darted from me to Gideon.

'Who do you think's behind it? Is it anything to do with the Moss case?' Mary queried.

'We're working on that,' Gideon answered. 'But we should have an answer later on.'

I added, 'Until further notice, everyone takes a phone, and make sure we have each other's new numbers. Until this is sorted, I want everyone to stay in constant touch, and give me the names of anyone who makes contact with you – socially or for work. I guarantee we're going to find out who's behind this.'

Chapter 59

COLLETTE WAITED UNTIL the others had left.

Her face had become flushed and blotches extended to her neck. She was rubbing an index finger over her thumbnail repeatedly.

'How long do you think someone's been spying on us?'

I slid into the seat next to hers.

'We don't know yet, possibly a few days.'

Her attention turned to rubbing her palms. 'I don't know if this is important, but I just sort of met someone.'

'How recently?'

'Couple of nights, but it feels like months. We just seemed to click.'

It had to be the man I'd spotted her leave with. That could have been their first date.

'Has he shown interest in your work?'

'No but I met him here. In the office, the morning the door was broken.'

The man I watched greet her that night wasn't one of the repairers. 'Was he with the glass company?'

'No, he was headed to his office early when I arrived and stopped to see if I was OK. He works in the next block. We got talking and he said he didn't normally ask someone out so fast, but he thought we had a –'

'Connection?' I doubted it was a coincidence. The timing of the computer virus, glass damage and 'accidental' meeting were too convenient. If the repairers didn't plant the devices, accessing Collette and gaining her trust could have been the purpose of the smashed door. 'Let me guess. You're interested in the same things, he likes what you like, maybe even grew up near you?'

The blotches on her neck reddened. 'He's from Tasmania. Devonport.'

Collette's family came from Launceston. Like anywhere, a link to childhoods was a strong one. It was an easy 'in' for a scammer to develop instant affinity with a target.

'What else do you have in common?'

'He learnt to drive on a VW.'

Collette owned one.

'And he listens to indie bands.'

'Like the ones you have on your phone?'

She swallowed hard. 'Is that how they knew about the raid at Dural? Has he been using me to get to . . .' Tears welled in her eyes.

I suspected they'd been intimate but it wasn't relevant. Whoever 'he' was could have accessed her phone when they were together or when she slept.

'This is all my fault.' She pushed the burner phone away. 'I'm sorry I caused you all this trouble.' Collette stood. 'The keys to the office are in my bag. I'll go get them.'

I rose and pushed the chair back into its place. I would bet money that Collette would never make the same mistake again. 'You're not in trouble and you still have your job. In fact, you're our best chance of catching this character and finding out who he's working for.'

She squinted, doubtful.

'He doesn't know we're on to him. When are you due to see him again?'

'Tonight. He is . . . I mean *was* . . . coming over for dinner.'

'Everyone's got to eat. Looks like you have a date to keep.'

Chapter 60

COLLETTE PASSED MARY on the way out.

'Eric Moss's personal pilot is headed to Contigo Valley later this afternoon.' She raised her eyebrows.

'Where's he leaving from?'

'Bankstown airport.'

'Any chance you can get us on the flight?'

'Hedge a bet?'

I laughed. 'Not when you're on the job.' If anyone could get us on the plane, Mary could. I was suddenly reminded how talented the team was. The office being bugged was a glitch. We still had work to do.

First, I needed to talk to Eliza Moss in person, without her phone. Ambassador Roden had implied she was being watched.

She agreed to meet in the foyer of her office building in twenty minutes.

I was there in ten.

A concierge sat behind a large marble desk answering queries from a constant stream of visitors. I watched from a black leather divan. The CIA would most likely have Eliza under surveillance. Once she arrived, from where I sat

I could see who followed in the lifts and lingered even for a moment.

Eliza eventually appeared, wheeling herself out. She was dressed in a short-sleeved silk blouse and navy skirt. A silver filigree locket sat on a short chain. Her face was drawn with a touch of darkness under her eyes. She couldn't have managed much sleep.

The concierge looked up and called out to her. 'Found your present.' He held up a pack of gum. 'Twenty-seven days today.'

'You and your lungs are welcome,' she called back before doing a half-circle to face me.

I kept my eyes on everyone exiting the lifts.

'Why the secrecy? Is Dad all right?'

I explained about the visit by Roden's crew and the fact that it was likely they were having her monitored and followed.

'Who'd want to follow me? It's pretty far-fetched, don't you think?'

'It isn't when the CIA could be involved. Someone planted spyware on my employee's phone and has been listening in to all conversations in the office. The break-in coincided with a virus on a computer as well.'

'Why would the CIA care about Dad? He worked in safety and recovery, for Pete's sake.'

People in suits, jeans, even a cyclist in Lycra and bike helmet filed out of the lifts. No one seemed to look twice at Eliza.

'He was obviously involved in defence contracts that were kept pretty quiet. Maybe he failed to deliver on time, or couldn't complete a contract for some reason. The US government definitely wants him found.'

She sat back in her chair.

A woman hovered by the concierge desk, glancing at her watch more often than necessary. She pulled out her phone and checked something.

'Well, why haven't they found him yet? People can't just hide from the CIA.'

The woman with the phone knelt down and a toddler ran into her arms. They exited with a man pushing a stroller. For a moment the foyer was empty apart from us.

'Not unless they have some kind of training in how to avoid being caught,' I explained. 'It isn't just your father who has disappeared. So has almost all the evidence that he ever existed.'

Chapter 61

ELIZA LISTENED INTENTLY. I'd noticed a man sit and start flicking through a four-wheel drive magazine on an adjacent lounge.

'Could Dad have been arrested by these people?'

'Not yet. Otherwise they wouldn't have come to me, or need to watch you. It makes sense; you're his only family. He may try to pass something on to you, or send you a message.' I looked directly into those intense green eyes. 'Has he?'

'No. I would have told you.' She dragged a piece of hair from her forehead and tucked it behind one ear. 'He would have warned me if something was wrong. That's why I'm scared for him.'

I instinctively reached out and took her hand. 'Maybe it happened too fast.' It occurred to me that Eric knew whatever he was involved in could endanger his daughter. Alternatively, he may have known she'd be under surveillance and was unable to get in touch safely. 'I suspect he may have known a time would come when he had to disappear. He just didn't know exactly when until last week.'

'Thank you for helping.' Eliza gently squeezed my fingers. 'What happens if the ambassador's people, or the CIA, or whoever, find my father? What will they do to him?'

'Honestly, I don't know. First I have to find out what they want from him.'

The magazine reader got up and headed to the stairwell.

'Can you think of anything he could have said, hinted at, or something he maybe gave you that at the time you thought wasn't important?'

She stared at her lap, concentrating for a few moments. 'Nothing stands out. We talked about going fishing again soon, or maybe a cruise. What if he did give me a sign and I missed it?'

'It's OK,' I assured her. 'Something might come back to you. For now, I want you to use this when we talk or meet.' I pulled out a spare burner phone. 'I'm the only one who has this but I've programmed in my staff's contacts as well as mine. Don't hesitate to call. What you may think is trivial could be vital in finding him.'

She put the phone by her side so it was hidden from view. 'You mean before anyone else gets to him.' Her voice wavered.

'Your father may have ticked off some pretty important people. From what I know of him, he's good at hiding. We have the advantage because we have you.'

She squeezed my hand again. 'I'll go through what I have. Cards, gifts, photos, messages.'

I felt a strange connection to this woman, one that I hadn't experienced in a long time. I put it down to her being a vulnerable client. Eliza Moss was no victim, but she could just be a target.

I stood and checked the foyer one more time. Apart from occasional glances, no one seemed particularly interested in us. 'I'll come see you when I get back from interviewing the Contigo Valley pilot. Whatever your father is involved in is serious. You need to be careful.'

Chapter 62

IN THE LAB, Johnny and Darlene sat on adjacent stools. He circled three recent billings on Louise Simpson's credit card, all for a radiology practice in Manly.

'Unless you know someone at a particular practice, why would you drive for what would be an hour-and-a-half round trip, with two small kids, just to get an X-ray?'

Darlene checked the billings. 'My mum said her world shrank after kids. She stopped going to doctors, shops and hairdressers who weren't near home or school.'

'My point exactly. There are two other X-ray places within a five-minute drive.'

Darlene flicked through a series of notes she'd taken. 'The GP says Louise didn't have any medical problems apart from reflux and sciatica after the second child that settled in a couple of months. No tests either, nothing except the kids' vaccinations.'

'Maybe she was a doctor shopper. It wouldn't be unusual if she wanted sleeping tablets or painkillers and didn't want her regular doctor to know. Maybe they ordered the X-rays.'

'That's easy to sort out then.' Darlene winked. She clicked

at the computer and then phoned Medicare, leaning across Johnny to read the credit card bill.

'I'm sorry to bother you, but I need to ask about one of my Medicare bills. Since my husband died, and the insurance company hasn't paid us, things are pretty tight for the kids and me.'

She instantly had the operator's attention.

'I'm trying to go over my medical expenses, to see if we qualify for the safety net but I can't remember all the tests I've had. I remember the last bill was for X-rays I had on the twentieth of last month. I paid $375.' Her voice dropped away just a little. 'My husband used to manage our finances.'

Johnny watched as she read out Louise's name, date of birth and Medicare number. It was enough to get the operator to answer her query. After a few nods and 'uh-huhs', during which she took copious notes, she finished the conversation. 'Thank you for this. You've been very kind.'

Johnny admired Darlene's phone manner. She could charm a politician into giving away his dirtiest secrets.

'Well,' Darlene turned to Johnny, 'Louise had three ultrasounds in a month, and six in the last three months. All of them were abdominal. She must have paid for some in cash if they're not all on her credit cards.'

'Don't suppose she said which doctor ordered them?'

'She did. The family GP – who has no record of them.'

'And we know Louise *wasn't* pregnant.' Johnny flicked through his notes. 'The Wallaces said they met the surrogate and paid a hefty deposit at Queenscliff. Which is . . .'

'Adjacent to Manly,' Darlene added. 'Chances are, the woman posing as Louise Simpson lives nearby.'

Chapter 63

I PARKED AT Bankstown airport with Mary and entered the small grey building with the blue passenger terminal sign. It was smaller than that of many regional airports.

Inside, the sole check-in counter was unattended. A couple near the exit was uninhibited about displaying affection. The septuagenarian would have been twice, possibly three times the woman's age, with a wispy comb-over.

A man dressed all in white entered from the airfield side, greeted the couple and collected their luggage. They headed to a Cessna on the tarmac outside. The woman struggled up the stairs in her six-inch heels.

'How long do you give it?' Mary asked.

'Not much longer than the trip,' I guessed.

'Hard to believe cynics like us are single,' she said as a thin gentleman in his fifties approached us.

'Ms Clarke?' He reached out his hand, first to Mary then me. 'Geoff Andren.'

'This is my boss, Craig Gisto,' Mary said. 'Thanks for seeing us.'

The pilot's silver hair was cropped short, nothing out of place. A white epaulet shirt bearing the Contigo logo was immaculately pressed, as were the navy belted trousers. Attention to detail was something I respected, especially in people who controlled the cockpit of a plane.

He escorted us through a security gate on to the tarmac. 'Bankstown specialises in charters, cargo and flight training,' he said, as if taking a tourist group for the hundredth time.

A plane landed on a distant runway as we approached a hangar. Sitting outside was a scaled-down version of Howard Hughes's Spruce Goose.

Mary stopped to admire it. 'Is that a Grumman Goose B49?'

Arms folded, Geoff paused and rocked on his heels. 'Yep. She's a beauty. Been here since it was built, in 1944.'

As we walked on, Johnny rang and I excused myself to answer. He said that Collette had agreed to meet the new boyfriend at her home tonight, with Darlene and Johnny outside monitoring the situation. I told him to keep me informed and get Collette out at the first hint of trouble. He also said he had a lead about the Simpson imposter he'd follow up first.

The pilot had become more animated.

'The hangars on this side are all original. They housed bombers in World War Two. In fact, when General Macarthur visited, this was the airport used by the US Army Air Forces.'

The enormity of the airport became apparent. It was amazing all this existed in the middle of suburbia. 'Did civilians object to having a military target so close to their homes in wartime?'

Geoff's eyes beamed. 'They disguised this place to look like farmland. Fake houses, fake roads, dummy roofs to hide the hangars.'

I thought it sounded a lot like Eric Moss. Something hidden in full sight.

A helicopter's rotorblades started up.

'Robinson R44?' Mary asked.

'You'd get on well with Eric. He loves military history and flying.' Our host pointed to a helicopter that landed on a pad in front of another hangar. 'Eric pilots the one we have at Contigo.'

I knew Eliza hadn't mentioned that skill. Maybe she didn't know. She had said that her father didn't like flying that much.

If Moss had access to a helicopter, the odds of us locating him just got a whole lot worse.

Chapter 64

ANY INFORMATION GEOFF Andren could give us was critical. He had vital knowledge no one else at Contigo was willing or able to share.

'It would help us to know a little about Mr Moss's routine, especially with travelling to and from Contigo,' I said, pleased Mary had gained his confidence.

'I always had the plane at the terminal, ready for take-off as soon as Mr Moss arrived.'

At the four-seater Duchess, Geoff hesitated. 'All staff were issued with advice from Sir Lang not to talk to private investigators.'

'We don't want you getting into trouble, but we have real concerns for Eric's safety.' Mary made the powerful point.

The pilot shoved both hands in his pockets and his eyes focused on the plane wheels. 'He gave me a job when I was let go from a commercial airline. He's been good to me from the start.'

Moss's intentions may have been noble, or he deliberately recruited people who were at a disadvantage and most likely to be compliant.

I asked why Moss chose the Duchess.

'His work was unpredictable. The Duchess is the most efficient way to get him around.' He proudly touched the wing. 'Extra instrumentation means she's more capable in rough conditions. We're over the Blue Mountains to and from Contigo, so he wanted something that could fly even in bad weather.'

The pilot asked Mary which military bases she had worked on, which quickly segued into which installations he had flown Moss to. The list was extensive.

'I thought he spent most of his time in Contigo Valley,' I ventured.

'True, but there are frequent short flights. Anything from one to four a week.'

'To the bases?' Mary was almost drowned out by a plane taking off.

Geoff explained, 'Often Mr Moss is in transit at the bases. Sometimes I see the other plane he's meeting. Otherwise I leave him alone to wait on the runway.'

The notion struck me as odd. 'How do you mean alone? With the people he was meeting?'

'Funny thing, I never saw anyone else. Not even the other pilot. My instructions were to wait in the lounge if he was gone for a few hours. Otherwise, I'd fly home and then go back for him. The longest he was away was three days.'

'Anyone return with him?'

'Not that I saw. He was always standing there alone when I arrived to pick him up.'

'What did he take with him? Luggage? Did he bring anything back?' The whole thing seemed highly suspicious to me.

'He only ever had the same duffel bag. Khaki, about so big.' He made a shape about 60 centimetres wide and 30 centimetres high.

The bag wasn't large enough to fit much of anything in apart from a laptop and maybe a change of clothes. 'Do you know what was in it?'

'Never saw. That thing didn't leave his side. He always insisted on carrying it himself.'

I now understood how Moss had managed to leave the country without a passport. He was using military planes, which meant there was no available record of where he'd been.

Yet we still had no idea who Moss actually was, or who he was really working for.

Chapter 65

JOHNNY FELT THIS was the break they needed to find Louise's killer, and baby Zoe. He entered the radiology practice in Manly where a series of ultrasounds had been billed to Louise Simpson's Medicare number and credit card. She was a victim of identity *and* medical fraud. Paying her bills automatically meant it could have gone on indefinitely if the amounts weren't enough to raise suspicion and Louise didn't scrutinise every transaction. Like most people, she seemed to have just scheduled payments to avoid late fees.

Johnny suspected the fraudster was using other identities as well. This imposter knew not to be greedy and risk exposure. Otherwise, she could have cleaned out Louise Simpson's account, taken out loans and financially ruined her for the sake of a quick pay-off. This woman had other plans. Surrogacy was her way of leeching money from desperate couples. They could hardly report her to the police if things went sour, given their involvement was illegal.

A soap opera blared on a large TV screen to a waiting room full of children and elderly people.

Johnny joined the queue at the reception desk, wondering if he should have done medicine after all. The radiology business was booming.

'Request form?' A middle-aged woman held out her hand without looking up.

'I'm not here for an X-ray. I need to see whoever's in charge,' Johnny began.

'I'm sorry. Doctors only see technicians and equipment reps with appointments. You'll have to wait until September.' She tapped at a keyboard.

Johnny showed his ID, leant over the counter top and said quietly, 'I'm investigating this practice's involvement in Medicare fraud in the case of a young mother who was brutally murdered.'

That caught the receptionist's full attention. 'I'll see what I can do.'

She wheeled back her chair and rushed off behind the scenes.

Nothing like the mention of murder and scandal to get action, Johnny thought.

A small man in a shirt and tie appeared with the receptionist. She was flushed and tugged at the hem of her shirt.

'I'm Dr Kwong,' he said. 'Please come this way.'

Johnny followed him down a corridor and into a large X-ray viewing room. Multiple lit boxes held films of chests, limbs and sections of a brain scan.

'How can I help you?' Dr Kwong offered a seat.

'You may have seen on the news,' Johnny said as he sat, 'a woman was murdered in Killara. Louise Simpson?'

The doctor lowered himself into a chair. 'My wife went to church this morning to pray for her and the baby. Do you know if she has been found?'

'Not yet. The woman who died supposedly had scans performed here recently and I need to see documentation of who did them and why.'

'With any patient and medical record, there are strict confidentiality issues. I have to check with the Medical Defence Association before we can speak about any cases, even a deceased patient.'

'I respect legality and ethics.' Johnny leant forward. 'There were a number of charges for ultrasounds billed to your practice. We believe Louise Simpson's Medicare number and credit card were used in those transactions. And because of that an innocent young mother is dead. A whole lot of trouble is about to rain down on this place.'

'I'll make a quick call,' Dr Kwong said. 'What do you need to know?'

Chapter 66

GEOFF ANDREN WAS taking replacement engine parts to Contigo Valley and agreed to take us there so we could see firsthand what Eric Moss had built. I wondered if it would give us any clues as to why the Americans were so desperate to find him. All things going well, Geoff estimated we'd complete his business and the three-hundred-kilometre round trip in four hours.

We climbed on board and were handed earphones with microphones. Geoff checked his flight plan and cleared us to taxi. Once the engines were on, my stomach felt unsettled. Lack of sleep, food and a neck ache were adding up. I also hoped Collette would be safe. I had no idea who we had been targeted by. I disliked putting a team member at potential risk without knowing who we were up against.

The one positive was that we'd be back in time to monitor her house and provide backup for Johnny and Darlene.

We were soon cleared for take-off. The engine hummed louder and we were seamlessly in the air.

Mary and Geoff chatted about the plane's technical features and I closed my eyes for a few minutes. I could fly in helicopters and large planes. It was the small ones that unnerved me. I'd known at least two people killed in them, both due to pilot error.

And for some reason, I couldn't get Eliza Moss out of my head. The feel of her hands, the smell of her citrus perfume.

The hum and vibration of the engine hastened the need to doze.

I was startled by Mary tapping me on the leg. 'You've got to see this,' she said into her mike.

We were flying west over the Blue Mountains. I'd never seen them from this perspective.

'Gillies Falls.' Our pilot pointed to the right side.

The site was spectacular even if clouds were moving in.

'We may be in for some turbulence,' Geoff warned.

With the plane buffeting, we passed Lithgow and came on a spectacular green valley, like something from a lost world.

'That's Contigovale, known locally as CTV. It isn't part of the organisation but is dependent on our staff to stay afloat.'

There were a small number of buildings on the ground, more like a village than a town, I thought. It had what appeared to be its own runway.

Mary asked, 'How much land does Contigo own?'

'Thirty-three acres surrounded by grazing land and national parks. The actual base sits above the valley, by the Casta River.'

This had to be the wealthiest non-profit organisation in the country. It made me more than curious to find out where Moss really got all the money.

Chapter 67

WE FLEW OVER a series of shipping containers, one of which was located next to a helipad.

'Did Eric ever invite guests out here with him?' I asked.

'Bankers, potential donors, celebrities, politicians. We've brought people who begged to come out and be photographed here.'

The engine buzzed and the aircraft dropped a couple of times.

'We fly everyone over this spot to show them what we're developing.'

'What's in those?' Mary pointed to the containers with helicopter access. There was nowhere else to land.

'Collateral, resources. Each is filled with millions of dollars' worth of high-tech equipment and can be opened if bankers need to see them before they approve loans. They view a couple at the base first, but they're free to see the others if they wish.'

I was curious about the funding. 'Did the GFC affect the organisation and make it more dependent on loans?'

Geoff checked the instruments and adjusted something I couldn't make out. 'The tours increased for sure, when donations slowed. Banks were banging on Mr Moss's door, throwing million-dollar loans at him. Mr Moss is good with people. A hands-on guy. He was on every tour, answered every question. Equipment sales and contracts repay the loans and all profits go straight back into research and development.'

Mary prompted, 'Were international businessmen interested in investing or donating?'

'Sure. Everyone from the Chinese, Russians, Indonesians and Americans wanted to invest, even a Bollywood actor. Not that I knew who he was, although Mr Moss said he was a superstar.'

'Do you know which ones shook on deals?' she pushed.

'Couldn't say. That was all done back at the base.'

I tried to elicit more on the secret trips. 'Did you ever wonder who he met on those other bases, or where he went?'

The plane shuddered a little. 'Wasn't my place.'

We were no wiser about the contracts missing from Moss's office safe.

I had to know what the pilot thought. 'Do you think Eric chose to resign?'

'I can't believe he would, and by email? This is a man who does deals with a handshake. He doesn't text or email you. He phones. It's all personal.'

'Do you have any idea where he might have gone?'

'Wish I knew,' Geoff admitted. 'This place was his life. He would never have given it up without a fight.'

We took in the near-vertical sandstone cliffs below; adjacent fields merged into dense forests. If Eric Moss hadn't absconded and instead met with foul play there were infinite places to dispose of a body out here.

Chapter 68

JOHNNY AND DR Kwong reviewed the scans and billings. The first was performed at eighteen weeks' gestation. The report by Dr Kwong's colleague described a foetus with significant abnormalities of the lungs, heart and brain. Dr Tan concluded that the developmental abnormalities were incompatible with life. The baby was unlikely to survive beyond twenty-four weeks. The second scan described an eighteen-week pregnancy. The irregularities were identical. Only this scan was performed three weeks later.

Dr Kwong pulled up the dates on the films and viewed the first. He then located the second on the computer and placed the video recordings on dual screens. The angles and close-ups were identical.

'If this is the same pregnancy,' Johnny asked, 'could the dates have been wrongly typed in?'

Dr Kwong's brow furrowed. 'Different ultrasonographers, different days should produce unique scans no matter the condition. Each ultrasound is like an original piece of art, dependent on pressure, position of the baby and mother, depth of abdominal tissue among a host of other variable factors.'

He searched computer records for another few minutes. Johnny checked his watch. All he wanted to know was who had access to the billings and who fraudulently presented Louise's details.

Dr Kwong used the phone and spoke in what sounded like Cantonese. 'My colleague will join us shortly,' he said and viewed the third scan. It looked exactly the same as the others.

An older gentleman wearing a green surgical gown and protective glasses entered the room. Dr Kwong introduced Dr Tan, describing him as their most experienced interventional radiologist.

Dr Tan took a seat at the screen as the videos were replayed. He moved closer and craned his neck.

'I remember this patient. From a couple of years back. She had already suffered a number of miscarriages. The baby died from a rare congenital condition not long after that scan.'

'Do you know the name of the syndrome? I mean, is there a database of cases like it, carriers, for example?'

He shook his head. 'I can tell you their name wasn't Simpson though. They were first cousins from a small village in Lebanon. I remember because the mother spoke English but the father needed an interpreter. She was too distraught to tell him.'

'Are you certain the scans are all identical?' Johnny needed to be sure.

'There is no doubt,' Dr Kwong answered.

So the doctors had just confirmed what they'd suspected – that the woman claiming to be a surrogate was using the same scan, with altered dates, to con couples.

The question was, how had she managed to pull it off?

Chapter 69

JOHNNY POINTED OUT that the unknown surrogate using Louise Simpson's identity was their only link to finding the missing baby. Dr Tan was keen to cooperate.

He explained that the only way to date the scans and patient details was within house. The machines themselves embedded the names and dates into the scan. Either someone re-entered details on to a copy of the scan, or had somehow managed to copy the videos and alter them on the main computer system.

Johnny wanted to know every other possible means. 'What about obscuring details for teaching purposes? If you send them to someone else, can they alter the information and print out images?'

'In theory, that's possible. However, most doctors obscure the patient details with a sticker or leave them blank.'

It still meant other doctors or ultrasound technicians theoretically could alter patient information.

As expected, the reports were even easier to change. The practice logo and wording could be done by anyone with a computer and printer.

The realisation seemed to hit both of the radiologists hard.

Because the original scan with the Lebanese couple had been performed in their practice, they had to consider that one of their employees was involved in a murder and baby kidnapping. They both wanted the source found and punished. Johnny doubted either of them was personally involved in the scam.

Dr Kwong provided a list of employees with accompanying photos that had been taken for ID badges. A total of forty-four full- and part-time staff. Nearly half were male, which left twenty-three potential female suspects. Johnny knew that the Wallaces could identify the surrogate they had met. If the woman had a male accomplice, he'd have to consider investigating the men and their partners. At least the photos were tangible.

What kept him positive was the fact that the other scans had been billed to the same practice. In case anyone checked, there would be a paper trail to suggest the scans had all been performed in Manly.

Johnny needed to be sure the location was significant. Given the Wallaces had met the supposed surrogate at the nearby Queenscliff Beach, he reasoned this was the most likely source of the fraudulent scanner. He knew that if he was wrong, the time wasted investigating the staff could cost baby Zoe her life.

Chapter 70

GEOFF ANDREN TAXIED to a hangar at the north end of Contigo's base. A security guard met us but didn't check our IDs or ask us to sign in, something I found surprising. We weren't provided with visitor badges either. That meant we were free to wander unmonitored.

The guard, Arnie Pymble, offered to show us around while our pilot disappeared to meet with the maintenance crew. From the air the place had resembled a university campus, with summer camp touches. Buildings were separate, connected by concrete paths. The corporate office was dwarfed by a research and development section. A basketball court, indoor swimming pool and gymnasium were featured on our brief tour.

Arnie informed us that Eric Moss may have worked 24/7, but he was adamant that employees stay healthy and fit in order to avoid work injuries and maintain efficiency. Eric believed that by coming out for a game of basketball, they could get together and exchange ideas while getting fit. It was the same reason they had weekly barbecues for staff. There was no alcohol consumed on the premises, so employees visited the

Contigovale pub, which maintained good relations with the residents as well.

'Did Eric attend the social functions?'

Arnie hoisted his trousers up. 'He does barbecues but rarely visits the pub, unless it's someone's birthday. He's usually working.'

As we walked around, Mary asked if the staff lived on the grounds.

'No, all hundred or so of us live in temporary housing in town. In fact, some of the staff were born and bred in the area.'

'Do you work in shifts?'

Arnie stared at his shoes and rubbed a scuff mark on the back of one leg. 'Most are gone by seven at night. Eric discourages hours longer than that. We pool cars and come back to get an early start.'

It meant the base was minimally staffed through the evening and night. 'How many guards do you work with?' Mary enquired.

'Four in the daytime – sometimes we act as tour guides to officials – and a couple at night.'

That seemed like minimal security for such a large organisation, particularly one with private government and defence contracts.

It also meant that flights could come and go without scrutiny or knowledge of staff. And so could Eric Moss.

Mary bent down and picked up a dead wasp. It was the only other form of life they'd seen, apart from Geoff and the security guard.

Arnie continued to sing Moss's praises. 'One of the first things he did was build a public pool in Contigovale. The local council gave us all these awards for service to the community. You see, the young kids were leaving town, businesses were closing. That changed when we came here. With all the training crews we get through, thousands of people bring money into the local economy every month.'

Clearly, Eric had ingratiated himself and Contigo Valley with local officials.

For a non-profit organisation, it seemed Moss was more than generous with borrowed or donated money.

Chapter 71

MARY AND I RETURNED to the plane, ready to head back to Sydney. Geoff wasn't there so we looked around the hangar.

I turned to Mary. 'Did you notice any security cameras?'

'None.'

It was alarmingly lax for an organisation with international interests and million-dollar equipment stored in shipping containers in the open.

The hangar next door contained a helicopter, a Robinson R44.

Geoff wandered in as I was checking inside the cabin.

'Is this the one Eric Moss flew?'

'Sure is. She's on stand-by for search and rescue now.'

Mary stepped back. 'How often would Mr Moss take the chopper up? If she'd been mine, I'd have been in her at every opportunity.'

'Come to think of it, not for a few months. We fly guests over the property in the Duchess.' He became serious, almost morose. 'Do you think Mr Moss is alive?'

The question took me a little by surprise. 'Are you worried he may not be?'

'Just that this all seems out of character for him. I can't shake this feeling something bad has happened. I saw him on Thursday and he seemed off. It was as if he was distracted. He didn't say anything, but I knew something was wrong.'

'We're going to find him,' I reassured the pilot.

He took a deep breath. 'You and Ms Clarke might as well grab a bite to eat at the canteen. I'll come and get you once I've refuelled and done the safety check.'

I mentioned again that I had to be back in Sydney as early as possible. I'd agreed to meet Eliza Moss and to be there in case the sting to catch Collette's boyfriend went awry.

Mary was waiting outside the hangar. We found our way to the canteen building, which was a large wooden log cabin, with tables on a verandah. Over freshly cooked burgers, we discussed what we'd seen.

It bothered me that Moss could fly a helicopter and there was a landing pad by the shipping containers they flew over. Geoff had said that he had flown all visitors over the area in the last six months in the Duchess. Moss obviously didn't want them landing.

'Or he developed something that stopped him flying,' Mary suggested.

One thing was clear. The CEO hadn't disappeared in his helicopter.

'Maybe he was hiding something in those containers,' I suggested. 'He didn't want potential investors finding out.'

Mary wiped her hands on a napkin. 'The only way to know for sure is to look ourselves before they're moved or emptied.'

The problem was, we were about to fly back to Sydney.

Chapter 72

WE WERE FINISHING our coffees when Geoff Andren walked into the canteen and grabbed himself a teabag and hot water from the urn near the ordering station. He slid into the chair next to Mary.

'We have to delay take-off until morning. I'm sorry to do this to you, folks, but safety is my prime concern.'

'Why?' I didn't understand. 'We just flew here without any trouble.'

'I found an insect lodged in the pitot-static tube.'

'One insect. How?' I wasn't convinced it was serious enough to ground the plane.

He sighed. 'It can affect instrument readings. Have to be sure there isn't a hive down behind it.'

'He's right, Craig.' Mary seemed unfazed. 'Better to make sure it's cleaned out. That's why they have such rigid safety checks.'

'Is there any other way of getting back to Sydney?' My first concern was Collette, meeting the man who bugged our offices without extra backup.

Geoff blew across the top of his drink. 'Someone might be able to give you a lift into Lithgow, and there's the train, but no guarantees you'd get there any quicker. All non-essential crew here have been given leave until Sir Lang replaces Mr Moss.'

'Explains why the place is so quiet.' Mary looked over the rim of her white mug.

'What about a hire car?' I had to try to get back. Somehow.

'No services around here.'

'We're better off staying.' Mary reached over and patted my hand then raised an eyebrow at Geoff. 'Anywhere we can sleep?'

'Trainees' accommodation. It's where the police and army troops sleep during survival training. Each one's equipped with gear and supplies.'

'Let me guess,' I said, 'Gillies cancelled all courses too.'

'No,' Geoff answered. 'From what I hear, trainees are the ones pulling out. In droves. Moss is the backbone of this place.' He glanced around. 'Hate to think what will happen to us all without him.'

He took his cup with him and walked out, shoulders a little more rounded than before.

As Mary finished her coffee, it became clearer.

'Any chance the insect blocking that tube was a dead wasp?'

She shrugged. 'Johnny and Darlene have Collette's boyfriend under control.' There was a mischievous glint in her eyes. 'And it'll be a long night for us if we're to get to that helipad site and back without being noticed.'

Chapter 73

I RANG JOHNNY and explained why we wouldn't be back. He filled me in on the ultrasound billings from the Manly radiology practice. I agreed there was a good chance Louise Simpson's impersonator had access to the facility or someone on staff. He assured me Collette was in good hands. They planned to see if the boyfriend tampered with her new phone, then track who he was working for. We should know then who had been bugging our offices.

Next I texted Eliza to let her know I wouldn't be back until the morning. I found myself looking forward to seeing her. I knew it had little to do with her disability. She was intelligent, resilient, high-achieving but down to earth with no pretences. I liked her quirky sense of humour. In my world of obscenely wealthy men, trophy wives, celebrities, models, pop and movie stars, she was intriguing.

I knew she was a client but it didn't mean we couldn't enjoy each other's company while it lasted. The thing that bothered me most was the feeling that the news about her father was unlikely to be good. The pilot's concerns echoed mine. If he was dead, chances were the body would never be found.

Especially if he were somewhere remote on Contigo's base or the parkland surrounding it.

Mary searched internet maps and discovered the containers were approximately five kilometres directly south-west of our location. Most of the terrain we had seen from the plane was manageable. She collected dark overalls, night-vision goggles, water and other essential supplies.

Geoff Andren was right. The cabins were equipped for any bush expedition.

We dressed and waited until dark to head out. Mary had gone for a light jog around the perimeter and noticed a guard who looked military. His walk and build suggested he was in charge. It wasn't unusual to have one professional and others to make up the numbers. Arnie was polite but hardly a threat if he challenged someone. He hadn't even checked our IDs. Without that attention to detail, the chances were we could leave the main compound without being seen.

Chapter 74

OUTSIDE COLLETTE'S HOME, Johnny and Darlene sat in his black V8 Commodore. Collette had asked to have the place to herself tonight, so her flatmates were headed to the movies. On cue, the pair wandered out the front door and drove off in a compact Mazda.

The target, who Collette knew as Callum Byrne, arrived early, carrying wine, flowers and a large gift bag.

'Our boy's a player,' Darlene declared. 'It isn't only information he's after. In my book that makes him a prostitute.' She raised her can of Diet cola. 'Here's to locating his pimp.'

Johnny made a mental note to hide the chocolates he'd bought for Darlene from the convenience store. He had ducked off for snacks while Darlene planted listening devices in the bedroom, bathroom and kitchen area in the hope Callum would give something away. It was more, though, for Collette's safety. First hint of a problem, they would enter the house and get her out.

Right now, the couple were in the kitchen. Callum was asking if she'd had any 'brushes with fame' in her work. She turned the question on him. 'You first.'

He started by telling her he'd met a few famous people. Jon Bon Jovi in New York once, Katy Perry down at Bondi, and taken a selfie with Russell Crowe when up near Byron Bay.

Collette gushed that Callum was more handsome than the actor.

He responded by wanting to know all about the famous people she'd met in her job.

Collette said she'd signed a confidentiality agreement when she joined the agency and couldn't possibly tell, but there were some *major celebrities* – she emphasised the words – who came to them for help.

'She's doing well,' Darlene said. 'Knowing how nervous she is, you can't pick it in her voice.'

Johnny hoped so. He opened a bag of crisps and offered some to Darlene, who declined.

As the sun set, they heard a pop and both went for their car doors.

Collette giggled. 'The cork almost hit the glass cabinet.'

Johnny and Darlene relaxed, knowing Collette was commentating for their benefit.

'That bottle's been opened pretty fast,' Johnny said. 'Maybe he thinks if she's drunk, she'll talk more or not notice him checking her phone.'

'I sent you a song today but it didn't go through,' Callum said as glasses clinked.

'My phone battery died,' Collette replied. 'Was thinking of getting it checked 'cause it's been running down really quickly.'

'No need for that – I can check on it. Why don't you heat up the butter chicken? I'm starving.'

Darlene grabbed a crisp from the pack. 'Didn't take him long. He's definitely the one who put the software on it.'

But Johnny's attention had turned to a dark Ford sedan that was pulling up a block down the road. No one left the vehicle. When a car turned into the street, its lights silhouetted two large figures inside.

He and Darlene slunk down, out of view. 'What do you think they're doing?' she asked.

'Not sure. Three of them makes serious muscle. Things just got a lot more complicated,' Johnny said.

Chapter 75

THE CAR'S INHABITANTS hadn't moved by the time Collette was ready to serve dinner. Alcohol flowed.

Collette pressed Callum about his work. 'How about we have lunch tomorrow? I can come to your office this time. Where is it exactly?'

'Sorry, babe. I'm outside on jobs tomorrow. All week, actually.'

The clang of forks on plates filled the silence.

'You've never said what it is you do. I'm betting human relations.' Collette sounded coquettish.

'It's pretty dull, really. I run a team of auditors. Your work sounds way more interesting.'

'Hold that thought while I get the cheesecake.'

'Indian food and cheesecake?' Darlene groaned. 'You did that, didn't you?'

Johnny shrugged. 'Protein and carbs, it's a good combo.'

'Mind if I step outside to return a call?' they heard Callum ask.

'No problem,' Collette answered.

Callum emerged from the front door, phone to his ear and one in his hand. He bent down and deposited something on the front step, seemed to finish his conversation then returned inside.

'We shouldn't talk politics or religion,' he began as glasses clinked again. 'What about that poor baby who got taken? My aunt lives right near there.'

Johnny sat a little higher, still watching the dark sedan. 'Here we go.'

The conversation inside continued. 'It's terrible. That poor mother. My aunt's really shaken up about some maniac randomly killing women and babies.'

'Maybe it wasn't random,' Collette said. A chair moved.

'Tell me your theory,' Callum said, '. . . on the lounge.'

'Hang on.' Johnny saw a man step out of the Ford. 'I don't have a good feeling about this.'

The pair waited as the man approached. Darlene dialled Collette's phone, which went straight to voicemail.

Then the man crossed over to Collette's side of the street.

Johnny grabbed a hoodie from the back seat and quickly pulled it over his head, with the hood up. He collected the chips, and slipped out of the car without closing the door properly. He punched Darlene's number into his phone so she could hear everything that transpired. Johnny loped along, hunched, stopping short of Collette's house.

The other man was holding Collette's gate when Johnny sauntered into the yard next door.

'Hey,' he said loudly, pulling a chip from the bag. 'They went to the movies. I can give them a message if you want.'

The man paused for a moment before saying, 'My mistake. I was looking for number 28.'

'That would be the next block down,' Johnny said and watched the man leave. The stranger headed straight back to his car.

Johnny had already memorised the number plate when the car started up, did a U-turn and left at speed.

'That was close. Didn't like the look of him.' Johnny spoke into his phone now.

'And the bastard was after Collette's phone. Loverboy left it on the step for his partner-in-crime. My guess is, the software was beyond him, which is why he had backup.'

Chapter 76

THE MAN SUPPORTED his injured arm by resting it inside his half-zipped jacket. After making a call with a burner phone, he walked slowly along Roseby Street. In the day, the historic Birkenhead Point shopping centre buzzed with activity. At midnight, Drummoyne resembled a ghost town. In many ways, the former rubber factory built in the 1800s belonged to the past.

He pulled in behind a tree when he saw movement in a doorway across the street. A car approached and the figure sat up. Headlights illuminated a small-framed male hugging a bag to his chest. The boy couldn't have been older than seventeen, dossing on the doorstep.

The man pulled his cap lower and donned dark glasses before crossing the road. His thoughts ran to the people he'd left behind. The family and friends he'd never see again. It was the only way to protect those he cared most about.

'Someone will appreciate knowing you're OK,' he said, bending forward to hand the teen his phone. The pain in his shoulder and wrist clipped his breath. He cradled the arm tighter. 'There's enough credit to call home. Maybe a shelter for the night.'

The boy wrapped filthy fingers around the offering. 'Hey –'

The man didn't stop and continued on his way.

He used his good hand to pull the jacket collar up to his ears. Avoiding the marina's security cameras he levered himself over the fence to the locked facility. With nearly two hundred boats moored, this was the largest privately owned floating marina on Sydney Harbour. Every berth had its own water access and power. Exactly what he needed.

The trawler-style hull made it easy to spot the boat he was after. A Riviera Clipper 34 motor cruiser. Water slapped between the boats and the pier. Ropes banged rhythmically on masts. The boats were covered in a cloak of darkness once clouds obscured the crescent moon.

If everything went to plan, he'd be cruising through Sydney Heads in the next hour or so. Away from the city and everyone in it.

Chapter 77

WITH HER FATHER still missing, Eliza Moss couldn't face people tonight. Relieved she could postpone a client dinner, she hoped to take advantage of the quiet to think and focus on where Eric could have gone. Using forearm crutches, she eased on to the lounge and sank into the large cushions, exhausted. Her shoulders and hips ached.

The question played on a loop in her mind. Why hadn't her father called?

The only answer was the one she didn't want to face.

He wasn't able to.

The thought made her heart beat faster and her breathing accelerate. Her father meant everything to her. He'd been the one to save her from an institution, made sure she was educated, cared for and loved. More than that, he taught her that she wasn't defined by her disabilities. They presented specific challenges, but everyone had some disadvantage to overcome. How she faced difficult times, like this, defined her.

Part of her wanted to scream at him for leaving. Abandoning her. If Craig was right, somehow he had managed to live without any proof of who he was. How? The question haunted her.

He drove cars but managed to do it without a licence? She couldn't face the possibility that he had lied to her and everyone else for all these years. The alternative was that his identity had been erased. Someone wanted every trace of him gone. Which meant something terrible had happened.

Hot tears dripped on to her shirt.

She consciously slowed each breath in, aware her lungs were already functioning well under capacity. Stress affected her physical resilience more than infection. She had to remain in control. Her father needed her to be strong now more than ever.

Felix was soon on her lap sleeping, as Eliza stroked his white fur. 'Everything's going to be OK. It has to be.' For the first time in years, she prayed before falling asleep where she sat.

A bumping sound in the bedroom roused her. She immediately thought of Felix, but the cat was still asleep on her lap.

Craig had warned her to be careful. Someone was monitoring her movements and contacts. It had to be something falling in the laundry. The clothes hanger wasn't that stable.

She lifted Felix off her lap and on to his own cushion and hauled herself on to her bare feet. Holding on to the lounge, then the wall, she listened from the corridor. Another soft thud followed.

Someone was inside. Heart hammering in her chest, she tried to stay calm. Maybe it was just a young kid looking for wallets, cash and jewellery. Her purse was in her bag on the kitchen table.

Her phone was in its charger, next to a marble Buddha statue on the hall table. She silently braced herself against the wall and reached for the phone to dial 000. Before she was connected, a large man in a dark jacket and black jeans appeared.

When Eliza saw the balaclava, she knew she was in trouble.

Chapter 78

ELIZA REACTED QUICKLY and grabbed the Buddha statue. Her best chance was on the floor. She was too unstable on her feet. Sliding down the wall, she flicked off the light switch and pulled the hall table over just as the man lunged. He tripped, hitting the wooden floor hard.

Eliza clambered backwards. A hand gripped her right ankle. With all her strength, she flexed her knee and lashed out. Her glutes may have been useless, but her quads were her strongest muscles. Her shoe connected with something solid, possibly a face. The intruder growled and released his grip.

She rolled over and commando-crawled to the kitchen in the dark.

The man was quickly above and flipped her on to her back. 'You'll save us all trouble if you tell me where you hid it.'

'I don't know what you're talking about!' She began to scream 'Fire' loudly, in the hope a neighbour might hear and at the least call for help.

He bent down and covered her mouth with his hand. He whispered, 'Tell me where you hid it and this will all go away.'

She could smell his sweat and garlic breath. What frightened her most was how controlled he sounded. She had to fight.

She bit hard on his hand and swung at his head. The Buddha made heavy contact as she let go. The intruder moaned and fell back. She rolled over and dragged herself on her stomach to the kitchen, heading straight for the cupboard under the sink. She opened the door and reached inside for something, anything.

He grabbed her shoulders. 'Tell me where it is or –'

She fired a prolonged blast of flyspray from one hand and oven cleaner with the other.

The man wailed. She kept spraying as he stumbled backwards. She felt his footsteps on the boards. He was headed to the front door. It opened and slammed. She tightened her grip on both triggers. What if he let someone else in to finish the job?

After straining to listen for what seemed like hours, there were no noises or footsteps. Eliza sat back against the cupboards and realised she'd been panting the whole time. Her fingers had cramped clutching the chemical bottles at the ready. Finally, she carried the oven cleaner with her as she crawled to the front door, pulled herself up and locked it.

With the lights now on, she held on to the wall and crept back to where she'd hit the man with the statue. There was blood spattered on the tiled floor.

'I'd call that karma, Felix,' she murmured and dropped the spray. Hands shaking, she called one of the numbers on the phone Craig had given her.

Chapter 79

AS MARY AND I trekked through dense bush, my burner phone vibrated. Not surprised that Moss had made sure there was reception out here, I answered but continued walking.

Before I could ask about Collette, Darlene told me there had been a break-in at Eliza Moss's home. I assumed she was out at the work dinner she'd mentioned.

'Anything stolen?'

'No,' Darlene said. 'The guy was after something specific. Tore her bedroom apart, then wanted to know where she'd hidden it. Whatever "it" is.'

My adrenaline surged. 'Wait. She was home at the time?'

'She cancelled plans at the last minute. My guess is this guy wasn't expecting to see anyone, though he was wearing a balaclava.'

I stood still. 'Is she hurt?'

Mary stopped in her tracks and looked at me.

'She's shaken, but fine. Turns out she packs a mean punch with marble and is a demon with kitchen chemicals.'

I wasn't sure what that meant but was filled with relief. Eliza was safe.

Darlene elaborated, 'Eliza says she has no idea what he was talking about but he was prepared to hurt her to get what he came for. She was lucky this time.'

The police were on their way but Darlene said she wanted to fingerprint the place before they arrived.

Heart pounding, I asked to speak to Eliza. The phone crackled and I heard her voice.

'I'm OK. Honestly. Darlene came straightaway.'

Mary tapped her watch. We needed to keep moving.

'To be on the safe side, can you pack an overnight bag, and take whatever is most valuable to you? There's a top-level security system at my place Darlene knows how to access.'

'I'd rather go to a hotel room. They have those locks –'

'They're too easy to override. It's how housekeeping gets in when someone's inside.'

There was a moment's pause. 'Then I'll stay here. After what I did to that guy, he isn't coming back tonight.'

'That's a bad idea,' I stressed. The intruder would most likely return. Maybe with back-up next time.

'Eliza, please trust me. You'll be safest at my place, even if you're being followed. Darlene can let the deputy commissioner of police know you're there. The police can watch your place, just in case.'

The wider implications of the attack seemed to stun Eliza. Suddenly her world would never be an entirely safe place again.

'This is insane. What was Dad really involved in?'

'I'm trying to get to that now.' The phone crackled. Reception deteriorated the further away from the compound we got.

Mary signalled we were almost there.

'You'll be safe tonight. Just stay there until I get home.'

'Hurry back,' she pleaded.

While I had Darlene on the line, I needed to know about Collette. She filled me in on the car with two inhabitants, one of whom was on his way to grab Collette's phone from the step when Johnny intercepted him. After that, the boyfriend took a call, excused himself and left.

I was relieved we at least had a lead on who'd put the malware on her phone. 'Can you trace the plates?'

Darlene was ahead of me. 'Sure did. It belongs to Craven Media, owners of *The Sydney Post*.'

Chapter 80

RANSACKING A HOUSE with the owner inside sounded amateur, or desperate. The CIA or ADIA should have known better. Unless they knew Eliza's schedule and expected her to be out. I wouldn't put it past some of the agents I'd met to be that incompetent. The physical risk to Eliza bothered me most.

What if her intruder was from the media group? If Craven Media were bugging our offices, it was a new low, even for them. There'd been phone hacking incidents in the UK, but nothing as overt in this country. Obviously, things had changed. It explained how Marcel Peyroni managed to get to the Wallaces' house in Dural before the Tactical Response unit.

Craven Media fed their scandal appetite via stunts like the one they pulled on Private. We looked after clients who wanted to hide scandal. They wanted to capitalise on that. Now we had a source for the malware, Gideon Mahler could trace it right back to Peyroni and Craven and prove the illegal bugging. Once we were back I'd let the police and federal agencies sort him out, along with his media magnate boss. A mere suggestion they were *suspected* of breaking, entering and threatening a disabled woman would be enough to irrevocably damage their business. Like the rot they printed, there didn't need to be truth in the accusation.

This late, the bush around Contigo Valley was eerily quiet. The only sounds were our feet crunching on twigs and rocks. I was perspiring heavily and stopped for a long drink.

Eliza's break-in preyed on my mind. I doubted even Peyroni and his team would have risked being caught in there.

For anyone chasing Eric Moss, Eliza was an easy target, given she was the only family Eric Moss had as far as anyone knew. Instinct told me it had to be someone from ADIA or the CIA in her home. Whoever broke in had to believe Eliza knew more about her father than she let on, or that he'd given her whatever it was they wanted.

That meant something tangible existed. Not just what Eric Moss kept to himself. A file, an object, papers? A code?

Further ahead, Mary checked her bearings.

'The containers should be just up here.' A hundred metres later, she unstrapped the boltcutters from her backpack. Mary was the fittest person I knew, but her endurance was exceptional. She seemed to function without sleep or rest until a crisis was averted. Even then she'd be back at work a few hours later.

We pushed through to the clearing. Searching with night-vision goggles, there was no suggestion of surveillance out here. No wires, no cameras and no power source.

We checked the helipad first. Small cracks had formed in the concrete. I wouldn't have wanted to land anything on a helipad that hadn't been maintained. It seemed odd, given Eric Moss's obsession with detail, cleanliness and presentation. I suspected nothing had landed on this for quite a while. It could have partly explained why Geoff Andren flew prospective lenders right over it. The question remained, *why* would Moss neglect this site?

The locks to both containers were rusted and didn't appear to have been recently disturbed.

Mary got to work with the boltcutters and the first padlock snapped with a loud crack. With a fair amount of effort we managed to creak open the door.

I shone the light inside.

Mary and I stood back in stunned silence.

Both containers were empty.

Chapter 81

PICKING THE LOCK on the boat would have been child's play, if not for his injuries. Just as the man thought he'd have to break in, the lock clicked and the hatch doors opened.

Down in the galley he went straight for the cupboard under the sink. He removed a tin marked 'herbal tea' and a bottle of gin strategically hidden behind it. Buried under the peppermint tea-leaves was a set of keys wrapped in plastic. He peeled them free with his good hand.

Next he unscrewed the cap from the gin and placed it on the small dining table before descending the aft stairs and lifting out a spare set of clothes from the storage area under one of the bunks.

Above and to the left of the sink was a latched cupboard containing a first-aid kit. He placed it on the saloon table. He unzipped his jacket and examined the still painful wrist. The shoulder ached but would heal. The spider bite still gave him grief. Sweats and nausea slowed him down more than he would have imagined. On the positive side, the lymph nodes under his arm were reducing in size. His body was slowly clearing the toxin.

He popped a pill from the kit to counteract nausea, washing it down with a sip of gin. He carefully washed his wrist with liquid soap, dried it and applied antiseptic cream before covering it with a bandage.

Thirty-six hours without sleep. He needed to rest so slid into the bench seat, closed his eyes and lay his head on the table while he waited.

Moments later a noise above deck disturbed the quiet.

He stayed silent and still. He was no longer alone. A light shone through the window, then a pause. Footsteps slowly descended the companionway. Fifth step, fourth.

He splashed the bottle's contents down his front and on the table.

Third.

He slid on the dark glasses.

A light moved through the crack above the hatch. The handle on the hatch moved.

The man gripped the flick-knife in his pocket with his left hand.

When the door opened, he was sprawled face sideways on the saloon table.

Chapter 82

FROM WHERE HE lay, he could make out the image reflected in the window. The intruder had a mouthpiece wired to a radio on his epaulette. Marina Security.

He moaned.

'Hey.' The guard stepped closer and poked the stranger's arm. 'You all right?'

The man snorted and sluggishly lifted his head off the table.

The guard recoiled. 'Jeez, you reek.'

The man licked his lips and slurred, 'Officer, I didn't do it.'

The guard lifted the half-empty bottle. 'How can you even drink this stuff? I need to see some ID.'

The man fumbled for his wallet, then pointed to a shelf. The guard turned his light to a framed photo of two men on a fishing trip. One currently stank of alcohol. The other was the boat's real owner.

'That was before my wife left with . . . our bastard of a lawyer.'

The guard hesitated and swung his torch around inside.

'I got a report someone broke in.' He kept the light on the boat's keys. 'Next time let us know you're coming. Save us all a lot of hassle. And, mate, I've been there. Alcohol is never the answer.'

The man folded himself down on the table.

The guard reported to base that the owner was sleeping off a binge, and was informed two kids had been spray-painting on the other side of the marina. The police were on their way. He sighed, took one look back and left.

The man quickly set to work.

Chapter 83

ELIZA GAVE HER statement to the police. Meanwhile, Darlene fingerprinted all drawers and doorhandles in the apartment. Eliza watched her use a swab to sample the bloodstain from the floor and store it in a clear plastic tube.

A female constable was asking Eliza if the assailant had made any physical threats. Eliza shook her head.

'No. It all happened so fast.'

'We can take you to hospital,' the female constable spoke softly, 'and have any injuries looked at privately?'

Eliza shook her head once more. Minor bruises on her elbows, wrists and knees would heal. Thankfully, nothing was broken so she still had her mobility.

'Is there anywhere you can stay for the night? With friends, in case . . .?' a senior officer enquired hesitantly.

Eliza's heart raced again. 'You really think he's coming back?'

'Only if he fancies another dose of flyspray and caustic burns,' Darlene said from the far side of the room. 'It's OK – she's coming with me.'

Eliza smiled weakly and wheeled herself to the bedroom to pack some things while the police took photographs of the mess in the hallway.

Felix rubbed against his owner's feet.

'It's just for one night,' she said. Before more loudly adding, 'I'll leave you plenty of food, don't worry.'

While Darlene saw the police out, Eliza wheeled herself towards the back door, stopping short in the laundry. She reached down into a sack of kitty litter and extracted a small sandwich bag containing a mini USB device. She quickly shoved it into her jacket pocket then levelled the pellets with a wooden spoon she kept next to the litter box.

'No one needs to know it was ever here,' she said to herself, and wheeled back out to the corridor.

Chapter 84

THE MAN REMOVED a panel from beneath the sink and pulled out a computer and cord. He tore the lining of his jacket and removed a USB from inside the hem.

So far he was still on schedule to meet his contact. He plugged in a series of passwords and broke through a firewall.

He tapped his fingers on the laminate, urging the program to open. The spinning wheel on-screen set his pulse rocketing. The computer can't freeze now. It should have been near-impossible to hack.

He forced quit and held his breath as the program restarted. His wrist had begun to throb again. All these years of planning his escape had almost been derailed by a spider. The icon finally appeared.

Two more clicks.

The waiting was more distressing than any pain. All these years distilled into this moment.

Attaching the USB, his finger hovered slightly over the enter button to transfer the program to the USB, then delete itself.

His other mobile phone jolted him out of the moment. He retrieved it from his trouser pocket and took a deep breath before answering.

This was the most important meeting he would ever have. At stake was his life.

Chapter 85

THE CALL DIDN'T go exactly as hoped. The contact wanted to meet in a cove only accessible by boat. The offer expired in twenty minutes. That left barely enough time to make it, and no chance of assessing the meeting place for signs of an ambush.

But if things went well, he'd be on a plane out of the country tonight.

He started the engine from the internal helm. As soon as the key turned, he could smell something burning. Plastic.

He scanned the gauges overhead. Water temperature, oil pressure, rpm on the tachometer were all in the normal range. The amp meter was erratic and read low but the engine was running. There was more than enough fuel to get there.

The smell dissipated as quickly as it came on.

His eyes darted back to the computer. The download was still in progress.

Seventy per cent.

Seventy-three.

There was no time to waste. He stepped out and around the deck to the fore and untied the mooring rope with his good arm. The boat butted against buffers on the pontoon as he hurriedly released the aft.

Back at the helm, he pushed the throttle forward and steered free. The hairs on his neck prickled. Something was wrong.

The laptop read eighty per cent downloaded.

Then he smelled smoke.

Eighty-four.

Beyond the laptop, a flash of light caught his eye. A fire had started in the aft.

If it took hold, the fuel tanks could ignite. In a split-second decision he grabbed the fire-extinguisher from the galley and rushed to the source. He pulled the pin and doused foam on the flames but the fire seemed to rear. Sweat pouring from his face and chest, he made one more choice.

He raced back to the computer.

Ninety-eight . . .

A loud whoosh sounded behind the cabin. Flames were out of control. And he was out of time.

Yanking the USB, he took off to the deck and levered himself over the safety rail. He leapt outwards. Midair, the explosion thrust him higher and further.

Intense pain as his shoulder hit the surface caused him to gasp. Water filled his burning lungs. Disorientated in the blackness, he struggled to find air. The surface had to be close. Fingertips broke through.

The next explosion propelled him backwards.

Deeper.

Into an abyss.

Chapter 86

I WALKED IN the door of my apartment clutching pastries and coffees from the local bakery. The sun had risen and streamed in the ocean-side windows. A wheelchair was parked behind the front door.

I wanted sleep after an exhausting night trekking through the bush but there were greater priorities. I heard the shower running and a quick check showed Eliza had spent the night in the spare room.

As I put breakfast on the kitchen bench, the bathroom door opened and Eliza appeared, dressed, hobbling on forearm crutches. Her legs swung wide from the hips as she moved forward. Her hair was wet and fell in soft waves around her face. She stopped when she saw me.

I'd never seen her stand, let alone walk. It struck me how tall she was.

'Good morning,' I said. 'Hope you were comfortable.'

'You were kind to let me stay.'

She looked drawn, as if she hadn't slept much.

'You should see the expression on your face. Surprised I can walk?'

I *was* a little taken aback, but didn't want to say something clumsy or insensitive. 'Maybe a little.'

'Don't get excited, I can't go far. The legs run out of oomph pretty quickly.'

Eliza deflected conversation, something I suspected she was very good at. There was no hint of the trauma she'd experienced last night.

I wouldn't normally open my home to a client but this case was bigger and more threatening than I'd imagined. And there was something special about Eliza.

'Hungry?' I nodded at the food.

'I am now.' She pulled herself on to one of the stools by the kitchen bench and placed her crutches in the corner.

I tore open the bags to expose cheese and bacon rolls, croissants and fresh bread. Plates from the cupboard went on the bench along with the two takeaway coffees.

Eliza asked if I had sugar. I rummaged through the cupboard but came up empty. Living alone, I tended to cook the essentials – meat and veggies, salads, sometimes roast a chicken.

'Sorry.'

'No problem. It's all about the caffeine.'

I thought about moving outside to the balcony, with the ocean view, but the chairs out there were low set. I joined Eliza, facing the ocean.

'We learnt some things last night.'

'Go on.' Her back straightened and she picked small pieces from the cheese and bacon roll and popped them into her mouth.

'With the visit from the US Ambassador, you being followed and then broken into, we have to think your father was involved in some kind of government organisation, overt or covert.'

'You mean like the CIA? You're kidding, right?'

I'd expected at best denial, at worst an argument. But Eliza had to believe last night was a targeted attack, irrespective of what the police may have said.

'I'm serious. It isn't unusual for government agencies to set up in other countries. These organisations sometimes use legitimate businesses as shopfronts. They call it "mutual advantage".'

Eliza listened intently.

'Operatives are paid by the business, or organisations, pay tax, and really believe they're contributing. It's an ideology as much as a job.'

'You think Contigo Valley is one of these fronts?'

'Honestly, I don't know. It could be that government agencies became interested because of the defence contracts and research and development projects your father initiated.'

'He is against war, of any kind. Everything he's done, with the surgical inventions, rehydration techniques, has been to save lives.' She became absorbed in a tiny piece of bacon. 'There's no way he is involved in war-mongering.' She looked directly at me. 'If you believe that, you're crazier than that guy who attacked me.'

Chapter 87

I KNEW ELIZA wouldn't take the theory well. Still, it had to be said.

'We have to consider the possibility your father was an agency operative. He didn't have any form of documentation. If it did exist before he disappeared, it has to have been wiped from every government database. No one else has that sort of power.'

Eliza stared out the window. 'We often talked about how the CIA overthrew dictators and replaced them with even worse despots. It was like a hydra – every time they intervened, the situation was made worse. Then there's South America, the Russians in the Ukraine; the list is endless. Those interventions never once ended well or made people safer.' She flicked her hair, almost defiantly, and the scent of coconut from her shampoo reached me.

'There's more,' I said. 'Your father was courting bankers for loans. He used containers that supposedly held high-tech equipment that could theoretically be inspected as proof of the organisation's value.'

Her eyes narrowed. 'Supposedly?'

'There were two shipping containers next to a helipad. Your father could have taken investors there and shown them, as collateral for the loans. He could fly them there anytime. He could pilot helicopters too.'

From the shocked expression, it was clear she didn't know that.

'Mary and I trekked out to them last night. The containers were empty.'

'Sir Lang must have had them emptied as soon as Dad left.'

I bit into a roll and shook my head. 'They hadn't been opened recently and were pretty much rusted closed. Contigo was on the fraud squad's radar.'

'Wait! Fraud? My father would never –'

I put a hand on hers. 'Just hear me out, please, and it may make more sense. We think he showed prospective lenders one container at the base, then flew them over others, which were supposed to house expensive equipment.'

'What was the point?'

'That's what I wondered. By then the bankers trusted him. Eric was accepting hundreds of millions of loans based on government contracts, which we can't confirm, and I can't see how he could have paid the loans back with interest. When the finance officer asked about some missing charity dinner tickets, I suspect your dad panicked.' I sipped my coffee. 'Once the in-house accounts team started auditing, they would have found evidence of much more substantial fraud. It's the only explanation as to why a missing receipt for ten thousand dollars triggered his disappearance.'

'But the organisation was financially sound.'

'If your dad was lying to bankers about non-existent tech-nology and equipment, something was very wrong. I suspect your father had built a house of cards that was about to collapse. It would explain why he disappeared in such a hurry, without telling you.'

Chapter 88

A KNOCK ON the door broke a long, tense silence.

It was Mark Talbot. He was alone and didn't apologise for the interruption. I wondered what bombshell he was about to drop by turning up at my home uninvited. I knew there was still no word on baby Zoe.

He wasn't forthcoming with the reason for his visit so I let him know about the phone hacking by Craven Media and how Collette's mobile was evidence. If they tracked the car that Johnny saw last night, the police would no doubt find illegal listening and surveillance devices.

'For what it's worth,' Mark said, 'I didn't think you'd risk a child's life for publicity or kickbacks. I know you better than that.'

Was that actually an apology? Maybe my cousin had been upset about his break-up and taken it out on me. I decided to let it go and offered to make him a coffee, but all I had was instant. He looked at the takeaway cups.

'I'll pass. I need to talk to Miss Moss. Alone.'

'I want him to stay,' Eliza said, reaching for my hand.

It didn't go unnoticed by Mark.

'Your prerogative,' he shrugged.

I offered him a seat but he preferred to stand. This wasn't just about the Zoe Ruffalo case or information leaks. Mark hadn't come to apologise or make peace. This visit was serious, and official.

'I've been asked by the commissioner to liaise with the Federal Police on Eric Moss's disappearance. He's asked me to personally update you on the case. And before you say anything, Craig, I'm as surprised as you. It's my area of command, but the investigation is being run by other agencies. My team has no official involvement.'

Eliza bit her top lip and I could see the pulse in her neck. We were both anticipating the worst news.

'We believe Eric Moss was using a false identity.' Mark let his words hang but there was no reaction from either of us. 'Evidence suggests he was a Swiss con man by the name of Hans Erikson Gudgast, born February 11, 1956. He was a mathematical genius who completed university by the age of sixteen and was recruited by a Swiss bank. He took bribes to set up bank accounts in false names for foreign nationals and was due to face trial for embezzlement and fraud. Something about skimming point zero, zero, zero, zero something cents from every account transaction. Made millions before anyone could notice.'

'Did he skip bail?' I asked.

'He was thought to have died in a kayaking accident on Lake Lucerne, at the ripe old age of twenty. A shoe and safety vest were all that washed up and they were positively identified as his.' He crossed his arms and leant back against the stove. 'A few months later, in June 1976, a man with a French passport entered Australia with the name Hans Gudgast. His mother was purportedly French so he had dual citizenship. Documents confirm he was six foot one and a hundred and sixty pounds. This of course preceded the European Union and digital records.'

I quickly did the maths. Gudgast would have been fifty-eight years old, the same age as Eric Moss. 'You think Gudgast flew here to avoid prosecution?'

'He was on the passenger manifest for a flight to New Zealand a week after arriving in Sydney and there were no further entries to Australia.'

'Then that can't be Dad,' Eliza said. 'Once you're confirmed on the passenger list, you have to board or they take your luggage off and stop the plane.'

'Not back then,' I remembered. 'You could get your boarding pass and leave the airport. If he didn't have luggage, no one would have noticed or recorded his absence.'

'We believe,' Mark said firmly, 'that Hans Erikson Gudgast and Eric Moss are one and the same person.'

Chapter 89

ELIZA SAT STARING out at the ocean as I escorted Mark out. I sat with her in silence for a few minutes.

'I don't believe any of it,' she said finally.

'It would explain why he didn't have a passport, or any documents about where he was born, went to school, why he didn't have a bank account. That wasn't lost on the police either.'

'That isn't true. Contigo paid him. You can't get a salary without a bank account. Non-profit organisations don't pay cash wages.'

Obviously, Eliza didn't know about the payout awaiting her. 'Actually, he didn't take the money. He negotiated a low salary and put it in a trust.'

She looked up, confused.

'The trust was for you. So you were always taken care of.'

Eliza's shock turned to anger. 'Are you falling for all the crap the police are sprouting?'

'Think about it,' I tried. 'It hasn't made sense from the start.'

She reached for her crutches, slipped her forearms into the open cuffs and stood, shakily at first.

'And you think that my father was defrauding Contigo Valley, the very company he built from nothing and which saved countless people's lives? You have *no idea* what my father is like. You just said he took no money, no salary.' She hobbled towards the spare room. 'Someone has set him up and you don't want to see it.'

I couldn't blame her for reacting this way.

'Where are you going?'

'Getting my things. Then I'll find Dad so he can clear his name.'

I paced, hands on hips. It wasn't safe for her to go out, especially if she were still being followed. But this was a determined, stubborn woman who needed to defend her father's honour. She couldn't go out alone.

'If you wait, I'll drive you,' I called out.

Through the open door I saw her crumple on the bed and the crutches drop to the floor. At first she began to cry quietly, then her body gave way to heavy sobs. I went in and sat next to her. I wanted to stop her pain but for now all I could do was hold her gently.

'Wait.' She sat up, eyes swollen. 'Someone wanted him out of Contigo Valley. It has to be Lang Gillies. He's the one capable of fraud. And he's rolling in cash.'

It was possible, but the police seemed pretty sure Moss was the Swiss man.

Eliza wiped her face. 'How tall did he say Gudgast was?'

'My height. Six foot one. 185 centimetres.'

'Well, that proves he isn't my father.' She composed herself enough to make complete sense. 'You can make yourself look taller, but it's hard to cut inches off. I used to measure him to see how tall I was getting in comparison. My dad is 180 centimetres. A whole *five* centimetres shorter.'

Chapter 90

I WONDERED IF the police genuinely believed Moss was Gudgast, or whether that's what they wanted us to think. I left Eliza to gather her things and headed for a quick shower. No sooner had I turned on the taps then I heard a scream. Towel hastily wrapped around, I ran out to find Eliza holding a hand over her mouth, staring at the TV in the lounge.

A badly damaged body had been pulled from Sydney Harbour. Sources believed it to be Eric Moss, missing CEO of the world-renowned Contigo Valley. The banner continued to scroll across the screen informing viewers that Moss had disappeared four days earlier.

I quickly dialled Mark Talbot and couldn't hide my contempt.

'Do you know what's blazoned across the TV right now?'

My cousin sighed heavily. 'As far as I know the body's still in the water and hasn't been identified. An anonymous caller told the Water Police they'd find Moss in the harbour. I needed confirmation it wasn't a hoax before I could tell Miss Moss. That's why I'm headed to the scene now.'

I watched Eliza.

'Craig?' Mark was still on the phone. 'I'm sorry she had to find out like that. If it isn't him, I'll let you know asap.'

I hung up, believing the media had found out before the local area command. The news report was on Craven's channel. I suspected we weren't the only office Craven Media had bugged.

Not wanting to leave Eliza alone, I dressed quickly and took her to the office, where Johnny promised to look after her. She hadn't spoken in the car and was still in shock when we arrived.

Darlene and I headed out straightaway to where the body had been discovered.

Police and media vans were already there and the scene had been cordoned off. Uniformed police and bystanders tried to block public view with rugs and space blankets. We bobbed under the police tape as the corpse was being placed in a body bag.

Darlene pushed through with her kit and began taking photos as I fended off challenges from officers who didn't know her.

The body was bloated. The face was darkish blue, swollen, unrecognisable. There was a foul stench, like rotting fish. Rex King was already on his haunches, examining the wounds.

His assistant instantly recognised Darlene. 'Fish have been at him,' he said enthusiastically. 'Nothing like fresh meat for a frenzy.'

Rex concentrated on a head wound. 'The state of the body is consistent with six to twelve hours in the water, which fits the time frame for the explosion reported back at the marina.'

A jet skier zoomed past about fifty metres from shore. 'This is a well-used stretch of water.' I wondered if the body had been dumped from another location. 'Is it surprising the body wasn't found earlier?'

'Not really. It would have sunk to start with. Decomposition produces putrefactive gases that make the body float. That, of course, depends on the water and temperature conditions.'

'Identifying the remains could prove difficult,' I said out loud.

Rex looked up. 'Police tell me they believe the victim didn't have medical or dental records.'

'And the only family member we know was adopted,' I added.

Under the circumstances the extensive facial trauma seemed a little too convenient.

Chapter 91

FURTHER UP THE bank, Mark was questioning a security guard from the local marina. I moved over to listen and Mark filled me in. 'Giorgio Kalafedes was on duty last night at Birkenhead Marina and says he saw the victim on one of the secured boats. He identified the man as Moss from a photo. Says he was drunk and stank of alcohol.' Mark turned to the witness.

'You're certain they're the same clothes he was wearing before the explosion?'

'Absolutely sure. He said his wife left him for someone else.' He looked to me then Mark. 'If I ever thought he'd take off drunk like that, I'd have grabbed his keys and called you guys.'

Something struck me. Geoff Andren and Eliza had said that Eric Moss never touched alcohol.

'Did he say if he was planning to head off the next day?' I asked.

'No. Just wanted to sleep it off. I thought it was his boat because of the photo.'

'What photo?' I asked.

'The one with the other man holding a fish.'

'Did the man you saw have sunglasses on in the picture?'

'Yeah. He had the same pair on inside the boat. I thought it was weird at night. And the beard was the same. That's why I thought he was the owner.' The guard looked over his shoulder at the scene, and the body. 'Can I go now? I don't feel so good.'

'Sure, have a seat in one of our cars. Someone will be with you soon,' Mark said, before gesturing for me to walk with him.

We stepped away from the action. 'Early indications would suggest an electrical short triggered the boat explosion.'

It had to be sabotage, I thought. 'You think it was a freak accident?'

'If it was, this character Moss, or Gudgast, must be pretty unlucky.' Mark raised his eyebrows. 'He resigns, goes away for a few days and happens to pick the only boat with an electrical defect.'

'Are you thinking he rigged it to blow and somehow stuffed up?'

'No, but I am suggesting you may not be the only one looking for him. Someone else got to him first.'

'Until you told us, Eliza had never heard of anyone called Hans Gudgast. Neither had I.' I didn't want to let on what Eliza had said about Eric's height. 'All we knew was that Eric Moss had no official documentation and wasn't big on having his photo taken without sunglasses. He kept a very low profile for all his public works.'

'I did some checking too, on the fire at Moss's friend's cabin. The local boys tell me magnesium was used to ignite it. Water only made it worse. So whoever lit it knew more than a bit about chemistry.'

'Or specifically fires,' I suggested.

Mark nodded, studying my face. 'And I suppose it was a coincidence that his daughter was assaulted in an attempted robbery and hid out at your place.'

I didn't want Mark setting off alarms with government agencies until I knew more.

'Is there anything else I need to know to get to the bottom of this?' he pressured.

'The less you know for now, the safer a lot of people will be.'

He clenched his jaw. 'I can't help if you keep me in the dark.'

'I guarantee I'll fill you in as soon as I work out what Moss was up to.'

'You're on extremely thin ice right now and can't afford to piss anyone else off. Me included.' He lowered his voice. 'I hear some pretty heavy hitters will be relieved Moss is dead. You expose what Moss was up to, you'll need to watch your back.'

Chapter 92

MARCEL PEYRONI CALLED my name. 'Hey, Gisto. Remember me?'

I felt the anger rise in me as I saw him behind the police lines. This time I didn't hold back and stormed over. 'You crooked scumbag!'

'Unusual metaphor, coming from an ex-lawyer who takes obscene amounts of money to make scandals . . .' he made a pfff sound, 'disappear.'

It took all my self-restraint not to hit him square in the face.

Peyroni made a rolling hand gesture at the cameraman who'd been slow to start recording. 'This is the second time in a week you've been involved in a death. The police have suggested you are implicated in Louise Simpson's death. I'm informed you were working on finding Eric Moss as well. Will you still be paid now he's dead?'

I clenched both fists and tensed my shoulders. The camera ensured there was irrefutable evidence if I thumped the pompous little git. The bastard had caused a lot of trouble and compromised at least one police operation. *And* he'd violated the privacy of my firm and clients. He deserved to be publicly exposed. I held back because footage of his eventual arrest would do far more damage than any punch I could deliver.

'What? No quips, no retorts?' He shoved the microphone close to my chin. I noticed an investigative reporter from an independent newspaper approaching.

I spoke loudly enough for the more respected journalist to hear. 'Who did you illegally bug this time, to get here faster than your rivals?'

It did more than pique her interest. I smiled as Peyroni refused to comment on the accusation I'd made.

Mark tapped my shoulder. 'You may want to intervene,' he said, pointing to a commotion near the body bag.

Darlene's arms were raised as two men in dark suits blocked her from the corpse.

'Who are they?' I leapt across a pine log and hurried over.

'No idea.' Mark followed me. 'But they look like Feds or spooks.'

Federal police or ADIA agents. They certainly had the arrogance to go with the jobs.

Darlene was assuring them she was here to help with the forensics investigation but they were physically pushing her from the scene.

'IDs,' Mark demanded, showing his own.

The dark suits retreated but said something I couldn't hear and Mark stood down to make a call. When he hung up, he turned to us.

'They override our jurisdiction. Only their authorised personnel are permitted near the body.'

'I'm not some ghoul off the street,' Darlene argued. 'This is my job, and Rex King can vouch for me.'

'I know,' Mark said, 'but they have their orders and I have mine. They'll formally identify the deceased. There's nothing more you can do here.'

I wondered how they could confirm whether it was Moss in the body bag without dental records or DNA. We needed to get some of Eric's DNA to compare to the body's. In exchange they could answer some of Eliza's and my questions about her father and his activities.

'Darlene, grab your gear. There's somewhere we need to be.'

Chapter 93

I GOT LUCKY with a parking spot in Hunter Street, close to Martin Place. If Moss used his workplace as a bedsit when he was in Sydney, Darlene should easily find DNA in his office or on toiletries to identify who he truly was, and if the body in the water was in fact him.

'Craig Gisto, private investigator,' I announced to the man standing guard outside the offices. 'I'm here on behalf of Eliza Moss to collect the personal possessions Eric left behind.'

'I'm not supposed to let anyone in,' said the tubby man with a face scarred by past acne. 'Sir Lang has to approve visitors now.'

Darlene waited beside with her bag as I stepped forward and lowered my voice. 'Look, I don't know if you knew Eric Moss well but a body's just been found in the harbour and the police think it's him.'

I let the news sink in. The guard turned an ashen hue. 'The poor man. And Eliza. He adored her.'

Darlene lowered her head. 'You can imagine how devastated she is.'

'They're having trouble identifying the body because it's been in an explosion,' I explained as he slumped back against the wall.

'He asked me about my holidays. Just last Thursday. He was never too busy to chat.'

We didn't have much time before Lang Gillies sniffed us out. 'We just need to get into his office and collect some things for Eliza. Things that he would have wanted her to have.'

'Of course,' the man said. 'It's only right. Go on in.'

'Thanks. We know the way. Your name is . . . ?'

'Barry. Please tell Eliza I'm real sorry. Eric was a good man.'

'I will.' I shook his hand as Darlene and I quickly slipped past Gillies's closed office door.

Inside Moss's office I had to look twice. The area had been gutted of furniture. The carpet had been ripped up and the walls freshly painted. Darlene entered the bathroom. 'Smells like it's been scrubbed with ammonia,' she said.

Lang Gillies had made damn sure there were no physical traces of Eric Moss in the building.

It was as if he never existed.

Chapter 94

'YOU PEOPLE ARE trespassing!' Lang Gillies was standing behind us, a mobile in his hand.

'We came on behalf of Eliza.' I turned to him. 'To collect her father's personal possessions.'

'Tell that to the police.'

'Or I could tell it to the media. Marcel Peyroni is particularly interested in this case.' I'd done my homework on the old man. 'Craven Media and I have a special relationship. He'd love to know about your penchant for visiting,' I made quotation marks with my fingers, 'a certain exclusive men's club.' I turned to Darlene. 'They have casual Fridays. And by casual, I mean butt naked.'

Darlene feigned shock. 'And what about this for a quote . . . "I was horrified to think he could have used the hard-earned donations of struggling families like mine who wanted to help make a difference"?'

'Don't forget the pensioners,' I urged.

Darlene ran with it. 'My grandmother is going to be devastated. She sacrificed so much to help people in disasters, through Contigo Valley. People who had lost everything.'

'Shut the hell up!' Gillies's face was ruddy and veins distended on his forehead and throat. He banged his walking stick against the wall.

'Why don't we take this to your office?' I said. When Lang didn't move, I led the way with Darlene.

Once inside, Sir Lang slammed the door. He looked on the verge of a stroke but he was obviously the master of temper tantrums.

I pulled up a chair, sat defiantly and placed both hands behind my head. The action irritated him even more. The power had shifted and he didn't like it one bit.

His entire face was engorged with blood. 'What do you want?' he spat.

'Simple. Eric Moss's personal possessions.'

Darlene offered him a chair as if it was her office.

He waved her away. 'The man walked out of here, abandoned everything. I had every right to dispose of them.'

'He was missing,' Darlene corrected, 'and those things could have helped find him.'

'There was no proof he was missing apart from the paranoia of his needy, unbalanced daughter.'

Darlene flashed me a warning look and I consciously relaxed both fists.

'If the press got wind of her erratic behaviour, she'd be humiliated. Just when her father's been dragged from the harbour.'

'You already heard?' Darlene sounded shocked.

'It pays me to know.' He sat now, facing me, walking stick held between his spindly legs. 'My job is to distance this organisation from that traitor.'

I wanted to see what else he knew. 'Your grief is choking us up. Can we count on you for a eulogy?'

'There'll be no one at the service once word gets out.'

I sat forward. 'About?'

'His lies, deceit, schemes to commit fraud.'

Crimes I suspected Gillies had known about all along. He could even have been behind them.

'You mean the containers scam.'

The colour in his face faded. He'd underestimated me.

'As chairman of the board, you are as guilty as sin. You'll be going down too. No more casual Fridays for you, old boy.'

'That's where you're wrong. Eric Moss was a con man. Or should I say Hans Gudgast? Or whatever the hell his name really was. Everything about him was a *lie*.'

Word travelled fast in police and business circles. Lang Gillies wasn't the complete fool I'd taken him for. Then again cockroaches were the ultimate survivors.

'You think the mighty Craig Gisto is the only one who was investigating Eric? The man was convincing. Look at Eliza. She thinks he's a saint. I can testify we had no idea who he really was or what he was capable of.'

That was it. Any responsibility Lang Gillies had in the fraud scheme would be buried with Eric Moss. He would be made the scapegoat for the entire organisation's corruption and ineptitude. Gillies was absolving himself of all responsibility.

Chapter 95

JOHNNY ARRIVED AT the Wallaces' home in Dural. A news team and station van hovered nearby.

The couple had been interviewed and released without Private being allowed to question them further about the woman posing as Louise Simpson. Johnny hoped the pair might recognise one of the women in the radiology staff photos as the woman they paid the twenty-five-thousand-dollar deposit.

Understandably, after the media coverage they were loath to leave the house and spoke through an intercom on the gate.

'Go through our lawyer,' the husband said coldly.

Johnny tried the soft approach. 'I'm so sorry about what you've been through. I know this is difficult but you are still the best chance of finding Zoe Ruffalo. All I'm asking is that you look at these photos and tell me if the woman you met claiming to be Louise is among them.' There was no reply, but the crackle on the line told Johnny Mr Wallace was still listening.

'You understand loss. We can only imagine what Zoe's parents are going through. But *you* know.' Johnny placed his forehead on the brick above the intercom and appealed one last time. 'All any of us want is to bring her home safe.'

There was silence, then a buzz and the gates separated.

Johnny made the sign of the cross and thanked God.

'Five minutes. That's all,' Wallace said. 'My wife can't take any more stress.'

'Thank you, sir.' Johnny walked briskly up the drive.

The couple had been embarrassed, harassed and arrested in full public view. Johnny could understand they would be reluctant to talk to anyone without a lawyer present. And, despite a police statement saying the Wallaces had helped in the investigation but were *not* suspects in the homicide or in the kidnapping of baby Zoe, they were still being hounded by journalists.

Alexandrus Wallace opened the door in tracksuit pants and a ragged T-shirt. Unkempt hair and a day's worth of stubble were indicators of a nightmare twenty-four hours.

'Thank you for your time.' Johnny pulled out the photos of the female staff.

Mr Wallace stood just inside the door, out of view from the road, keeping his visitor on the step.

He looked carefully at each image, shaking his head, then arrived at the final photo. 'She isn't here.'

'Are you certain?' Johnny was sure the woman worked at the radiology centre. He produced the photos of the male employees, including the two doctors he'd spoken to. 'Do you remember seeing any of these men on the beach when you met with that woman, or any other time?'

Wallace exhaled but took the next set of pictures. 'I'm sorry. I don't recognise anyone.'

'OK. Well, I appreciate your time,' Johnny said.

'People say time heals. Nothing can heal the pain of losing a child.' He part-closed the door. 'For everyone's sake, we hope you find the baby.'

Johnny trudged back up the drive, painfully aware that without any other leads Zoe Ruffalo might never be found.

Chapter 96

JOHNNY WASN'T ABOUT to give up, however. He headed back to Manly. This time he wanted to know about any practice employees who had left in the last year. Ones who could have printed out X-rays in advance.

One had married and moved to Glasgow with her new husband. A radiography student, Felicity Wenham, had begun a rotation with them but failed to return after the fourth week. No one had heard from her since. Dr Kwong explained that wasn't unusual. Sometimes students didn't fit in, or wanted to work closer to home. According to the practice manager, the student was a fast learner and was eager to know how the business worked. If Felicity had finished her rotation, she might have been given a job after graduation.

Johnny found her name on the electoral roll and was pleasantly surprised to see she was living in Balgowlah, close by. He drove straight to the address and parked a short distance from a blue weatherboard home set back from the street. A separate garage down the drive looked like it had been converted into a studio or office.

A woman in her forties answered the door. He asked if it was possible to see Felicity Wenham.

The mother enquired, hesitantly, 'Are you a friend from college?'

'No. I'm investigating the disappearance of a young baby and a possible link to the radiology practice Felicity spent time at. We're interviewing current and former staff members in case they came into contact with the kidnapper.'

Mrs Wenham was shocked. 'I saw that on the news. My daughter may have met the kidnapper? The person who killed that poor woman too?' She grabbed Johnny's arm. 'Is Felicity in danger?'

Johnny patted her hand. 'No. I just need to talk to her. She may know something she doesn't realise is significant. Is she home?'

After a few moments, seemingly deep in thought, Mrs Wenham looked up. 'Our daughter has always been a hard worker, good at everything she ever tried. Out of the blue, she developed anorexia at fourteen.' She swallowed. 'We thought it was all behind us. Then she found out her boyfriend was seeing someone else. Our daughter is just so hard on herself.'

'I understand and I'll be very sensitive to that, but a child's life is at stake.'

A man appeared behind Mrs Wenham. 'The answer is no. We're sorry for the child's family, but we can't risk you upsetting Felicity. She's all we have.'

The door slammed in Johnny's face.

Chapter 97

DESPITE BEING STONEWALLED by her parents, it wasn't difficult to find Felicity Wenham. There were a limited number of treatment options – psych, acute medical or a facility for anorexia. Twenty minutes and three phone calls later, Johnny entered the cardiac ward at the Royal Balgowlah Hospital. A slim young woman with short layered hair sat by the window of her private room. Leads extended beneath her pyjama top to a monitor on the wall above the bed.

He knocked on the open door and she continued gazing into the distance. 'Felicity? My name is Johnny Ishmah.'

'I'm done with shrinks.' She curled her lip in disgust.

'Don't blame you,' Johnny grinned. 'I'm a private investigator. Psych is my major. The criminal kind.'

This time she made eye contact. 'Has my father sent you to see how crazy I really am?'

Johnny mentally noted 'father issues' but quickly moved on. 'I wanted to ask you about your Manly radiology rotation.'

'Yeah, well, flunked that.' She opened her buttoned pyjama top just enough to reveal a well-defined, square lump under her collarbone. The wound looked fresh.

Johnny looked at the pulse rate monitor. 'Is that a pacemaker?'

She stared at the implant, as if still in disbelief. 'Attractive, don't you think?'

'Sounds serious.' Johnny knew how much damage anorexia could do to vital organs.

'When the defib kicks in and you're awake, it's a blast. The ultimate accessory.' Felicity's sarcasm couldn't hide her anger.

She looked back out the window overlooking a patch of garden. 'What are you investigating the radiology practice for?'

Johnny pulled up a visitor's chair.

'There were some X-rays that had false dates and names on them. I'm trying to work out who could have got into the system and changed them, before printing them out.'

He watched for a reaction. Her heart rate on the monitor remained consistent at sixty beats per minute.

'Theoretically anyone with a code to the system could.'

'Who has access to the X-ray codes at Manly?'

'The doctors. The radiographers. Receptionists can't normally enter patient data on the machines.'

'Were any of the staff interested in the machines who maybe shouldn't have been?'

She thought for a moment then looked up. 'Only Sigrid.'

Johnny flicked through his notes. 'I don't have that name on my employee list.'

'She works at night. Sometimes I'd stay back so she could teach me.'

Johnny thought office hours were eight am to five pm. 'Is she a doctor?'

Felicity wrapped a lock of hair into a small curl. 'Only in Norway. Sigrid researched radiation exposure in people with chronic bone disease. Then married a boy from the northern beaches and followed him here. It didn't last. She was left with no money and no job.' She seemed to soften. 'It's tough. The government doesn't recognise her qualifications and she couldn't afford to sit the medical exams all over again.'

'Do you know her last name?'

'Hale? Holt? No. Hall. That's it. Sigrid *Hall*. She said her ex had a used-car business.'

'If she couldn't work as a doctor, what was she doing at the practice?'

'She's in charge of the contract cleaners. It was either that or drive a taxi.'

Chapter 98

I GOT THE call from Johnny. He was at Balgowlah and had a strong lead this time. Sigrid Hall. A woman who was medically trained and knew her way around X-ray machines. *And* who worked nights cleaning at the Manly radiology practice.

While he was on the line, I searched for her business. All I could locate was a post office box for her contracting company along with a phone number. I dialled the landline but was sent straight to voicemail.

There was no one with the name Sigrid Hall listed in the White Pages. All the usual databases came up short.

Johnny mentioned an ex-husband with a used-car business.

'That's something. We can call them all if we have to, to find him.'

There were multiple entries with the surname Hall in that postcode area.

'Bingo,' I said aloud. 'Hall's Honda is on Military Road.'

Johnny wasn't far and I told him I could be there in minutes. We pulled up at the same time and entered the office.

A friendly receptionist said Tony Hall was with a client. 'We'll wait, thanks,' I said.

Johnny phoned Mary and told him where we were. She wanted to be kept in the loop the second he got an address for the radiologist-cum-cleaner.

A toned man in his thirties in a red polo shirt and black trousers greeted us.

'I was told to ask for Tony,' I said.

'At your service,' he grinned. 'What are you after today? It's a great time to buy. We do fantastic deals on trade-ins.' He glanced at Johnny. 'And can provide instant finance at competitive rates.'

The white toothy smile and spiel were well practised.

'Actually, this is about your wife.'

'Ex.' The friendly persona instantly vanished. 'Piss off,' he said, storming back towards the show room. 'Tell her the goddamn well is dry. I don't care if she can't make bail. She can rot in hell.'

Johnny followed. 'We're not here for money. A baby is missing and Sigrid could be at risk.'

'Boo hoo,' he mocked. 'Let me guess. One of you screwed around with her; she got knocked up. You did the right thing and paid all her expenses. Well, wake up and smell the bullshit. She never was pregnant.'

A female staff member in heels, black dress and red scarf came through the sliding glass doors and asked if everything was all right. Her badge said 'Marianne'.

'This guy wants to know about Sigrid. He was just leaving.' Tony turned to go inside. The employee rested her hand on his upper arm.

'Isn't it enough she almost bankrupted him?' She threw her hands up. 'You people are unbelievable. They are divorced and Tony isn't legally responsible for her debts.'

I interrupted. 'Sigrid could be in serious trouble. Right now. We need to find her before someone else gets killed.'

Marianne rolled her eyes. 'You really bought into the whole drama, didn't you? Poor little Sigrid? What about the people she's hurt?'

'We're private investigators, working on a police investigation,' Johnny tried.

'Then why don't you talk to your police colleague? I gave him Sigrid's address to get rid of him.'

Someone else was after her. Before us. 'Who else was here?'

She folded her arms. 'The detective. He said Sigrid had ripped off the wrong person. I figured the police had finally caught up with her.'

'How long ago was this?' I pressured.

'About an hour.'

'Can you give me the address? This is important!'

The ex-husband didn't hesitate. 'Gladly. 17/22 Rolfe Street in Manly. I can't wait to see that bitch finally pay.'

Chapter 99

JOHNNY AND I RACED to the address Tony Hall gave us. In the car I phoned Mary to fill her in.

'Don't spook her yet,' she suggested. 'We don't know if she has the baby, and can't afford for her to do a runner. Wait,' Mary said, 'Darlene just came in. I'll put you on speaker phone.'

'Where's Eliza?' I asked.

'Working from your office. She can't hear us.'

I sped through an orange light as Johnny gave details. 'Sigrid Hall is Norwegian. Blonde. Scammer, pretends to be pregnant to get money, according to her very angry ex. She's familiar with X-ray equipment and had the contract for cleaning at the Manly radiologist.'

'I'm on my way,' Mary said. 'Where are you now?'

'Turning into the street. We'll wait for you.' Mary was invaluable in a confrontational situation. If there was time, she was worth waiting for. There were no cars parked near the home.

'Be careful,' Darlene warned.

'We will be. Martyrdom never ended well,' Johnny replied.

I asked Darlene where we were at with the IP address used for the emails our imposter sent to the Wallaces.

'We've narrowed it down to Manly. It's the closest I could get for now.'

'So far we've only got circumstantial evidence. Anything specific I can use for leverage will help.'

'I'll try to get the account name, but it may take time,' she said.

'Do what you can from there and keep an eye on Eliza.'

As I hung up, Johnny frowned. 'Do you think it was a detective ahead of us?'

That's what bothered me. Neither Hall nor the receptionist asked to see our IDs and had merely assumed we were police.

'We need to be careful how we play this.' I referred to the GPS for directions. 'If the police arrest her, she'll lawyer up and is likely to use what she knows to bargain with the prosecutors.' I was talking to myself as much as to Johnny. 'That could take days. And we don't have time to mess around.'

We finally had the chance to find Zoe and Louise Simpson's killer. If the man claiming to be a detective hadn't beaten us there.

Chapter 100

I PARKED A good two blocks from the house and didn't have to wait long for Mary. A caravan and trees along the kerbside obscured the view of my car from Sigrid Hall's house.

I told Johnny to sit tight and call the police if there was trouble. Mary and I walked towards the gate.

So far it was quiet apart from cockatoos squealing in the trees.

Mary scouted around the side of the house. I did up my suit coat and knocked three times on the front door.

A small woman opened the chained door, revealing only half her face in the gap. She was blonde, as Johnny had described.

'Sorry to bother you, ma'am, I work for Reed Armstrong Real Estate and we have buyers keen to move into this area.'

'I'm not interested in selling.' She tried to close the door but my foot was already blocking it.

'I could give you an obligation-free quote on the spot. I think you'd be surprised what homes like yours are selling for in the current market.'

She part-turned at something behind her. I glimpsed marks on the side of her face.

'I'm not interested,' she said. This time she slammed the door. I only just got my foot out in time.

She had looked scared. Someone else had to be inside.

I headed back down the drive and into the street before doubling back via the neighbour's yard. All the curtains and blinds were closed.

I signalled for Mary to find a way in. She climbed on the rubbish bin and managed to lift the screen of the open bathroom window.

I kicked off my shoes and pulled myself up through the window while Mary took off around the back. I had just climbed through when something crashed inside.

From the bathroom door I caught a glimpse of the living room. The woman was now tied to a chair, crying.

And a man a lot larger than me was standing over her.

'You destroyed my daughter!' He wrenched hard on her ankle ties.

Sigrid Hall winced. 'I never hurt anyone, I swear.'

I pulled out my phone and quickly hit record.

'You're a liar! My son-in-law was tested. He has *no* genetic defects. He doesn't carry the condition you say the baby had.' His tone suddenly calmed as he bent down, right in his captive's face. 'At first I thought it was you who had it and knew you could pass on the defect.'

'No!'

'Then I got to thinking . . .' He gave her a long calculating look. 'I saw a specialist who said the gene was dominant. Do you know what that means?'

She closed her eyes, tears spilling down her cheeks.

'You claimed to have two healthy children but we both know that's not possible with a dominant gene.' He paced in front of her. 'The specialist thought it was odd my daughter didn't get to see the body. That all we had was your word.'

She flicked hair from her doe-like eyes. 'If you untie me, I'll tell you everything.'

The man gave her a hateful smile. 'No need. I *know* the baby didn't die. There was never anything wrong with her.'

He cocked his head and raised his hand.

Sigrid blurted, 'Wait! The scan could have been confused with someone else's. It happens sometimes.'

'Wrong answer.' He landed a slap to her left cheek. She slumped to the right and he pulled her up. 'Try again.'

'All right!' Her breathing became shallow. 'I lied about that.'

'So you admit it. You and that other woman planned the whole thing. You kept my grandchild.' He raged. 'Is there a standard fee for a white baby girl? Or is there some kind of bidding war?' He stormed into the kitchen and I could hear drawers slamming.

Sigrid's eyes widened with panic.

Chapter 101

I TEXTED MARY: *escalating. stand by. tall male 120 kg.*

'There is no baby,' Sigrid Hall screamed. 'You've got it all wrong.'

The man returned; this time his expression was even more menacing. 'You would have sold my grandchild like a piece of meat.' He raised a hand and struck her across the face again. Not hard enough to knock her over, but solid enough to cause pain.

I tensed, ready to intervene at any second.

'I wasn't pregnant!' she shouted. 'I'm infertile!'

He stepped back, looking at the woman. 'You're doing exactly what the other bitch did. She acted all shocked and innocent. Until I heard the baby cry. Then it became clear. You kept my grandchild so I took her back.'

'Oh my God. You killed Louise Simpson!' Sigrid tried to scream but he clamped one hand over her mouth.

'That's when I realised that Simpson woman must have faked the scans. She would have needed an accomplice. Someone at that X-ray place. I watched all day yesterday. I was ready to leave when I saw something through the windows. What sort of cleaner uses the computers and leaves with envelopes?'

Sigrid couldn't talk back. His hand gripped her reddened face even tighter.

'I lost you in traffic when you left but your car has a yard sticker on it, same last name as your cleaning company.'

She spluttered and tried to writhe free.

'Letting parents think their baby died and allowing them to grieve. You two are evil.' His rage was building with every word. 'You *both* deserve to die.'

I searched again for something to use as a weapon. There was a hot curling iron on the bathroom bench. I flicked its power point on.

Sigrid was sobbing. He took his hand away.

'I'll tell the police everything. You can call them now.'

'And see you just get a slap on the wrist? I don't think so. What you did to my daughter, to my grandchild . . . You need to be punished.'

I looked through the gap in the doorway again and saw the flash of a carving knife in the man's hand.

Chapter 102

SIGRID HALL BEGGED for her life.

'I didn't sell a baby,' she cried. 'There never was a baby. It was a scam. That's all it was. I didn't even *know* Louise Simpson. I just used her name. The ultrasound your daughter saw was fake.' She sniffed. 'I swear to God, there never was a surrogate pregnancy. Your grandchild never existed!'

The man straightened to his full height.

'I found an abnormal scan in the X-ray archives,' Sigrid continued, tears streaming down her battered face. 'I changed the name and date. If you let me go, I'll give you back the twenty-five thousand. Every cent. *Please* just let me go.'

He ran a hand through his hair. 'You expect me to believe my daughter lost everything because of a baby that *never existed*?' He was mumbling to himself and pacing.

I knew as soon as he realised he'd killed an innocent woman and taken someone else's child, Sigrid was dead. I grabbed a towel and wrapped it around my left arm then I texted Mary.

NOW.

I snatched up the curling iron and rushed down the corridor.

The man swung around, slashing at me. I deflected the knife with the hot iron and clamped it on to his hand. He screamed in pain as his flesh burnt.

At that moment, Mary kicked in the back door and knocked the woman and the chair out of the way.

The man, distracted, didn't see her right cross coming. As he staggered back, she kicked him hard in the chest. He landed heavily and she trapped him, straddling him and pinning both arms with her knees.

He struggled to breathe.

I held the hot iron to his face. 'Where's the baby?'

'I want a lawyer!' he yelled, face engorging.

Mary put more weight on his biceps. 'What did you do with the baby?'

He refused to answer.

'Sigrid is telling the truth,' I said. 'She never was pregnant. The baby you took isn't your grandchild.'

As realisation hit, the man looked winded. He'd murdered Louise Simpson for nothing.

'My daughter, Majella, has her. Oh God. She thinks that's her child.'

Chapter 103

MARY SECURED THE man with cable ties while I scoured his pockets and extracted a wallet. Evan Piper was his name. The baby was at his daughter's Mosman home.

I phoned Mark Talbot. 'We've got Louise Simpson's murderer, and the woman who took her identity,' I told him. 'I'll explain the specifics later, but we have detained them and have a recorded confession. They're at 17/22 Rolfe Street, Manly. I'm going for the baby.' I gave him the Mosman address. He was sending a team here and heading to the daughter's house.

I moved over and sat Sigrid Hall up but I refused to release her ties. She was a liar, a con woman and had committed the cruellest act, letting couples think their unborn children had died of an incurable condition. She'd also stolen an innocent woman's identity, and money. She may not have foreseen the danger she was putting Louise in, but she still had blood on her hands.

I phoned Johnny and told him to back Mary up. No one was to leave. The police were minutes away.

Then I sped all the way to Mosman. Majella Piper believed the baby was hers. She wouldn't just give Zoe up.

I pulled up outside the house just as Detective Sergeant Kristen Massey, in plain clothes, was climbing out of her unmarked car. She let her hair out of its ponytail, stripped down to a singlet and unselfconsciously slipped off her skirt. She grabbed some khaki shorts from inside the car and stepped into brown Blundstone boots. A sweat-stained cap finished the look.

'We don't know how suspicious the woman will be.'

'So what's your plan?' I deferred to her.

'She may open the door to me like this. You're my husband in case you're wondering.'

'Good to know.'

Kristen knocked and a young woman answered.

I took the detective's hand.

'Hi there. We live down the street and have been admiring your roses. Can we ask what you feed them with? Ours keep dying.'

The sound of a baby crying came from inside. The woman looked around, then back again. 'I'd love to help you but I'm sorry, I have to go.'

'Wow,' Kristen said. 'How old's your little one?'

'Eight weeks.' The woman didn't seem at all suspicious. If anything, she was bursting with pride.

'That is so exciting. We're expecting ourselves. Ten weeks.'

I touched her belly as if confirming the fact.

Majella seemed to hover for a second, then said with a grin, 'She's due for a feed. Wait there.'

Kristen moved her leg forward even though the door was ajar. Majella was soon back, with the baby clasped tightly at her chest.

She exposed its face.

'She is so tiny,' I said. 'What's her name?'

'Elspeth. It was my grandmother's name.'

'You are a cutie,' Kristen cooed. 'Can I hold her?' She reached over and took Zoe before Majella had the chance to object. I admired the baby, placing myself between the two women.

Within seconds, two squad cars pulled up and six officers ran towards the house, weapons drawn.

It all happened so fast Majella Piper didn't appear to react. Until Kristen turned back and said to her gently, 'My name's Detective Massey,' and flashed her police badge. 'I'm sorry, but this child is not yours.'

Chapter 104

'LEAVE MY BABY alone!' Majella thrashed to break free from my grasp.

The child began to cry.

'These people are stealing my daughter!' Majella Piper was panic-stricken.

I had the woman in a vice-like grip and locked eyes with her. 'Listen. That baby isn't yours. The police are here because your father took someone else's child.'

The fight went out of her at the mention of her father.

'You're wrong. She's mine. The surrogate is the one who should be arrested. She was going to sell Elspeth.'

Mark was now at my side. 'I think we'd better go inside,' he said softly, 'where we can talk. Paramedics are checking the baby. She's safe and they're not going anywhere unless I say.'

His soothing, rational tone seemed to calm her down, at least enough to walk into the lounge room and sit.

Only her hands, clasped tightly together, betrayed the emotions she was battling to keep in check. She focused her attention on the portacot that had been set up next to a rocking chair.

Mark broached, 'A simple DNA test will clear all this up. For now, your father's talking to us about Louise Simpson.'

'Have you arrested her? All this time we thought she'd been stillborn.' Her face became animated. 'I couldn't believe my baby was alive.'

Mark cleared his throat. 'Have you seen the news in the last two days?'

'No. Elspeth and I have been getting to know each other.' She began to fold a crocheted rug from the lounge. 'Did you know she loves classical music?'

Mark rubbed his hands on his trouser legs.

Majella Piper was in denial. She needed to hear the full truth.

It was up to me. 'I just left your father with the surrogate you met with. Her real name is Sigrid Hall. She stole Louise Simpson's identity, feigned being a surrogate and took money from couples like you and your husband. She faked a pregnancy then pretended she'd miscarried.'

'No.' Majella was adamant. 'The pregnancy was real. I saw our baby's heart beating on the video of the scan.'

'That was part of her scam. She used the scan of a child who died two years ago, with the names and dates changed to look like she was a surrogate mother.'

Majella's eyes narrowed as the truth began to sink in.

'But Dad said she admitted it was my baby.'

I pieced the story together for her, and the police. 'He went to the house of the real Louise Simpson, whose identity had been stolen. She was innocent and didn't know anything about the fake surrogate. She was babysitting an eight-week-old girl, Zoe Ruffalo, for a friend.'

Majella's eyes flashed from Mark to me, confused.

'Your father admitted to murdering the real Louise Simpson and taking Zoe Ruffalo. If it's any consolation, he really believed she was yours.'

'*Murdered* . . .? No. That can't be,' Majella pleaded, as the truth slowly sank in.

This poor woman had already grieved for a child that never existed. Now she'd lost a child who was never hers.

Mark stood. 'You'll need to come with us to the station for a formal statement,' he said, with a hint of regret.

Kristen Massey came in and took Majella Piper formally into custody. It was up to the Director of Public Prosecutions as to whether or not she'd be charged with conspiracy after the homicide.

'Don't answer any more questions,' I advised, 'without a lawyer present.'

I handed Mark my phone with the recorded confessions. There was nothing more I could do here.

'I'll make my statement later.'

Mark nodded. 'Give you the heads-up. There'll be a press conference shortly on the Moss case.'

It was his way of thanking me for today. And letting me know Eliza would need all the support I could offer.

Chapter 105

I DROVE BACK to the office. Exhaustion was hitting me hard. Any relief at finding baby Zoe safe and well was countered by the pain and grief Eliza was going through.

We still had no DNA to compare with the body from the water, even if we could extract a tissue specimen. Darlene was denied access to the autopsy even as an observer.

Mark Talbot texted my usual phone number.

Televised press conference 4 pm. Family NOT briefed.

That was barely enough time for the autopsy to be performed. Toxicology results and microscopic examination of the body were impossible to complete by then. This reeked of a cover-up. Relatives should be told before information was made public. Eric Moss's only family member was being frozen out. The instructions had to be coming from the highest level. But from whom?

I decided to leave Eliza in my office. She had only just fallen asleep. According to Darlene, she hadn't received any calls from the police.

The rest of us gathered around the TV in the conference room. The police commissioner was confirming the death of Eric Moss in a boat explosion.

'We are satisfied there were no suspicious circumstances surrounding Mr Moss's death. The coroner has released Mr Moss's body for burial. There will not, at this point, be an inquest. I'd like to take this opportunity to offer my condolences to his family and friends.' He looked up from the podium. 'Any questions?'

'Can you confirm an investigation is underway into fraud at Contigo Valley?' a reporter asked.

He cleared his throat. 'An investigation was conducted into alleged fraud at Contigo Valley. I believe Mr Moss was aware he would face charges. As a result of that investigation I can confirm the name Eric Moss was in fact an alias for a Hans Gudgast, a Swiss national who fled Switzerland before being tried on embezzlement charges. At this stage I would like to stress that Contigo Valley is in no way implicated in the fraud perpetrated by the man we now know to be the fugitive, Hans Gudgast.'

That was news to my team and me. The investigation into Contigo's finances was still pending. This had to be a stitch-up, with Eric Moss being tainted with guilt when he could no longer defend himself.

'Now we know why Eliza wasn't briefed,' Mary said coldly. 'She was blindsided so she couldn't refute any of it.'

'Did Moss commit suicide?' a TV broadcaster queried.

The commissioner sighed, and became more sombre. 'We never know what was going on in someone's mind in the moments before death. Mr Moss resigned from the organisation on Friday afternoon and was reported missing by a family member. It appears Mr Moss was intoxicated when he started the boat and may or may not have intentionally set the fire that caused the explosion. Only he and God know what he was thinking that fateful night when the police were closing in on him.' He went on to add further insult. 'The coroner has released Mr Moss's body for burial. As I said, there will not, at this point, be an inquest.' He abruptly ended the press conference.

I sat in complete disbelief. The commissioner had implied that the investigations into fraud and Moss's death were both closed, exonerating Contigo Valley and Lang Gillies from any wrongdoing.

I stood up, replaying in my mind what we had just witnessed.

'Eliza's going to be devastated when she finds out,' Darlene said quietly.

I turned to see Eliza in the doorway.

Chapter 106

I DROVE ELIZA back to my place. She didn't speak at all on the way and her withdrawn state concerned me. Once back home, I tried to get her to open up. Even a little.

She used her crutches to step out on to the balcony. Hair gusted across her face as she stared at the waves pounding on the sand. I placed two hot mugs of tea on the table.

'If you like, I can organise a funeral home. The coroner's releasing –'

'Dad didn't drink. Why was he on that boat?' She seemed bewildered. 'And how could he be Hans Gudgast? I thought they were different heights.'

I suspected we'd never get to the truth behind who Eric Moss really was but he'd officially been declared dead. Everything had happened so fast, even for a high-level cover-up. Perhaps Moss did go to the boat that night to get drunk. Whether it was suicide or an accident, the result was the same.

'Maybe he was so tired from running and pretending to be someone he wasn't.'

'This can't be happening.' Eliza covered her mouth with her hands. 'He can't be gone.'

With that, her emotions erupted and she buried her face in my chest. I held her, and felt every ounce of her pain.

The doorbell rang and I ignored it. It rang again. Next thing, Mark Talbot was calling out from below.

I waved for him to come up and eased away from Eliza to answer the door.

'This is an official visit, I'm afraid.' He fidgeted on the spot. 'You saw the press conference?'

'Someone could have warned Eliza.'

Mark paused. 'I had no say in that. I need to speak to her if she's here.' He lowered his voice. 'How's she doing?'

'How do you think?'

Mark headed to the balcony. Eliza looked up, soulfully, as if hoping he had good news.

'I'm sorry for your loss,' my cousin began. 'But there are some questions about the trust fund your father established on your behalf.'

'Seriously, Mark, this can wait. Eliza didn't even know about the trust.'

Her eyes didn't leave his face.

'Well, she needs to know the account has been frozen, as it may contain the profits from crime,' he said to me. 'I'm sorry, but Lang Gillies and some pretty high-flyers are rapidly trying to distance themselves from anything your father was involved in.'

'You mean his *alleged* criminal activity.' Eliza was curt.

Mark looked out towards the sea. 'I met your father and believe he was a good man. If there's anything I can do to help, please don't hesitate to let me know.' He placed his card under the mug closest to Eliza.

Outside, I challenged him. 'What the hell was all that about? What were you fishing for?'

'Craig, you need to bury the guy and move on. It's *over*.'

All my frustrations came to the boil and I shoved him against the wall.

'What are you going to do now? Burn me with a curling wand?' he snapped.

'Cut the crap, Mark. This is a cover-up and you're part of it.'

He raised both hands in surrender. 'I'm telling you this as a favour. To you and Eliza. You're in way over your head. This is bigger than any of us and some serious players are pulling the strings.'

I stood back. 'Who exactly?'

'All investigations into Moss's activities are being dropped. He made idiots out of people who can't afford to be embarrassed. Not when national security is such a vote-winner.'

'Doesn't anyone want to know how a guy with zero credentials or documentation got access to restricted military bases?'

Mark pushed back. 'Think with your head, not your dick for a change. A contact in the Prime Minister's office told me the US Secretary of State had Moss on speed dial. *Do you hear what I'm saying?* For your sake and Eliza's you need to drop it. You had a win today finding Zoe Ruffalo. You'll never get lucky with this. Trust me. Bury the guy and let it go.'

Chapter 107

ELIZA WAS FINALLY accepting the fact her father was no longer with her. She said he would want to be cremated and his ashes released over Contigo's forest valley.

Thankfully, the grisly task of choosing a coffin was one she didn't have to perform. She had just taken a call from Lang Gillies. He'd already made the arrangements, to 'save her the pain at such a time'.

The service would take place the next morning at the Northern Suburbs Memorial Gardens on Delhi Road, North Ryde. Ten am. It smacked of a rush job. Moss being dead clearly wasn't good enough for some. They wanted him cremated as soon as physically possible.

I thought about what Mark had said. Was he trying to warn me, or protect me? Or both? He didn't agree with what was happening but he had become more of a pragmatist lately. Every fibre in me sensed a cover-up by authorities and it had to do with his supposedly secret contracts.

I stood in the lounge, watching Eliza for a moment. She had already been through so much, and I didn't want anything to compromise her safety.

Time was running out to discover who, if anyone, had murdered her father. There were too many unanswered questions. Ambassador Roden's determination to find Moss, the US Secretary of State's close ties with Moss, who was really behind any fraud at Contigo and what the secret contracts involved.

First, I wanted to call Rex King and ask about the blood alcohol level in his system. It was a quick blood test and would confirm whether or not Moss had been drinking or was just acting drunk for the security guard.

Rex didn't answer his phone. I left a message.

The best way to delay the service was to call the coroner and request a second, independent autopsy. As a family member, Eliza had that right. That way we could access any report on the cause of the boat explosion. Any physical evidence and test results would have to be kept until then. Eliza could make a public statement saying that if there was a fault with the boat the manufacturer needed to be aware and safety measures put in place to prevent another death. It sounded reasonable and focused on the mechanics of the boat, not the politics of the death.

I talked to her about making the calls. She agreed. It was our only chance to buy time and maybe get some answers.

Chapter 108

I COULDN'T REMEMBER the last time I'd slept in a bed. I dozed for short periods until morning, unable to shake the feeling Lang Gillies wasn't doing Eliza any favours by rushing to put Moss to rest. Eliza had remained holed up in the spare bedroom since sending emails to the coroner's office and the department of forensic science at the morgue. She was now leaving voicemail messages, stressing the urgency.

Time was running out for a response.

Darlene had kindly collected clothes from Eliza's home for the funeral. Not knowing what she'd need, she brought multiple changes of outfit, some dark, with bright accessories.

By six am I had the desperate need to get out and clear my head. I changed into running clothes and left a note saying when I'd be back. Closing the door, I noticed dark grey clouds blanketing the sky. A cold front had hit and storms were brewing from the east.

I didn't bother stretching, just began jogging. Soon I was sprinting along the beach. Waves pounded and sprayed me as my leg muscles contracted and extended against the sand's resistance. Trying to make sense of the past few days, I pushed harder, until my body ached with fatigue and lactic acid. Short of breath, I stopped and bent over, hands on knees. My chest heaved trying to get air.

I had to face facts. Someone had attacked Eliza in her own home. She defended herself then, but opening up the mystery of Eric Moss to public scrutiny could get her hurt, or worse. Maybe Mark was right. I hadn't been thinking clearly. What good was truth if it got people you cared about killed? Nothing would change who Eric Moss was to his daughter. Or how much he cared for her.

One thing I did know. I had feelings for Eliza and wanted to protect her from any more hurt. The cost of exposing any cover-up could be too great. And would it really do any good? Her father was still gone.

Chest still heaving, and shirt soaked with sweat, I headed back home, knowing what I had to do today.

Chapter 109

WE ARRIVED EARLY at the crematorium, hoping to avoid the media. Eliza met the minister who would conduct the brief service. As far as we knew, his would be the only eulogy, with a small group paying their respects.

As Eliza sat, one hand on the coffin, in a private moment, a man with a wreath asked to say goodbye to his old boss. Within seconds he'd pulled out a camera from inside the wreath and was photographing Eliza in her wheelchair beside the coffin.

I didn't waste time evicting the man who, coincidentally, resembled a poorly fed vulture.

Eliza turned to me, barely holding it together. 'Is this ever going to stop?' I'd reluctantly talked her out of an inquest for that very reason. It would raise more questions than it answered and what was left of Eric and Eliza's reputations would be destroyed by Gillies and his cronies.

I stood guard next to her from then on. A handful of people filtered through. Lang Gillies wasn't one of them. Moss's assistant, Oliver Driscoll, and the former financial officer, Renee Campbell, came forward and hugged Eliza. The pilot, Geoff Andren, took a seat without fuss.

Mary quietly let me know there was a horde of press outside, like red fire ants at a barbecue. I told her to remind them this was a private service, for family and close friends only.

I moved forward to take my seat next to Eliza and felt my phone buzz in my jacket pocket. I checked caller ID. It was Darlene. I walked towards the back of the church and answered.

'Craig, we don't have much time. I need to access the body.'

'What?' I couldn't believe her timing. 'The minister is about to start.'

'I'm five minutes away. Trust me. You have got to stop the service!'

'I need specifics, and they'd better be good,' I told her.

'Jack Morgan can explain. He's calling in a minute. I'm almost there.' The phone cut out.

As if on cue, my mobile rang again. I recognised the caller ID.

'Jack, what the hell is going on?'

'When you told me about Eric Moss, something didn't sit right. I did some digging and a CIA contact came through. A US air base has been extracting a number of undercover operatives from the Asia-Pacific region, codenamed Eagle-watch. There is supposed to be one rogue agent.'

'You think it was Moss?'

'Looks like he went off the grid, vanished. My contact just sent through a photo of Moss. CIA had him as deceased in a boat accident until a surveillance camera snapped him at a car rental place in Mascot. Time and date stamp registered six am today.'

'After he was supposedly killed.' I knew there was little picture documentation of Moss. 'How can you be sure it's him?

We haven't been able to establish facial recognition in anything we have.'

'Beard's shaved, glasses are gone. Craig, I've met the guy. It's him.'

'Then we're about to cremate the wrong body.'

'Sorry about the timing. The image just came through.'

There was one thing I needed to know, unequivocally. 'How sure are you about the timing of the photo and your source?'

Jack didn't miss a beat. 'I'd trust him with my life.'

I closed my eyes.

Somehow I had to stop the funeral. I watched Eliza as she nodded for the minister to begin.

'I'd like to welcome everyone on this sad day, to celebrate the life of a man few people knew as well as you who are gathered here.'

It was now or never. I took a deep breath, then shouted: 'Stop! There's been a bomb threat and we need to evacuate the building.'

Chapter 110

THE MINISTER AND the dozen or so mourners turned around. I ran forward, arms outwards.

'We need to clear the building. Bomb squad are on their way.'

I didn't look directly at the mourners. I couldn't bear to see the distress on Eliza's face.

The minister urged people to grab their bags and move quickly and quietly towards the back doors, which Mary held open. Darlene and Johnny slipped in via a side entrance.

We had to move fast. With the media outside, someone was bound to call the police. This could turn nasty.

Eliza had refused to budge.

'A bomb threat?' she demanded. 'Is this some perverted joke?'

'I'm sorry, Eliza. There is no threat. I just needed to buy some time. There's reason to believe the body in that coffin isn't your father's.'

'What?' She appeared hopeful at the news until Johnny approached the coffin clutching a handheld drill and crowbar.

'You're insane!' she shouted. 'Get away from there.'

Johnny began removing screws on the lid while Darlene set up her mobile kit.

Eliza was yelling at them to stop. She flinched with every whir of the drill. I could hear sirens outside. Time was running out so I grabbed the crowbar. Together Johnny and I began to lever off the lid.

Eliza wheeled herself back in horror.

I knew she would never forgive us for what we were doing.

The lid gave way and a putrid smell seeped out.

Darlene was wearing surgical gloves and a surgical mask and handed me the same as I looked down at the body. The face was badly bloated, more decomposed. A section of cheek was missing.

The body was shrouded in a white sheet. No one had bothered to dress it. Darlene cut through the sheet with scissors before ripping it apart. She was looking for anything to suggest another cause of death.

In his left side, irregular chunks of flesh were missing in small sections. On the upper left arm was a straight-edged mark.

'See this wound?' Darlene said. 'The others look like they were caused by fish or trauma. This one's a surgical excision.'

Johnny snapped images with his phone.

Loud banging on the wooden doors stopped us momentarily.

Mary was still on guard at the back doors. 'Craig, what do you want to do?'

The police had arrived and over a loudspeaker we could hear them demanding we evacuate immediately.

Darlene scraped a small piece of skin and dropped it into a half-sized tube. She quickly shoved it under her shirt at the back.

I closed the coffin lid and we all stepped back.

'We need to do what they say,' I instructed.

Mary opened the doors and Eliza wheeled through first. I quickly followed to explain about Jack's call.

'Why?' Eliza said to me through clenched teeth.

Two police in protective gear were feet away. I had to explain later. There was one thing I needed to know.

'I know what you're thinking. But did your father have a tattoo or skin lesion removed from his left arm? Any kind of minor operation?'

She wheeled herself away, Mary close behind. I waited until they were clear.

'There was no bomb scare,' I shouted, hands raised in the air. 'I made it up and acted alone.'

Darlene and Johnny followed, passing Eliza in her chair.

'Craig, you were right,' Darlene whispered.

Right now that wasn't much consolation. We'd unleashed a shitstorm I had no way of controlling.

Chapter 111

ELIZA TRIED TO fathom what had just taken place. Had Craig completely lost his mind? Lying about a bomb to break into the coffin at the service attended by the few people who still had any respect for her father.

Numb, she watched bulbs flash as police handcuffed Craig and ushered him into the back of a marked car.

A team of heavily padded police entered the building.

Johnny was clearly shaken by what they had done. He squatted on his ankles as police questioned him. Darlene stood defiantly, casting sympathetic looks towards Eliza.

None of this made sense. These people had been so kind until now. The last thing she could do for her father was to make sure the service was dignified. He had died alone, in a violent explosion. Everything he'd worked for, his innovations and dedication to helping others was instantly erased. More than that, he had been publicly vilified, now physically desecrated.

A man who never drank would be remembered for dying in a drunken stupor trying to avoid charges for stealing from the charity organisation he'd dedicated his life to.

'All clear,' the police announced and left the crematorium.

Eliza wheeled herself inside right up to the casket.

She placed a hand on the polished wood and tried to connect with the man she thought she knew better than herself.

Had his life been one giant lie? Part of her wanted to hate him for leaving her without an explanation, or even the chance to say goodbye. If he had met her one last time, how could she have believed anything he had to say, knowing everything up until now was a lie?

Anger surged through Eliza's veins and her heart accelerated. Her breathing became shallow and rapid. Air. She needed to get outside and get some air.

She moved and felt something dig into her thigh. A plastic specimen tube had dropped into her chair. She picked it up and thought of what Craig had asked her.

Did her father have any tattoos or skin lesions removed?

The last time she'd seen him was in the city office. He'd spilled tea on his shirt and changed before a meeting. He always wore a white Bonds singlet underneath. She thought back. His skin was pale to the elbows and tanned below the level of his sleeves. There were definitely no lesions, marks or scars on his upper arms.

Eliza took a series of slow, deep breaths, counting to four with every exhalation. The heart flutter slowed and she was finally able to speak.

She glared at Johnny, who was blessing himself in the entrance. He opened his eyes and met her gaze. 'I am so sorry, but we had good —'

'Tell me what Darlene saw. Inside the . . .'

He took a step towards her. 'A mark that didn't appear natural. I mean it didn't look like a fish —'

She wheeled closer. 'Tell me exactly what it was.'

He seemed to hesitate.

'I'm sick of being protected. Lied to. Tell me the *truth*, Johnny.'

'It looked like a wide section of skin had been excised.' He pointed to the outer, upper part of his left arm. 'About here.'

'Why did Darlene sample it?'

'To see if it was done before death. Microscopy would show if it had healed.'

Eliza spun around and raced out the doors. When she realised Johnny was still behind, she held up the specimen.

'Are we going to get this to Private or not?'

Chapter 112

MARY PICKED ME up from the police station. I was escorted out the front of the building to run the media gauntlet. Public humiliation was part of the punishment for trying to stop a cover-up, it seemed. I just hadn't figured out who was directly involved.

My lawyer had hoped to label me a whistleblower who would be legally protected from prosecution. The problem was, we were only protected if we actually worked for the government institution we were trying to expose. Laws recently passed under the guise of anti-terrorist measures were more likely to bury whistleblowers. It also gave secret agencies unprecedented powers without scrutiny or recourse.

That worried me more than charges pending for interfering with a body. If Eric Moss's corpse had been substituted – either while still in the water or while in the morgue – someone had wanted him cremated quickly and with few questions asked. The ambassador's cronies could have murdered Moss with impunity, if he'd offended or compromised the US government. The question was whether the Australian government was involved as well. What was Lang Gillies's involvement? It would explain the rush to funeral service and cremation.

The other possibility was that Moss was still alive and managed to somehow fake his death. But that meant he needed access to a body, or killed a man to take his place.

With police and authorities satisfied the case was closed and would remain that way, there was little chance of getting to the truth.

On top of that, I'd just put a giant target on Private Sydney's back.

Mary brought the car around and I climbed into the passenger seat, unable to forget the horror on Eliza's face as we broke into the coffin. Jack Morgan's intel had to be accurate. But I'd never be able to prove it.

Mark Talbot had realised this was far bigger than any of us knew.

Mary dropped me outside Private's building and I headed inside. Collette greeted me with a long hug.

'I'm so proud of you.' She wrestled back a tear but didn't elaborate. 'You better get to the lab.'

I was confused when Johnny appeared in the corridor outside, face beaming.

'Lucky we have a Gene-IE to grant us wishes,' he said.

Darlene brushed past in her white coat.

To my surprise, Eliza was at the computer desk behind the lab door and looked up at me.

'You took your time,' she said with a glint in her green eyes. 'Leaving us to do all the work.'

I had an overwhelming urge to hug her, which I didn't fight. She responded very tightly, then slowly broke away.

'What are you doing standing around? I'm still paying you to find my father.'

Her smile made the morning's events worth it. 'All right then.' I stepped back, fully realising Eliza was the reason I cared so much about the case.

'First, though,' she added, 'there's something I need to tell you.' Her tone was suddenly grave. 'And I don't think you're going to like it.'

Chapter 113

I SUGGESTED WE talk outside. My paranoia about surveillance meant Eliza and I left our phones at reception. This time, I didn't want to take any chances.

'Keep all the doors locked,' I advised Collette. 'Don't let anyone in we don't already know and trust, and don't accept any deliveries.'

'I won't let you down,' she said, locking the doors behind us.

Whatever it was Eliza wanted to reveal had me concerned. I opted for a café we hadn't been to before.

I had no idea what this morning could have triggered. If ADIA or the CIA had murdered Moss and had switched his body in the coffin for some reason, they'd be mighty pissed off with this morning's events. And if they had nothing to do with the death, they'd be back on Eric's tail now they knew he wasn't dead. Which meant on Eliza's tail too.

The hissing of the machines and grinding beans made eavesdropping almost impossible. We found a seat in the corner and ordered two lattes, and a chicken salad on sourdough to share.

As soon as the waiter left, Eliza began.

'A couple of days ago, flowers arrived for the accountant in the office next to mine. Inside the envelope that came with them was something addressed to me, asking him to hand-deliver a micro USB.'

Whoever sent it had to know all mail and deliveries to Eliza would be monitored. 'Is it from your dad?'

'It has to be. It contains a file with the text of a kid's story he used to read to me, word for word. I knew it by heart, so Dad didn't need to remind me.'

'Was there anything else on it? Maybe some encrypted files?'

'I asked my neighbour, who's an IT whiz. He said there was nothing else on it.'

'Who else knew you read that book together?'

She moved the salt and pepper to the side of the table to make way for the coffees. 'No one.'

It was also plausible there were encoded or encrypted files that couldn't be readily deciphered. Whoever sent the USB didn't want it seen by the authorities.

'What's the book?' I asked.

'It was part of a series. *Oh, The Things You Can See*. This one was about Asia and highlighted exotic animals, costumes and landmarks. You know the sort of thing, orangutans and rainforests, panda bears, warriors and the Great Wall of China. I loved the intricacy of the pictures. They were works of art in their own right.'

If Eric Moss wasn't Hans Gudgast, maybe this was a clue to where he had been, or where he intended to go. Even so, Asia encompassed a broad range of countries.

'Did anywhere seem to mean something special to him? Or did he talk about any of those places?'

'Dad insisted I learn about the world, not just our backyard.'

I swallowed a mouthful of coffee. 'Why didn't you tell me this before?'

She poured sugar into hers. 'I was going to, only that guy broke into my house. Then I saw the TV news.' She looked around the café. 'If this is how Dad wanted me to remember him, I didn't want anyone taking or –'

'Dissecting it like a piece of forensic evidence.'

'I know, it sounds stupid now to have kept quiet.'

I understood completely the need to keep a part of someone to one's self, especially when they were gone.

'Where is it now?'

'I'll have to go to the bathroom to retrieve it. And before you raise an eyebrow . . .' She reached into her oversized handbag and removed, of all things, a sewing kit with a fine-tipped pair of embroidery scissors. 'I had to hide it somewhere no one would think to look.'

Chapter 114

I SUGGESTED WE go straight to Eliza's and pick up the book. Maybe there was a subtle message pointing to something in the text. And she could also extract the USB from her clothing in private.

My car was parked in the underground garage. I opened the passenger door and pain immediately exploded in the back of my skull. I hit the roof forehead first. Dazed, my head was suddenly in an arm lock.

'You need to stay out of things that don't concern you,' a gravelly voice ordered, his grip tightening.

'Like hell.' I managed to pull more upright and jammed the heel of my shoe down his inside leg. The second he loosened his grip, I thrust my elbow hard into his solar plexus. He lost contact, staggered back. Using momentum, I spun around and struck. The crack echoed as my right fist made contact with his jaw.

He stiffened and dropped backwards on to the ground. He wasn't getting up soon so I turned to Eliza. She was still in her chair, stunned.

'Are you all right?' She wheeled closer.

'Better than him right now.' A lump on my forehead throbbed. At least we were both alive. Bending down to check the pulse in his neck, I noticed red marks around his eyes. They looked like chemical burns. 'I think this is the guy who attacked you the other night.' I rifled through his pockets and found the wallet. Inside he had an Australian Department of Defence pass with his photo and name on it. Graydon Knight. I'd seen IDs like this before, different from ones carried by defence force members or public servants. 'He's Defence Intelligence,' I said, as tyres squealed somewhere on a floor below.

'ADIA was in my house?'

'This time he didn't mention handing anything over from your father.'

I suspected the Australian government wanted Eric Moss to stay dead as much for their own reasons as the CIA's.

'Craig?' Eliza said. 'Don't move.'

I felt the sting of cold metal on the back of my neck.

Chapter 115

THE VOICE BEHIND me instructed, 'Get him up.'

Knight had begun to rouse. I glanced sideways at Eliza, who nodded for me to do it. I wasn't about to argue with the barrel of a gun at such close range.

A black van pulled up alongside us. The man with the gun aimed it now at Eliza. 'Put him inside.'

It took what strength I had left to drag the semiconscious lug to the van. The man with the gun used his spare hand to open the van's sliding door without his weapon losing its focus. I levered the dead weight of the agent in.

'I've done what you wanted so let her go.'

'Not so fast,' he said. 'I want Ms Moss to get in. We'd like to ask her some questions. Off the record, of course.'

He turned his back on Eliza for a moment and trained the gun on my chest.

'Don't hurt him,' she pleaded. 'I'll go with you.' She wheeled towards us.

Then I saw a silver glint in her hand. With one swift action, she lurched at the back of the man's knee. He instantly buckled and I seized the gun.

Face contorted, he reached behind, yanked out the weapon and held up a bloodied pair of embroidery scissors.

Now I had the gun, I wanted answers. 'What does Moss have that you need so badly?'

The man winced as blood gushed from his wound. 'We thought he died in that blast, just like you.'

'Who was behind the explosion? Moss can't have acted alone.'

'Ask her.' He gestured with his head at Eliza. 'She knows more than she's letting on. That's why we need to question her.'

I tightened my grip, aware the van had a driver I hadn't seen yet, who could be armed. No one was taking Eliza. 'Is ADIA acting alone or is the CIA pulling the strings?'

'You already know Moss was privy to defence contracts.' He tried to stem the bleeding with his hand. 'Disabled or not, she's dangerous. Next time it could be you she stabs.'

He wasn't going to give me anything useful and his colour was fading. He needed medical attention.

I kept the gun steady. 'Slowly get in the van and leave us alone, or we'll go public with what we know. Ambassador Roden's friends won't be impressed at your cock-up.'

He limped to the open door and slid in, nursing his leg. The driver gunned the engine and sped off towards the exit. If they wanted Eliza, they had to be desperate. I dropped the gun to my side and moved to her.

'Is there anything you can't do?' I asked in amazement.

'The "YMCA" dance is out of the question. Can't lift my arms above my head, remember?'

She was shaken but hadn't lost her sense of humour. I pulled her to standing position, arm around her waist and eased her into the passenger seat. She drew the seatbelt across with her left hand.

I grabbed a packet of cleaning wipes from the side door and wiped blood from her hands.

'Did I just commit grievous bodily harm?' she asked.

I bent down so our eyes were level. 'You stopped yourself from being kidnapped. They would have used you as a bargaining chip to get to your father.' Or worse. They could have held her as a terrorist because of her father and his defence contracts. From what the agent had said, it sounded like ADIA really *did* think Moss had died in the explosion. So they weren't part of any cover-up. They'd been duped like the rest of us. Maybe that was true of the US too. And if ADIA and the CIA didn't switch the bodies, who did?

I closed the car door and folded her wheelchair into my boot, senses heightened for other potential threats.

We needed to find out what message Eric sent Eliza before anyone else tried to stop us.

Chapter 116

I PULLED OUT of the garage at top speed and called Mary on the hands-free about the ambush and threat. I warned them all to be alert and go to their cars in pairs for safety right now.

Darlene came on the line.

'Craig, our little Gene-IE came through. The data from the DNA sample of the body was compatible with one on record.'

I flicked a glance at Eliza who held her breath.

'All I got was a name, Bobby Sim, but he left a trail of media reports and public records. Fifty-nine years old, multiple convictions for drug possession, one for trafficking and a couple for aggravated sexual assault. This guy drugged and assaulted his victims.'

Eliza looked relieved it wasn't her father.

'How and when did he die?' I asked.

'Two weeks ago from lung cancer.'

'Did he have any identifying features?' I was thinking particularly about the arm lesion.

'A press shot showed him in a t-shirt with a jacket over his face. He had a tattoo of what looked like an angel on his left upper arm.'

'Great work, Darlene. Remember, we all need to be careful. This isn't over. In fact, it just got a whole lot worse.'

As soon as we arrived at Eliza's house, she collected her spare set of crutches and headed to the bedroom. I followed. A double bed was raised higher than normal, easier to get down from, I assumed. A bookshelf in the corner only had books on the middle shelves, at a functional height for Eliza. The top and lower shelves were filled with photos, vases and trophies. I couldn't help noticing the multitude of swimming awards, including a gold medal in one corner. There was so much I didn't know about this woman.

'Wait a minute. This is gold from the 2008 Paralympics!'

'For breaststroke. As you know, butterfly wasn't an option.'

I had done a quick background search on Eliza and this wasn't something she promoted in her company or online.

'You won this and never think to mention it?'

'It doesn't make me any better than anyone else. It was a personal goal I set and got to achieve it. It doesn't define me. That blue ribbon,' she pointed to a small wide ribbon with faded writing, 'for running twenty-five metres in first grade means far more. Doctors said I'd never walk, and it took me longer than anyone else, but it was my proudest moment. Dad's too. It showed me life was about potential not limitations.'

She leant across and removed an old, faded picture book. 'Here it is.'

We sat on the bed and she lovingly stroked the cover. I noticed there was minimal dust on it.

'When was the last time you looked at it?'

'Couple of years, maybe.'

Someone else had touched it since.

She opened it and flicked through the pages. 'Every page is here.'

'May I?' I ran my hands over the cover and binding. 'We need to pull it apart.'

Eliza hesitated then agreed. 'Do whatever you need to.'

I used a knife from the kitchen. The lining inside the back cover came away more easily than expected. I opened the binding and separated the cover, exposing a thin piece of paper.

Chapter 117

ELIZA READ THE letter slowly, then handed it to me.

My dearest Eliza,

These words are my legacy to you. I see you rolling your eyes because you have heard all of this before, many times, in various forms over the years. These are my firm beliefs. If we are separated, this is what I pray you remember.

I have always been the best person I could be. I beg you never forget that.

It isn't who you are in life that matters. It is what you do and WHY that counts. Intentions are paramount. I have always believed that inaction is more harmful than well-intentioned actions that fail.

Life is a series of illusions. Things aren't always what they seem.

Each of us is the hero in your own story (and you in mine). However, we may equally be viewed as a villain in others' stories, for genuine or perceived crimes. Despite holding different views, looking or sounding different, originating from another place, one truth is certain:

We all strive to live in a just world, and to see that our loved ones are safe and cared for.

If events occur beyond your control, accept them. You were neither complicit, nor responsible. You should never be shamed by them. Hold your head high for the woman you are. Innuendo, supposition and accusations of others have no role in your life.

Anger, hatred and bitterness are lethal poisons. They cause a slow, painful emotional death that only you suffer. Self-destruction will never defeat an enemy or create justice.

Be prepared to live with the consequences of your actions. If you will not be proud of an act, don't commit it.

In times of struggle, always remember that when the pupil is ready, the teacher will appear. You will always have help should you need it.

Words can start wars, so be careful what you say and whom you say it to. Again, if you are afraid to own those words in a public forum, they are best never said.

Remember these things and you will have a safe, fulfilling and satisfying life.

Be true to yourself, my darling Eliza. Let each step bring you closer to your ultimate destination.

You are the greatest inspiration a man could have, and the dearest child. I love you forever, in this life and the next, from Questacon to Timbuktu and beyond.

This was a farewell note. Wherever he was, he was sure he would not be back.

Eliza slid off the bed and rested herself against the tallboy. She held a photo in a frame and handed it to me. In the faded image, a toddler grinned with pure joy at being held high in the air. The back of a man's head was in the frame, as the child looked down adoringly.

'I thought I could fly when I was in his arms.' She wiped a tear from her cheek.

The letter referred to wars, crimes and self-destruction but I had to ask if Eliza had picked up anything else from his words. I re-read the final sentence.

'Is there any significance to the phrase "from Questacon to Timbuktu and beyond"?'

'Timbuktu was the silliest word I'd ever heard.' She smiled. 'It made me laugh every time Dad said it.'

'Could he be letting you know he's going to Africa?'

Eliza studied the photo again. 'He'd ask me where it was, tickle me every time I got the answer wrong.' She half-smiled. 'I knew exactly where it was, so I mentioned every other city I knew, just to make the game last.'

Maybe the letter was a confession of sorts. Jack Morgan said CIA intelligence believed one of their operatives had turned. But who was he turning to?

There had to be something vital in the message. Questacon was a hands-on science centre in Canberra, the home of parliament.

As we headed back to Private so Darlene could examine the USB, I began to quiz Eliza, hoping to prompt a memory or association.

'Did you ever visit Questacon with your dad?'

'A few times. I loved that things were at wheelchair height and I could use almost every exhibit. But that was years ago.'

I thought about the buildings around that site on Lake Burley Griffin. The High Court, Old Parliament House, the National Gallery, government departments.

'Did you visit any other places when you were there?'

'We went to the zoo, the Australian Museum, the War Memorial. I always wanted to go in those paddling bikes, but Dad didn't think it was safe for me.'

'She who became a Paralympian swimmer.'

'He was just protecting me.' She looked out the window.

'Did he ever go to meetings or stop for business when you were there?'

'When we were together, he left work behind. It was just him and me. Unless there was a massive bushfire or floods or something he needed to be involved in, which was rare when we were on a road trip.'

'Where did you stay?'

'Close enough for us to get to Questacon without a car. He got a good deal, I think, at the Hyatt, the one on Commonwealth Avenue.'

I knew the hotel. It was a favourite for visiting politicians and dignitaries.

Eliza reflected, 'I remember the first time he took me around the embassies. I loved the different types of architecture but one was my absolute favourite.'

Eliza's eyes widened. She reached out and gripped my left arm tightly.

'Oh my God, Craig. I know where my father is.'

Chapter 118

'DAD'S AT THE Chinese Embassy. He has to be.'

I didn't need proof. Eliza's revelation made complete sense now. So much so, we were quickly back at the Private office. I stopped Eliza from mentioning our destination in the car or in the office. We had no idea who could be listening in. First, we needed to know if Darlene could extract any useful data. She put it straight in her computer.

'I can't see anything else on here apart from the kids' book,' she admitted, defeated. 'Not even encrypted or corrupt files.'

I had been sure there was something else on the USB. Otherwise, Eric Moss could have sent his daughter a card or note making reference to the text. I hid the USB in a zippered compartment in my belt, something Becky had bought me for when we travelled. At the time I'd humoured her by wearing it. Now it might just come in handy.

We needed to get to Canberra asap. If Eliza's hunch was right, her father could be preparing to leave the country with the help of the Chinese. And after the fiasco with his supposed funeral, he couldn't afford to wait much longer. Thanks to us, the police, ADIA and CIA now knew he hadn't died in that boat explosion.

He could have already gone, but I believed the only reason he'd left the letter and USB was to give Eliza a chance to find him.

There were two major operative rules, both of which Moss had broken. Adopting Eliza was a complication he was supposed to avoid. He'd also failed to walk away and not look back when he had the opportunity.

But how to get to Canberra? Three hours on the road was too dangerous. We'd be followed for certain. I contacted Geoff Andren and explained the situation. Within half an hour Eliza and I were seated behind Geoff, in one of his friend's private planes.

'I just wanted to thank you for everything.' Eliza leant over towards me. 'I couldn't have had this chance to find Dad without you.'

'We haven't found him yet, and we may be too late. Not to mention the trouble we could be in if we try to get into a foreign embassy.'

The engine started and I placed my palms flat on the armrest. Not knowing what we'd face, Eliza seemed keen to talk.

'I loved seeing the variety of architecture among the embassies. Weird, for a child, but hey, I've always been different.'

I smiled. 'I see you more as a stand-out. For all the right reasons.'

She looked down and pulled a section of hair behind her ear. I had to admit, from someone so confident and accomplished, the action was more than a little endearing.

'We've got about forty-five minutes,' I said. 'We should rest while we can.'

Within minutes she was dozing. I watched her, wondering what the next few hours had in store. Eliza had made it clear that no matter the consequences, she'd seize any chance to see her father again. I consciously hadn't asked what she would do if Eric wanted her to join him.

When the wheels finally hit the tarmac Eliza opened her eyes and stretched her neck. 'Are we here already?'

'Better grab your things. We don't know when we'll be back.'

The keys to a rental car awaited us at the terminal and we were soon headed north-west towards the city. Extensive road works slowed us. I obeyed every speed zone to avoid unwanted attention.

Within a few kilometres, it became apparent – two cars were tailing us. One was a marked police car. I accelerated, it accelerated. I slowed, it slowed. The Feds already knew we were here, and had to be still after Eric Moss.

We passed the Royal Military College on our right. Neither car turned off.

I had two choices. One was to drive somewhere else and throw them off the scent. But that may cost Eliza the only chance to see her father.

I took the second option.

Chapter 119

'HOLD ON,' I WARNED Eliza as we approached the Kings Avenue exit ramp.

Seizing the opportunity, I slammed the accelerator to the floor. The Commodore engine screamed to life, letting us overtake an elderly couple in a Mazda.

The police kept pace as we sped across the bridge. Without sirens, they were likely to follow us all the way. Traffic ahead pulled to the left. I capitalised on the extra lane space and wove between lanes, gaining some distance.

The Chinese embassy was only minutes away. Once we were inside its walls, we would be safe – temporarily. The problem was, Eliza couldn't make it out of the car quickly and the Chinese didn't know who we were, or that we were coming.

'Call the embassy, tell them who you are and see if they'll open the gates,' I urged.

She used her smartphone to find the number.

We were fast approaching the Parliamentary Triangle, an area rife with tourists, workers and the highest concentration of police. And the biggest security response to potential terrorist threats. I needed to put time between us and our pursuers. We had no chance of losing them.

The traffic lights on to King George Terrace remained green. I tapped the brake, then accelerated on the orange and swung right, barely missing an ACTION bus. The police lost time slowing at the red. But not enough.

Clinging to the left verge, the rear wheels barely hung on. A furniture truck loomed just ahead and indicated right. I took it on the inside, thumping up the kerb, then swung hard right.

Tyres squealed as the back wheels slipped. I took my foot off the pedal and steered out. The truck stopped mid-turn, buying me precious seconds.

I crossed two more sets of traffic lights and found myself behind the Hyatt Hotel. The police were gaining.

I looped around to the embassy but the gates were closed.

On the phone, Eliza continued to plead for someone to open them. We needed more time. I passed the embassy and swung left on to Commonwealth Avenue then dog-tailed into the Hyatt entrance, barely missing a row of parked cars. Accelerating out of the bend, I turned hard left as the police car entered the drive, close behind, carefully steering past a Lamborghini and Porsche. Our pursuers weren't so lucky. Eliza spun her head around at the crash.

In the rear-view mirror, I saw the mess. The marked car clipped the Lambo and pushed it into the Porsche.

I flinched at the carnage, cornered left and floored it to the embassy, metres away. 'We're outside now!' Eliza shouted, and the gate began to open.

I braked and spun hard. The car slid into the driveway as an unmarked car jumped the kerb and cut off my path, blocking our access to the gate. I put my left arm out to protect Eliza.

Our car squealed to a sudden stop, just short of the vehicle that had swung in to block us. Eliza's seatbelt locked but her head was thrown forward and back against the headrest.

I unchecked my belt and saw a gun pointed in at me through the window.

Chapter 120

THE POLICE OFFICER yelled at me to raise my hands, as he opened my door.

'Slowly exit the car!' he ordered.

As I stepped out, hands raised, I saw the Glock aimed at Eliza.

'Get out, ma'am, with your hands up.'

'She can't physically lift her arms,' I shouted. 'And she needs a wheelchair. It's in the boot.'

Two plain-clothes men assisted her and she stood, propped against the car.

There were sudden shouts in Chinese, and three armed guards appeared in the drive from within the embassy.

Guns were pointed at the police now, who diverted their attention to the new threat.

'Stand down!' a voice behind me shouted.

A well-groomed gentlemen gave an order in Mandarin. His men lowered their weapons as he stepped through the gate.

'Sir, this is Federal Police business.' The officer who still had his gun trained on us did the talking. 'I ask you and your guards to step back and away.'

'This has just become official business of the People's Republic of China,' the other man answered, now switching to perfect English.

I noticed cameras on the brick fence, recording every minute. A fleet of police vehicles began filling the street.

'Sir, you don't understand. These two are wanted for aiding a fugitive, and are suspected of illegally selling classified information. Their crimes are covered by the Terrorist Act.'

'What?' Eliza demanded. 'This has to be a sick joke.'

The senior officer announced, 'You two are under arrest.' He gestured for us to be taken away.

The Chinese official put himself between the gun and Eliza. 'I'm afraid you will not be taking anyone from this embassy.' He handed the officer a card.

I lowered my hands a little. Eric Moss had to be inside.

'Mr Chin, is it? They are on Australian not Chinese soil.' The officer stood firm.

'Technically, yes. Your laws allow you to arrest suspects, even on embassy grounds. However, it is customary to do so with the permission from the relevant ambassador. That would be Ambassador Xing. He is currently in Beijing but will return next week.' He pulled out a notebook. 'May I have your name please?'

'Detective Sergeant Scott Wilson.'

Chin wrote it down.

'With respect, Mr Chin, we don't need your boss's permission. We are on a public street, outside your gates. Federally owned land.'

'I am afraid you are mistaken. You are standing on our paved drive, which is very much part of our embassy.'

The police looked at each other. We were at a stand-off.

Wilson tried again. 'Sir, we don't want to concern you or your staff. We just need these two to come with us and we'll be out of your way.'

Chin stepped forward. 'Forcibly removing anyone from within this perimeter will create – how do you say? – an international incident. Is that something you have authority to do?'

The detective sergeant looked furious. He ordered his men to make sure no one moved then stepped away to make a phone call.

Eliza and I were trapped. If we did manage to get inside the embassy, the Feds would be waiting for us the second we showed our faces.

We were trapped with no way out.

Chapter 121

WE WERE IN limbo. No longer on 'Australian soil' yet outside the protection of the embassy, on a small patch of asphalt, metres from the Federal Police. Without so much as Eliza's chair.

Eliza leant heavily against the car. Her legs were fatiguing quickly.

Tense minutes passed before the senior detective returned. The other officers still had their guns drawn on us.

And all this time, the Chinese guards hadn't altered their positions.

'Mr Chin, I have been instructed to comply with your request.' The Fed looked like he'd choke on his words as he directed his team to pull back, out on to the road.

'I'm glad we could come to an arrangement,' the embassy official said.

I moved around to support Eliza and she wrapped her arm around my waist as I took some of her weight.

'The wheelchair's in the boot,' I said. 'Can someone get it?'

Wilson clenched his jaw. 'No. The car comes with us,' he said. 'And everything in it.'

I looked at Chin, who shrugged.

'My bag,' Eliza said.

'If it's in the car, we're taking it.' Wilson stood ramrod straight.

'But the car and its contents are on embassy grounds,' I argued.

Mr Chin walked over, reached into the car, removed Eliza's bag and dumped it at my feet.

'Thank you,' Eliza said. 'I need my wheelchair.'

'You will not require it,' Chin said, matter of factly.

'We'll be here when you get hungry or thirsty,' Wilson declared before reversing the hire car on to the road.

Mr Chin called his guards inside and the metal gate began to slide closed in his wake. With us on the outside.

Chin raised a hand and the gate stopped, before he turned to us.

'Miss Moss, Mr Gisto, you are very welcome to come in.'

Chapter 122

'ARE THEY ARRESTING us?' Eliza whispered as I helped her walk. Two more military guards had appeared.

I wasn't sure. They knew who we were so they had to have been monitoring us. We were ushered through a door, down a corridor and into a lift. We were underground, no windows and no natural light. They searched us both at gunpoint. Our phones, watches and personal effects were immediately confiscated. A handheld metal detector beeped at my belt. I had to remove it, with the USB still inside. It was then handed back, thankfully without being searched. I quickly replaced it around my waist.

Next we were each photographed against a wall and moved to what looked like an interrogation room. A scratched wooden table sat in the centre, with two sealed bottles of water. Two metal chairs on one side, one on the other.

I helped Eliza into the first chair and she almost flopped into it with exhaustion.

'Dad must be here. Why else would they let us in?'

'They need to confirm our ID. Maybe they want to know why the Federal Police were on their territory.' The thought occurred to me: the only possible reason for the Chinese government to harbour Eric was that he worked for them.

I walked around the small room. Reflective glass inside, viewing room behind it. I was convinced we were being watched and possibly filmed. None of this felt right. I hoped we hadn't walked into something far more dangerous than Detective Sergeant Wilson and his mates.

'I'm sorry I got you into this,' was all I could say.

'I'm the one who got you into this . . . I just couldn't let it go. Let Dad go.'

I kept thinking of the Federal Police in the street. Even if there was a secret exit to this place, and we managed to evade them, we would be arrested as soon as we were recognised, anywhere in the country. There was no way to let Mary or the others know where we were.

'Eliza, they may know of your dad but it isn't clear if he's with the Chinese or against them.'

She unscrewed the lid on a bottle and stared at the label. 'He kept so many secrets. What sort of person can be that deceitful? I didn't know him at all.'

I sat beside her and held her hand, aware we were being monitored. 'Not his birth name, maybe. Or what he was involved in but the man loved you, read to you, cared for you. That was him. That wasn't an act.'

'Thank you, Craig. For everything.' She squeezed my hand. 'No matter what happens, I'm glad we met.'

A bang on the door interrupted us and an armed soldier marched through. He was shouting in Chinese and English. 'Where is USB?'

Chapter 123

THE DOOR OPENED further and a man appeared dressed in a navy jumper, grey tracksuit pants and ill-fitting slippers. He had a sling that positioned his hand over his heart. He looked thinner but, at five foot eleven, was still stocky. This time there were no reflective glasses, no dark lenses. Even in humble clothing, it was easy to appreciate the charisma he exuded to staff and politicians.

Eric Moss spoke softly to the soldier, in Mandarin. He lowered the gun and the unlikely pair exchanged further words before the soldier left the room, closing the door with a bang.

Wide round eyes glistened when he saw us.

Eliza slowly lifted her face and wiped her eyes. 'Daddy?' She saw the sling.

I slipped out of my chair and stood in front of the glass, to give them some modicum of privacy.

'You're hurt,' she said.

'Not as much as I've hurt you.' He reached forward to touch her face.

A thud on the glass made it clear. Contact was forbidden.

'This is Craig –' she tried.

'I know who he is. I figured you'd contact Jack Morgan again, who would refer you to Private Sydney. Months ago I put a small tracking device on your chair so I could monitor your whereabouts on computer. I'm sorry, but I had to know you were safe.'

That was why the Chinese embassy hadn't seemed that surprised we were on our way. I couldn't hide my frustration that he'd put his daughter at risk. 'Did you know Eliza was attacked at home? And ADIA tried to detain her earlier today? She could have been killed.'

'I was informed by my contact here. I'm sorry. If I could have stopped them from hurting you, Eliza, I would have.'

Somehow 'sorry' didn't seem to make up for all the lies and deception. If it were my child threatened, I would have been beyond angry. He didn't show any emotion or remorse for what she'd suffered.

I watched Eliza, studying her father's face as if meeting him for the first time.

'Do you know what they wanted with me? And that USB?' she eventually asked.

'I couldn't just abandon you after things changed at Contigo. Unfortunately, my selfishness made you a target.'

I felt protective of Eliza and didn't want her being deceived anymore. Selfishness? 'You mean when your illegal account keeping and secret contracts were about to be exposed?'

He slipped into the chair I'd vacated. 'All these years of work compromised by a few missing event tickets. The internal audit would have found more discrepancies. I'd managed to keep the fraud squad at bay. Time ran out.'

He wasn't going to worm his way out of what he'd done. 'You're not just talking about a routine audit,' I interjected.

'I had a visit from Jim Roden who was eager to find you, dead or alive.'

He sighed. 'I broke their rules with what I did to keep Contigo afloat. There was no going back once I became an embarrassment to the US and Australian governments. The simplest solution was the one they chose.'

'Are you saying the Australian government tried to assassinate you twice?'

'The assassination attempts were CIA. The Americans had a mole in with the Chinese who warned them I was meeting at a bay only reachable by boat. The exact location was secret even from me, until twenty minutes before time. Obviously, the boat was the best way to make sure I didn't make it to that meeting. Only I got lucky.'

I couldn't let Eliza be taken in by him again. I stepped forward and slapped the table hard.

'You're a liar! You've been playing us all right from the start.'

Chapter 124

ACCORDING TO JACK Morgan, the CIA had suspected a rogue agent, which is why they were pulling operatives out of the country. Moss was that rogue agent. I guessed the missing tickets were incidental, and didn't set off the series of events.

'That isn't true,' he pleaded with Eliza. 'You know me. Better than anyone.'

'The fire at the cabin,' Eliza concluded. 'I knew you'd been there.'

'You just happened to have magnesium on you, and get into an escape hatch which happened to be beneath a friend's cabin?'

He didn't blink at the accusation.

I leant forward. 'You set a trap for them, didn't you?'

He sighed and looked up towards the glass. 'I did what I had to to survive.'

'You're a regular MacGyver,' I mocked.

'Craig,' Eliza warned. 'Stop it.'

'And the boat,' I said. 'Did they get lucky assuming you'd go there and rigged it to blow?'

He pulled the chair close to his daughter, without touching her. His sole focus became Eliza. 'I need to know where the USB I sent you is.'

'Oh my God, it's the only thing you care about.' She covered her mouth. 'You used me to get it here?'

'I know you can't understand. But it is our ticket to safety. Without it . . .' His voice trailed away.

'I can't believe you worked in secret for the Americans, then made a deal with the Chinese.'

'It isn't that simple. It was only through sheer luck I survived that explosion.' He moved the fingers on his right hand in the sling. 'The Americans and the Australians wanted me dead. They still want me dead. By running, I confirmed their suspicions that one of their agents had turned rogue. That put you at risk. It made sense to have people think I was dead and it ended the attacks on you. The man who took my place was part of a Chinese drug syndicate. His relatives couldn't afford the burial. Chinese agents witnessed the explosion and pulled me from the water. They came up with the idea of substituting and the family signed over the body. I had to protect you, Eliza, and this was the only way.'

Eliza shook her head, suddenly defiant. 'Don't make this about me. You've been lying my entire life. Hans Gudgast? Is that your real name?'

He shrugged. 'Gudgast was an embezzler, but in death he gave me a chance to do good.'

I understood. He couldn't fake the height difference, so wasn't Gudgast at all. 'You took his identity to enter Australia with the help of the CIA.'

He lowered his gaze. 'I came here from Europe, where doesn't matter, after being recruited as a university student interested in biomedical engineering. I had no family and was idealistic back then. I saw it as an opportunity to do good.

And the CIA offered to fund lifesaving research in exchange for information about foreign defence force bases and technologies. That's why I developed training programs.' He rubbed darkened eyes. 'I never agreed to hurt anyone.'

'Except the people who lent or gave you money,' I said. 'They won't be seeing it again, after you conned them out of it.' This man was either phenomenally naive or extremely manipulative.

He flashed me a quizzical look as if the answer were obvious. 'I did that for the staff. The CIA were starting to funnel their funds elsewhere, to their latest projects, and sucking the business dry. If I didn't borrow more, the staff and Contigo would have lost their jobs. We had sold so many of our assets, I had to be creative in presenting to the banks. The employees were like family after all those years. I couldn't let them suffer for something I started.'

I couldn't work Moss out. 'You must have known it would eventually unravel.'

'I had to buy time. Until the last series of secret projects was complete. Now, Eliza, I need that USB.'

'I'm sorry, Dad. I can't give it to you.'

Chapter 125

MOSS'S EXPRESSION HARDENED. 'Eliza, how is your breathing?'

His daughter made no comment.

'You know it's seventy per cent normal. There is a clinic in Zurich that specialises in degenerative neurological diseases like yours.'

The word 'degenerative' was like a blow to my chest. I had no idea Eliza's condition would deteriorate. I moved and sat at the desk opposite her. She would not make eye contact with me.

'Why didn't you say anything?' I tried to process what that meant.

She bowed her head. 'I couldn't.'

'You're already at seventy per cent lung function,' her father continued, 'and stress speeds the disease process. Who knows what the last few days have done to your immune system. Again, I'm truly sorry for that.'

He placed his hand on the table, next to hers. 'You just book in for an assessment when you're ready. They do stem cell therapy.' He lifted his hand, revealing a card. 'It's all been taken care of.'

A long silence hung in the room.

Eliza then spoke, a quiver in her voice. 'Is that part of the deal you brokered with the Chinese?'

'I had two conditions. In exchange for my research they get me out of Australia safely, and you get the very best medical care. The genetic testing has been paid for in advance. Eliza, this clinic could have the answers no one else does.'

Eliza began to tremble.

I wasn't buying it. 'So what's on the USB that makes it so valuable? Our computers couldn't detect anything.'

'The USB is half of a complex series of systems that will change the face of warfare. That means limiting civilian deaths and carnage.' He looked at both of us. 'I developed an advanced encryption code, which is why you couldn't decipher it. It needs to be paired with the other USB to be read.' He took a deep breath. 'Contigo Valley started out as an altruistic, forward-thinking company but in the last ten years it became overrun with agendas I could no longer influence, or stomach. War is a powerful industry and makes certain interests extremely wealthy. Resources and politics are the endgame. Power of the worst kind.'

'All this because you're disillusioned with American foreign policy?' I was incredulous.

'The West continues to prop up militants who overthrow those who would keep the US, UK and Australia away from oil and other resources. Inevitably, the underdog rises to fill the power vacuum and, morally corrupted, becomes the monster it fought. Look at Iraq, Iran, Afghanistan, the list is endless.'

'The proverbs we used to talk about,' Eliza argued, 'like the one about the teacher coming to the pupil. They're fiction. Buddha never said those things. China is no different from anyone else. It's a superpower and equally prone to corruption.'

'I disagree. China is looking to the future to break old habits. They are leading the world in commercialisation of renewable energy, and are proving giants in the manufacture of those technologies.'

Eliza shook her head. 'This can't be about solar energy, Dad. It's too far-fetched. And you're going to sell your life's research to another superpower. How can you be sure you can trust them with it? How do you know you're not selling your soul to another devil?'

'Think about it. The Middle East is a debacle, in many ways trapped in the Middle Ages, still obsessing about crusades and infidels. China is on the rise and will have the economy, trained workforce, political influence and autonomy to orchestrate a better way. We're not talking about a larger version of North Korea, like propagandists would have you believe. Without the West dependent on oil, Middle Eastern wars won't have to be fought. If oil isn't in demand, the power of Saudi Arabia will dissolve.'

For the first time, he made a reasonable point. The industry behind wars would need to look for new sources of income.

'Finally, armies can save lives, not take them.' He sounded like a politician campaigning for election.

Eliza paused, then spoke firmly. 'I'm lucky, happy, and prepared to let fate take its course. I won't accept you doing this for me.' She pushed the card back at him.

'The old ways aren't working. The spy game doesn't work. This is my way to make a positive difference.'

Despite his motives, I was concerned what would happen to us all if the USB wasn't located. After all, it was the reason the Chinese were helping him escape. I reached into the zipper on my belt and pulled out the tiny device, still mulling over what to do. I eventually slid it across the table.

'Thank you, Craig.' He stood. 'I have a clear conscience for what happens from here on. Eliza, you've made me a far better person. I will always love you.'

Eliza and I both realised that this was the last time we'd ever see the man known as Eric Moss.

Chapter 126

A KNOCK ON the door broke the tearful silence. 'Time is up. I have to go,' Moss said.

'Please ask for more time, *ask them*.' Eliza grabbed her father's hands.

He looked at her with eyes full of love.

'You couldn't make me happier, or more proud.'

'What about Lang Gillies?' I asked. 'How is he involved?'

'Lang likes to think he's involved in secret work. Truth is, Jim Roden has him in his pocket, for his own reasons. He would have let the ambassador know the second I sent him the resignation email.'

I wanted to know one more thing. 'Was he complicit in the fraud?' Seeing him pursued by the fraud squad would give me a certain satisfaction.

'He can't tell his left from his right. Subterfuge is beyond his minimal talents.' Moss smiled to himself, then looked again at Eliza.

'When will I see you again?' she asked. 'How will I contact you?' She reached for his arm and he bent down, tenderly kissing her forehead.

'I have to go somewhere no one will find me. While we've been talking, a deal has been brokered with the Australian and US governments. You will be free once you leave here. Fortunately, Ambassador Roden and his friends at the CIA won't want it getting around that a man with no records and no passport conned the CIA, defence forces, even the Secretary of State into providing intimate knowledge of highly classified defence contracts and bases. The Australian government wouldn't be proud of it either. The only price you pay is silence.'

'Please, Daddy, don't do this. We can work something out.'

An official entered the room with the guard.

'It's time.'

Eliza's hands gripped him tightly and she cried softly in his arms. 'I love you. Please don't go.'

After a couple of minutes of silence, the guard moved to separate the pair.

I blocked him and took Eliza's hands. Her father walked slowly towards the door. He turned and blew a kiss. 'I hope you'll see me one day as a hero in your story, not a villain.'

He didn't look back.

Chapter 127

AS ERIC MOSS predicted, we exited the embassy via the front gates. The police were nowhere to be seen and Eliza's wheelchair had been returned. We sat in the back of a diplomatic car, with a Chinese driver separated by an electric screen. I had no doubt he was listening to everything we said on the way to the airport.

She gripped my hand tightly in the back seat, all but emotionally spent.

I ran over what Moss had told us. Eliza would never know his true identity, for his own reasons. The lack of documentation was deliberate. He was a CIA operative and didn't leave a paper or digital trail. Anything else could have been wiped by the CIA once he went rogue.

Eliza placed her head on my shoulder. 'Do you think he was lying?'

I watched the view from my window.

'I think he honestly believes he's doing the right thing. It sounds as if he's been disillusioned with his work for a long time. Maybe it was time for him to stop lying.'

She lifted her head and turned her face to mine. 'He's still trying to look after me. Swiss treatments? Wasn't stopping wars enough?'

I smiled at her resilience. 'Maybe that's how he justified it to himself – his last act to make sure you're taken care of.'

'Craig, he's a traitor, isn't he?'

To be honest, I wasn't sure. 'It depends on which side you're on. Julian Assange, Edward Snowden polarise opinion all the time. If he does change the face of warfare, he'll be a hero in a lot of people's stories.' Although I suspected it was more likely the regime he was defecting to would be just as disillusioning. 'One thing is clear,' I added. 'He loves you more than anything and wants you to get the best possible treatment.'

'About that. I didn't know how to tell you. There never seemed to be a right time.'

I kept painful secrets myself and couldn't blame Eliza for shielding her privacy. If disability didn't define her, a progressive condition wouldn't either. I looked into her eyes and our faces touched. I kissed her softly at first, then with increasing intensity. For a few minutes, the world went silent.

Chapter 128

THREE MONTHS LATER

We'd arrived at the international airport early and were outside the departures gate. I couldn't believe the day had come so quickly.

'I can always tag along if you change your mind, carry your bags?'

Eliza held my hand and smiled. 'Kiss me like Peyroni and the paparazzi are watching,' she joked.

'Think he's a little busy preparing for that court case of his. Now talking of cases . . .'

'We've been over this. I have to go alone. If they think I'm suitable for the trial and there's a chance of improvement, I'm going through with the treatment no matter the risks. I don't need Mr Logic here muddling my thinking, or kissing me to cloud my senses.'

I bent down and kissed her again. These months had been memorable. My apartment would be lonely without her. That incredible smile, the raucous laugh and her zest for life, in spite of the loss and heartache.

'The genetic testing should be able to – I mean, before things go any further between us, I need to know.'

Eliza had no idea if her condition could be passed on to children. Before committing to any long-term relationship, she deserved the chance to find out.

I kissed her button nose.

'Well,' she held up her passport, 'love you and leave you.'

She wheeled away, then spun around. 'Hey, you'd better get practising the "YMCA" dance. It's the first thing we're doing when I get back.'

I raised both arms in a Y-shape and she laughed before disappearing through the departure gate.

THIS HOUSE WILL COST YOU ... YOUR LIFE.

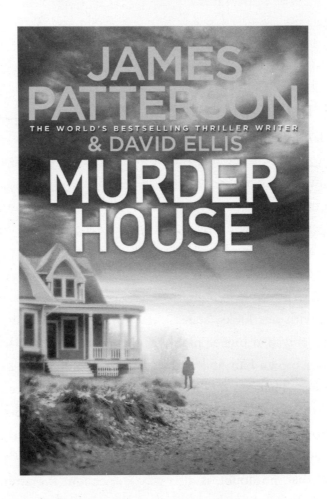

THE FUNERAL FOR Melanie Phillips is heavily attended, filling the pews of the Presbyterian church and overflowing onto Main Street. She was all of twenty years old when she was murdered, every day of which she lived in Bridgehampton. Poor girl, never got to see the world, though for some people, the place you grew up *is* your world. Maybe that was Melanie. Maybe all she ever wanted was to be a waitress at Tasty's Diner, serving steamers and lobster to tourists and townies and the occasional rich couple looking to drink in the "local environment."

But with her looks, at least from what I've seen in photos, she probably had bigger plans. A young woman like that, with luminous brown hair and sculpted features, could have been in magazines. That, no doubt, is why she caught the attention of Zach Stern, the head of a talent agency that included A-list celebrities, a man who owned his own jet and who liked to hang out in the Hamptons now and then.

And that, no doubt, is also why she caught the attention of Noah Walker, who apparently had quite an affinity for young Melanie himself and must not have taken too kindly to her affair with Zach.

It was only four nights ago that Zachary Stern and Melanie Phillips were found dead, victims of a brutal murder in a rental house near the beach that Zach had leased for the week. The carnage was brutal enough that Melanie's service was closed-casket.

So the crowd is owed in part to Melanie's local popularity, and in part to the media interest, given Zach Stern's notoriety in Hollywood.

It is also due, I am told, to the fact that the murders occurred at 7 Ocean Drive, which among the locals has become known as the Murder House.

Now we've moved to the burial, which is just next door to the church. It allows the throng that couldn't get inside the church to mill around the south end of the cemetery, where Melanie Phillips will be laid to rest. There must be three hundred people here, if you count the media, which for the most part are keeping a respectful distance even while they snap their photographs.

The overhead sun at midday is strong enough for squinting and sunglasses, both of which make it harder for me to do what I came here to do, which is to check out the people attending the funeral to see if anyone pings my radar. Some of these creeps like to come and watch the sorrow they caused, so it's standard operating procedure to scan the crowd at crime scenes and funerals.

"Remind me why we're here, Detective Murphy," says my partner, Isaac Marks.

"I'm paying my respects."

"You didn't know Melanie," he says.

True enough. I don't know anyone around here. Once upon a time, my family came here every summer, a good three-week stretch straddling June and July, to stay with Uncle Langdon and Aunt Chloe. My memories of those summers—beaches and boat rides and fishing off the docks—end at age seven.

For some reason I never knew, my family stopped coming after that. Until nine months ago when I joined the force, I hadn't set foot in the Hamptons for eighteen years.

"I'm working on my suntan," I say.

"Not to mention," says Isaac, ignoring my remark, "that we already have our bad guy in custody."

Also true. We arrested Noah Walker yesterday. He'll get a bond hearing tomorrow, but there's no way the judge is going to bond him out on a double murder.

"And might I further add," says Isaac, "that this isn't even your case."

Right again. I volunteered to lead the team arresting Noah, but I wasn't given the case. In fact, the chief—my aforementioned uncle Langdon—is handling the matter personally. The town, especially the hoity-toity millionaires along the beach, just about busted a collective gut when the celebrity agent Zach Stern was brutally murdered in their scenic little hamlet. It's the kind of case that could cost the chief his job, if he isn't careful. I'm told the town supervisor has been calling him on the hour for updates.

So why am I here, at a funeral for someone I don't know, on a case that isn't mine? Because I'm bored. Because since I left the NYPD, I haven't seen any action. And because I've handled more homicides in eight years on the force than all of these cops in Bridgehampton put together. Translation: I wanted the case, and I was a little displeased when I didn't get it.

"Who's that?" I ask, gesturing across the way to an odd-looking man in a green cap, with long stringy hair and ratty clothes. Deep-set, creepy eyes that seem to wander. He shifts his weight from foot to foot, unable to stay still.

Isaac pushes down his sunglasses to get a better look. "Oh,

that's Aiden Willis," he says. "He works for the church. Probably dug Melanie's grave."

"Looks like he slept in it first."

Isaac likes that. "Seriously, Murphy. You're looking for suspects? With all you know about this case, which is diddly-squat, you don't like Noah Walker for the murders?"

"I'm not saying that," I answer.

"You're not denying it, either."

I consider that. He's right, of course. What the hell do I know about Noah Walker or the evidence against him? He may not have jumped out at me as someone who'd just committed a brutal double murder, but when do public faces ever match private misdeeds? I once busted a second-grade schoolteacher who was selling heroin to the high school kids. And a candy striper who was boning the corpses in the basement of the hospital. You never know people. And I'd known Noah Walker for all of thirty minutes.

"Go home," says Isaac. "Go work out—"

Already did this morning.

"—or see the ocean—"

I've seen it already. It's a really big body of water.

"—or have a drink."

Yeah, a glass of wine might be in my future. But first, I'm going to take a quick detour. A detour that could probably get me in a lot of trouble.

AS THE FUNERAL for Melanie Phillips ends, I say good-bye to my partner, Detective Isaac Marks, without telling him where I'm going. He doesn't need to know, and I don't know if he'd keep the information to himself. I'm not yet sure where his loyalties lie, and I'm not going to make the same mistake I made with the NYPD.

I decide to walk, heading south from the cemetery toward the Atlantic. I always underestimate the distance to the ocean, but it's a nice day for a walk, even if a little steamy. And I enjoy the houses just south of Main Street along this road, the white-trimmed Cape Cods with cedar shingles whose colors have grown richer with age from all the precipitation that comes with proximity to the ocean. Some are bigger, some are newer, but these houses generally look the same, which I find both comforting and a little creepy.

As I get closer to the ocean, the plots of land get wider, the houses get bigger, and the privacy shrubs flanking them get taller. I stop when I reach shrubbery that's a good ten feet high. I know I've found the place because the majestic wrought-iron gates at the end of the driveway, which are slightly parted, are adorned with black-and-yellow tape that says CRIME SCENE DO NOT CROSS.

I slide between the gates without breaking the seal. I start up the driveway, but it curves off to some kind of carriage house up a hill, which once upon a time probably served as a stable for the horses and possibly the servants' quarters. So I take the stone path that will eventually lead me to the front door.

In the center of the wide expanse of grass, just before it slopes dramatically upward, there is a small stone fountain, with a monument jutting up that bears a crest and an inscription. I lean over the fountain to take a closer look. The small tablet of stone features a bird in the center, with a hooked beak and a long tail feather, encircled by little symbols, each of which appears to be the letter *X,* but which upon closer inspection is a series of criss-crossing daggers.

And then, *ka-boom.*

It hits me, the rush, the pressure in my chest, the stranglehold to my throat, I can't breathe, I can't see, I'm weightless. *Help me, somebody please help me—*

I stagger backward, almost losing my balance, and suck in a deep, delicious breath of air.

"Wow," I say into the warm breeze. *Easy, girl. Take it easy.* I wipe greasy sweat from my forehead and inhale and exhale a few more times to slow my pulse.

Beneath the monument's crest, carved into the stone in a thick Gothic font, are these words:

Cecilia, O Cecilia
Life was Death Disguised

Okay, that's pretty creepy. I take a photo of the monument

with my smartphone. Now front and center before the house, I take my first good look.

The mansion peering down at me from atop the hill is a Gothic structure of faded multicolored limestone. It has a Victorian look to it, with multiple rooflines, all of them steeply pitched, fancy turrets, chimneys grouped at each end. There are elaborate medieval-style accents on the facade. Every peak is topped with an ornament that ends in a sharp point, like spears aimed at the gods. The windows are long and narrow, clover-shaped, with stained glass. The house is like one gigantic, imperious frown.

I've heard some things about this house, read some things, even passed by it many times, but seeing it up close like this sends a chill through me.

It is part cathedral and part castle. It is a scowling, menacing, imposing structure, both regal and haunting, almost romantic in its gloom.

All it's missing is a drawbridge and a moat filled with crocodiles.

This is 7 Ocean Drive. This is what they call the Murder House.

This isn't your case, I remind myself. *This isn't your problem. This could cost you your badge, girl.*

I start up the hill toward the front door.

ABOUT THE AUTHORS

JAMES PATTERSON is one of the best-known and biggest-selling writers of all time. Since winning the Edgar™ Award for Best First Novel with *The Thomas Berryman Number,* his books have sold in excess of 300 million copies worldwide and he has been the most borrowed author in UK libraries for the past eight years in a row. He is the author of some of the most popular series of the past two decades – the Alex Cross, Women's Murder Club, Detective Michael Bennett and Private novels – and he has written many other number one bestsellers including romance novels and stand-alone thrillers. He lives in Florida with his wife and son.

James is passionate about encouraging children to read. Inspired by his own son who was a reluctant reader, he also writes a range of books specifically for young readers. James is a founding partner of Booktrust's Children's Reading Fund in the UK.

KATHRYN FOX is a medical practitioner with a special interest in forensic medicine. She is the author of seven internationally bestselling novels, most recently *Death Mask*, *Cold Grave* and *Fatal Impact*. Her debut, *Malicious Intent*, won the 2005 Davitt award for adult fiction. She has twice been short-listed for the prestigious Ned Kelly award. Her books have also been selected in the '50 Books You Can't Put Down' Australian reading initiative and are published in over a dozen languages.

Kathryn lives in Sydney and combines her passion for books and medicine by actively promoting the links between literacy and health, particularly in disadvantaged communities.

Also by James Patterson

ALEX CROSS NOVELS

Along Came a Spider • Kiss the Girls • Jack and Jill •
Cat and Mouse • Pop Goes the Weasel • Roses are Red •
Violets are Blue • Four Blind Mice • The Big Bad Wolf •
London Bridges • Mary, Mary • Cross • Double Cross •
Cross Country • Alex Cross's Trial (*with Richard
DiLallo*) • I, Alex Cross • Cross Fire • Kill Alex Cross •
Merry Christmas, Alex Cross • Alex Cross, Run •
Cross My Heart • Hope to Die • Cross Justice (*to be
published November 2015*)

THE WOMEN'S MURDER CLUB SERIES

1st to Die • 2nd Chance (*with Andrew Gross*) •
3rd Degree (*with Andrew Gross*) • 4th of July (*with Maxine
Paetro*) • The 5th Horseman (*with Maxine Paetro*) •
The 6th Target (*with Maxine Paetro*) • 7th Heaven (*with Maxine
Paetro*) • 8th Confession (*with Maxine Paetro*) •
9th Judgement (*with Maxine Paetro*) • 10th Anniversary (*with
Maxine Paetro*) • 11th Hour (*with Maxine Paetro*) •
12th of Never (*with Maxine Paetro*) • Unlucky 13 (*with Maxine
Paetro*) • 14th Deadly Sin (*with Maxine Paetro*)

MICHAEL BENNETT NOVELS

Step on a Crack (*with Michael Ledwidge*) • Run For Your Life
(*with Michael Ledwidge*) • Worst Case (*with Michael Ledwidge*) •
Tick Tock (*with Michael Ledwidge*) • I, Michael Bennett
(*with Michael Ledwidge*) • Gone (*with Michael Ledwidge*) •
Burn (*with Michael Ledwidge*) • Alert (*with Michael Ledwidge*)

NYPD RED SERIES

NYPD Red (*with Marshall Karp*) •
NYPD Red 2 (*with Marshall Karp*) •
NYPD Red 3 (*with Marshall Karp*)

STAND-ALONE THRILLERS

Sail (*with Howard Roughan*) • Swimsuit (*with Maxine Paetro*) • Don't Blink (*with Howard Roughan*) • Postcard Killers (*with Liza Marklund*) • Toys (*with Neil McMahon*) • Now You See Her (*with Michael Ledwidge*) • Kill Me If You Can (*with Marshall Karp*) • Guilty Wives (*with David Ellis*) • Zoo (*with Michael Ledwidge*) • Second Honeymoon (*with Howard Roughan*) • Mistress (*with David Ellis*) • Invisible (*with David Ellis*) • The Thomas Berryman Number • Truth or Die (*with Howard Roughan*) • Murder House (*with David Ellis, to be published September 2015*)

NON-FICTION

Torn Apart (*with Hal and Cory Friedman*) •
The Murder of King Tut (*with Martin Dugard*)

ROMANCE

Sundays at Tiffany's (*with Gabrielle Charbonnet*) •
The Christmas Wedding (*with Richard DiLallo*) •
First Love (*with Emily Raymond*)

OTHER TITLES

Miracle at Augusta (*with Peter de Jonge*)

FAMILY OF PAGE-TURNERS

MIDDLE SCHOOL BOOKS

The Worst Years of My Life (*with Chris Tebbetts*) •
Get Me Out of Here! (*with Chris Tebbetts*) • My Brother Is a Big,
Fat Liar (*with Lisa Papademetriou*) • How I Survived Bullies,
Broccoli, and Snake Hill (*with Chris Tebbetts*) • Ultimate
Showdown (*with Julia Bergen*) • Save Rafe! (*with Chris
Tebbetts*) • Just My Rotten Luck (*with Chris Tebbetts,
to be published October 2015*)

I FUNNY SERIES

I Funny (*with Chris Grabenstein*) •
I Even Funnier (*with Chris Grabenstein*) •
I Totally Funniest (*with Chris Grabenstein*)

TREASURE HUNTERS SERIES

Treasure Hunters (*with Chris Grabenstein*) •
Danger Down the Nile (*with Chris Grabenstein*) • Secrets of
the Forbidden City (*with Chris Grabenstein, to be published
September 2015*)

HOUSE OF ROBOTS

House of Robots (*with Chris Grabenstein*) •
Robots Go Wild! (*with Chris Grabenstein, to be published
December 2015*)

KENNY WRIGHT

Kenny Wright: Superhero (*with Chris Tebbetts*)

HOMEROOM DIARIES

Homeroom Diaries (*with Lisa Papademetriou*)

MAXIMUM RIDE SERIES

The Angel Experiment • School's Out Forever •
Saving the World and Other Extreme Sports •
The Final Warning • Max • Fang • Angel •
Nevermore • Forever

CONFESSIONS SERIES

Confessions of a Murder Suspect (*with Maxine Paetro*) •
The Private School Murders (*with Maxine Paetro*) • The Paris
Mysteries (*with Maxine Paetro*) • The Murder of an Angel (*with
Maxine Paetro, to be published October 2015*)

WITCH & WIZARD SERIES

Witch & Wizard (*with Gabrielle Charbonnet*) •
The Gift (*with Ned Rust*) • The Fire (*with Jill
Dembowski*) • The Kiss (*with Jill Dembowski*) •
The Lost (*with Emily Raymond*)

DANIEL X SERIES

The Dangerous Days of Daniel X (*with Michael Ledwidge*) •
Watch the Skies (*with Ned Rust*) • Demons and Druids (*with
Adam Sadler*) • Game Over (*with Ned Rust*) • Armageddon (*with
Chris Grabenstein*) • Lights Out (with Chris Grabenstein)

GRAPHIC NOVELS

Daniel X: Alien Hunter (*with Leopoldo Gout*) •
Maximum Ride: Manga Vols. 1–8 (*with NaRae Lee*)

For more information about James Patterson's novels, visit
www.jamespatterson.co.uk

Or become a fan on Facebook